D1630238

THE
G-STRING
MURDERS

GYPSY ROSE LEE

With a foreword by DONNA MOORE

Afterword by RACHEL SHTEIR

And selected correspondence between
Gypsy Rose Lee and her editor, LEE WRIGHT

CONTRABAND

Contraband is an imprint of Saraband

Published by Saraband,
Suite 202, 98 Woodlands Road
Glasgow
G3 6HB
Scotland

www.saraband.net

This edition published 2017

Copyright © 1941 by Gypsy Rose Lee
Afterword copyright © 2005 by Rachel Shteir
Originally published in 1941 by
Simon and Schuster, Inc., New York
Published by arrangement with
The Feminist Press at the City University of New York

All rights reserved.
No part of this publication may be reproduced,
stored in a retrieval system, or transmitted, in any form
or by any means, electronic, mechanical, photocopying,
recording, or otherwise, without first obtaining the written
permission of the copyright owner.

ISBN: 9781910192504
ebook: 9781910192511

10 9 8 7 6 5 4 3 2 1

Typeset by Iolaire Typography Ltd. Newtonmore.

Printed and bound in Great Britain by Clays Ltd, St Ives plc.

MIX
Paper from
responsible sources
FSC® C018072

FOREWORD

I am a huge and unapologetic fan of pulp fiction, especially that written by women. I have a small (but perfectly formed) collection of my own and I was lucky enough to curate an exhibition and collection of women's pulp fiction at Glasgow Women's Library. I own three different editions of *The G-String Murders* by Gypsy Rose Lee, so being asked to write the foreword for this wonderful Contraband edition was a real joy.

The pulp fiction of the mid-twentieth century often exposed women's lives in a way that hadn't been seen before, allowing women to step out of the everyday humdrum and into a different world, and perhaps fantasize about an alternative identity. Bored suburban housewives could discover they were lesbians after reading Tereska Torrès' *Women's Barracks* or Vin Packer's *Spring Fire*; teenage girls living in Nowheresville, Minnesota, could dream of life in the big, bad city after reading Valerie Taylor's *The Girls in 3-B*; bedridden grandmothers could experience palpitations reading Arlene Hale's *Private Nurse*.

In the case of *The G-String Murders*, the brave new world we are exposed to – quite literally, in fact – is the world of the ecdysiast, the take-it-off artist, the stripper, the burlesque performer. But don't expect sexual titillation on these pages. These pages promise "FULL NET PANTS. NO BUMPS. NO GRINDS. KEEP YOUR NAVEL COVERED." So what you'll actually get is a full-on caper of a murder mystery, set in a run-down theatre that needs a new toilet, and in a world where a burlesque performer grabs at the security of a twenty-week guarantee of folding money and a chance to get her laundry out of hock.

Burlesque has its origins in using performance to satirize social conventions. The theatre in the book promises not only "GIRLS! GIRLS! GIRLS!" but also "LAFFS! LAFFS! LAFFS!" And that's definitely what the reader gets, with a plot as outrageous as some of the acts, and a cast of characters that includes "Golden-Voiced Goddess" Lolita La Verne, racketeer Louie Grindero, "Dynamic" Dolly Baxter, and the mysterious Princess Nirvena.

But *The G-String Murders* is also a wonderful slice of social fiction, giving a glimpse into a life that is all gilt and feathers on the surface, but long hours and hardscrabble underneath. A raid on the theatre, for example, shows us the shocking treatment of the performers at the hands of the police and the squalid conditions in a police cell. We also see the true friendships and loyalty that form amongst the backbiting and vying for position; the sharing of food and money; and the importance of labour unions and working class solidarity.

The G-String Murders doesn't take itself too seriously, but its engaging heroine gives us a glimpse into an alien and intimate world – a world of candy butchers, grouch bags, and pickle persuaders – where life is a struggle, and where the diamond in the rough might only be a rhinestone, but it's still worth fighting for.

Donna Moore,
January 2017

Donna Moore is a crime fiction author, blogger and aficionado. She works at the Glasgow Women's Library and is a co-organiser of the annual Crimefest convention.

ONE

FINDING DEAD BODIES SCATTERED ALL OVER A burlesque theater isn't the sort of thing you're likely to forget. Not quickly, anyway. It's the little things, incidents that don't seem important when they happen, that slip your mind.

With me, for instance. As long as I live, I'll remember seeing that bloated, bluish face, the twisted, naked body, and the glitter of a G-string hanging like an earring from the swollen neck. Sometimes, even now, I wake up in a cold sweat with the sound of a body squashing on the stage, and Dolly Baxter's screams in my ears.

The things that are harder to remember are the incidents leading to the murders. The raid is a good example. How was I to know it wasn't just another pinch?

Then, Dolly Baxter and Lolita La Verne. They were always fighting anyway, so how could I guess that their ordinary hair-pulling, name-calling differences of opinion were leading to death?

I'll admit I should have known something was up when the Princess Nirvena opened at the Old Opera. She must have seen the signs backstage; they were all over the place: FULL NET PANTS. NO BUMPS. NO GRINDS. KEEP YOUR NAVEL COVERED. You couldn't miss seeing them. But when she did her specialty and took off her last pair of pants, I was definitely going to hand in my notice.

I didn't, of course, but …Well maybe I'd better start from the beginning. Not when I first went into show business, but from the time I received the telegram in Columbus, Ohio.

```
GYPSY ROSE LEE, it read,
GAIETY THEATER, COLUMBUS, OHIO
YOU OPEN FEBRUARY TWELFTH OLD OPERA THEATER,
NEW YORK CITY. SALARY 125.0 NET. THEATER REAL
SHOWCASE FOR BROADWAY DEBUT. WIRE CONFIRMA-
TION. RUSH PHOTOS.
    H.I. MOSS
```

The wire was typical of him. H.I. Moss, owner of six burlesque theaters and undisputed impresario of burlesque, wouldn't wire, "*Can* you open?" And although I'd been working for him for two years, he wouldn't sign it "Best regards," nor would he write "Herbert" or "Isadore Moss."

"Burlesque is the poor man's *Follies*," was one of his expressions, but I'm sure he didn't feel that way about it. He was convinced that an H.I. Moss production meant not only "clean entertainment for the whole family," but also stood for the very best Broadway could offer. If he thought Eugene O'Neill could write a good burlesque blackout, then O'Neill was the man for him. If he couldn't write anything but *Dynamo* and *Strange Interlude*, Moss would shrug his shoulders and say:

"Who wants to know from such corn? Girls! That's what the public wants!"

He might have been right at that.

Of all this theaters, the Old Opera was the favorite. It had survived a good many depressions and the policy was girls! girls! girls! In smaller print they advertised LAFFS! LAFFS! LAFFS! Next in prominence, BOXING THURSDAY NIGHTS.

Moss emphasized the "clean entertainment" part, too. The night I met him, he impressed it on my mind. That was the night he changed my name from Rose Louise to Gypsy Rose Lee.

"That Louise is too refined for a stripteaser," he said. "Refinement in burlesque we must have, but not too much."

I really didn't want to join a burlesque troupe. No vaudeville actor does. If you find one in burlesque you can be sure he got in through the starvation route. I certainly did. Maybe not exactly starvation, but when there's only one punch left on your meal ticket, it's close enough. Not only that, but I'd been locked out of an egg crate of a hotel in the thriving city of Toledo!

H.I. Moss didn't care much whether I wanted to be a stripteaser or not. He thought of himself as a star builder; a sort of cross between David Belasco and Flo Ziegfeld, with a little Napoleon thrown in as an added attraction.

"I will personally see to it that your name is in lights on Broadway," he told me exactly one half minute after I met him.

It was my closing night in a comfort station that the defunct owners playfully called a night club. The lights were dim and a five-piece orchestra pounded out tune after tune while my new boss outlined my future to me. From the routine he was giving me, it sounded like I was going in training for the ballet, or at least the Olympics.

"Experience. That's what you need." His eyes, peering at me through bifocal glasses, closed dreamily. "And clothes; velvets with feathers, diamonds in your hair." The red and blue overhead lights reflected on his bald head as he raised his voice above that of the singer with the band.

When he really interested me was when he got down to cases, a play-or-pay contract. Diamonds in my hair is well and good, but at the moment I was a little hungry.

"First you play my circuit, then you play a year in stock here in Toledo. If at the end of that time I, H.I. Moss, feel that you are ready for Broadway, you play the Old Opera!"

He waited for me to gurgle, "*Not* the Old Opera!" with awe in my eyes. Unfortunately, I had never heard of the theater, so all I could give him was, "What is the salary?"

"With a twenty-week guarantee, and H.I. Moss personally grooming you for stardom, we don't talk money." With a grand gesture he handed me the contract. It was a blurred carbon copy, the salary the blurriest part of all, but I signed it. Twenty weeks is twenty weeks and it sounded like a chance to get my laundry out of hock.

That had all happened two years before the telegram arrived. In that time I had signed many more blurred carbon copies and, with the exception of a raise every six months, the contracts were all alike.

One hundred and twenty-five dollars! That was folding money. And I had also learned to get the awed look in my eye when the Old Opera was mentioned. My hand shook a little as I reread the wire. At the time I thought it was from the excitement of reaching a goal. Now I know it was a presentiment.

Not that I try to live up to the name of Gypsy, but I do occasionally read tea leaves. And aside from having the Girdle of Venus in my right palm, I was born with two cauls.

That very morning I had seen a knife in the bottom of my cup!

"Violent death," I said to Gee Gee Graham, my roommate and best friend. She laughed at me as usual. "And a trip," I said.

She didn't laugh at that. With a quick gulp she finished her tea and handed me her cup. "Tell mine, Gyppy. No knives, but see if you can find a trip for me, too."

"If it's there or not," I said, "a trip for me is a trip for you."

We had worked together since the year ...Well, it was when we were kids that Gee Gee and I both joined the "Seattle Kiddies Revue." We had done boy-and-girl team numbers then. Because Gee Gee was small and blonde and dainty, she was the girl. I wasn't as graceful as I might have been, and the braces on my teeth didn't help my beauty any, so I was the boy.

Since then Gee Gee had gone through several transformations. At the moment she was a redhead and she had developed a temper to go with it. But I could still only think of her as the Gee Gee who had trouped with four guinea pigs, a white rat, and a chameleon.

4

There was no knife and no trip in her cup, but the tea leaves aren't always true. We sent H.I. Moss a wire describing Gee Gee's versatility. Naturally she got the job. A singing, dancing, guitar-playing stripteaser is a good bet at seventy-five a week in any business.

We packed happily for our Broadway debut.

THE OLD OPERA wasn't exactly the show place that Moss had affectionately called it, but it was one of the choice burlesque theaters. In the nineties, when only opera was performed there, it must have been considered elegance personified.

The façade was gray marble, the lobby long and spacious. To the right, there was a wide staircase that led to the balcony and loges. The red carpeting was frayed and worn, the gold leaf peeling symbolically enough from the cherubs that decorated the ceiling. In places, the marble had cracked and had been repaired clumsily with plaster. Full-length, hand-tinted pictures of girls in various forms of undress graced the walls. The one of me, wearing a sunbonnet and holding a bouquet of flowers just large enough to bring the customers in and keep the police out, was third from the left.

Opposite the staircase was the candy butcher's counter, piled high with cigars, cigarettes, and candy bars. An automatic Coca-Cola dispenser stood next to the counter. Moey, an ex-racketeer, ran the concession. He had never been an important racketeer, just a relative of one who found it cheaper to put Moey to work than to support him. He wore a white washcoat when he was working, dazzling checks when the show was over. Strictly a green-fedora guy, but he gave us a ten percent discount on our cokes, so he was popular enough backstage.

Some pretense had been made toward keeping up the front of the theater, but, aside from an occasional sweeping backstage, no one gave much thought to the actors.

The entire chorus dressed in one room just off the stage, the principal women and show girls in a room upstairs, and the men's dressing room was on the top floor. A ventilating pipe ran from the basement room, a small, damp, airless, unused place, through the chorus dressing room, ours, the men's, and right up to the roof of the theater.

We used this pipe as a sort of telephone when we had something to shout from one floor to another, but when we were talking among ourselves we would stuff a makeup towel in it. Otherwise our voices would carry to every room in the theater.

It was Friday of my twenty-eighth week at the Old Opera when we were talking about how to romance Moss into installing a new toilet. It was a subject that came up from time to time, but never before as urgently, and we hadn't thought it confidential enough to stuff the ventilating pipe.

None of the girls had had a really bright idea when Biff Brannigan, the first comic, yelled down, "Look. To keep you tomatoes from squawking so much, we guys are chipping in a buck each for the down payment on a new throne. How's that strike you?"

If Biff had been in any other business and I had been anything but a stripteaser, we would be going steady, or he might have been my beau. In burlesque, romances seem to be different; we eat night lunch together. But that didn't mean that I felt unromantic about Biff. Only at that moment I felt, well, sort of funny. Having him talk about a throne. Even if it had to be talked about.

The old one was by rights a museum piece. It was probably the first one to be built indoors; a collector's item but we weren't collectors, so Biff's suggestion was greeted with enthusiasm. Fourteen of us gathered around the pipe and shouted our thanks to Biff and the boys. The fifteenth, Lolita La Verne, billed as "The Golden-Voiced Goddess," started writing down the names to see how much of a contribution we could depend upon.

"I'll start with the men," she said. It sounded natural coming from her. Moey, the candy butcher, was the only man in the theater she hadn't given the glad eye to and I can't see why she skipped him. He certainly was prettier than Louie Grindero, her saloonkeeper favorite.

Not that I object to a girl taking her sex life seriously, but La Verne overdid it. Maybe it was all right when she was younger, but even though she kept herself well groomed and dressed to the teeth, the bags were under the eyes and the neck hung like an empty salt sack. Her hands gave her away, too. They were bony, greedy-looking hands, and they clutched the pencil as though it were diamond studded.

"Russell Rogers," she said as she wrote.

He was our new straight man, a "Meet chu in the moonlight, m'boy" type. Thought he was too good for burlesque, and made Sardi's his hangout instead of the Peerless or the Baron's, where we all went. He always carried a briefcase full of scripts. "A sensational play that is being tried out in Woodstock this summer," or "the American rights to a terrific thing they did in London last year."

I never saw the manuscripts and always suspected the briefcase bulge of being a couple of old telephone books. But I'm naturally skeptical.

"Russell Rogers," La Verne repeated, with a little twist to her mouth.

Gee Gee looked up from a bedspread she was crocheting. "You said that once, dear. We all caught it."

"Then there's Mandy," La Verne said quickly. He was the second comic and had been shell-shocked in the war. He had a round, happy face and a wife and three kids. La Verne made a fast job of writing *his* name.

"And there's Joey, and Phil, and—oh yes—Biff." She paused and gave me a look as though we were sharing some secret.

"Biff ought to pay double," she added with a sly smile. "He's in here all the time."

"If you're going to figure it that way, don't forget Louie, even if he doesn't work here. And while you're at it, you'd better put

Russell down for his whole salary," I said. "The guys upstairs are forgetting what he looks like."

"Is that so?" La Verne said sarcastically. "Well, someone else had better forget what he looks like, too. Some dames never know when a guy is fed up."

I would never have mentioned Russell's name if I had seen Dolly Baxter standing in the doorway. She was still jealous of him, even though they had sort of split up. The first week La Verne was in the theater she had marked him as her "next." During the weeks following, she had dropped hints that they were splitting their room rent.

Up to now Dolly had ignored them, but tonight there was a tenseness to her mouth and bluish splotches on her cheeks that made me nervous.

I said, "Er—I was just joking with La Verne about how much money we can get out of upstairs for the…"

"Yeah. I caught the end of it." Except for those two splotches, Dolly's face was ashen. She had just finished her number and the skirt of her costume was thrown over her shoulders. Crisp, pinkish hair fell over her puffy eyes and her body paint was streaked with sweat. She was known as "Dynamic Dolly" because she worked so hard and fast, with bumps and grinds that shook the second balcony.

There was something pathetic about her as she unpinned a grouch bag from her G-string and took out a five-dollar bill. "I'll put up the money for Russ," she said, glaring at La Verne. "I've sorta got the habit."

"Good thing you have, girlie," drawled La Verne. "You sure couldn't hold a guy unless you did pay up."

Dolly moved so fast that we couldn't have stopped her if we'd wanted to. All I could see was her arm flashing through the air, the dull gleam of a nail file, then a streak of blood on La Verne's shoulder.

"You baby-faced bitch! I'll mash you to a pulp!"

Gee Gee and I grabbed her, pulling her toward the hall.

La Verne slumped over the makeup shelf, the blood dripping into a powder box. A photograph of a woman, posed like the Saint Cecilia painting, even to the veil and the roses falling on the organ, smiled up at her. La Verne directed her remark to it.

"She tried to disfigure me," she whimpered. "She's always been jealous of my beauty. Oh, my face, my face."

If it had been anyone else but La Verne, it might have made a touching picture. We all knew the picture was her mother, who had died when La Verne was born. La Verne never let the photo out of her hands. When she left the theater at night she took it with her and brought it back the next day.

The picture wasn't the only memento she carried around. Aside from her bankbook which was her Bible and Koran rolled into one, she had her mother's gallstones preserved in alcohol and they were on the shelf, too. At first the gallstones made me a little sick. Later I pretended they were marbles and let it go at that.

This wasn't the first time La Verne had talked to the picture, either. Whenever she was tight, she had long, intimate conversations with it. She wasn't the type for sentimentality, but maybe she was sincere about this one thing. I don't know. I do know that it got pretty tiresome at times and this was one of the times.

Dolly was struggling to get free and shouting so loudly that even Stachi, the doorman, was alarmed enough to join the crowd at the door. Most of the stagehands were in the group and I asked one of them to help me hold Dolly. Gee Gee had to go down to do her number so we were short of hands.

"Jealous of her beauty," Dolly shouted. "Who in the hell would be jealous of a sewer-mouth son of a bitch like her?"

A couple of men grabbed Dolly, but then we had La Verne to handle. She had jumped up from her chair and was making a dive for Dolly.

"It's only an expression," I kept saying. "She doesn't mean that your mother was…"

9

La Verne winced with pain as I touched her shoulder. She dropped weakly into her chair. Sandra, one of the strippers, handed me Gee Gee's bottle of gin.

"Here. Clean it with this," she said. "It's alcohol. You know, like they use in the hospitals."

When I poured on the gin, La Verne's screams were partly for the sting, but mostly to keep the center of the stage for herself. Dolly was getting altogether too much attention from the men who were trying to restrain her from rushing back into the room.

"Dirty hypocrite!" Dolly yelled. "Carrying her mother's picture around all the time. You don't see any sign of a father, do you?"

One of the men put his hand over her mouth but it was too late. They started dragging her upstairs, urging her to have a drink and forget it.

Her voice, hoarse with anger, came through the ventilator. "She's a whore and her mother was a whore."

I quickly stuffed a towel in the pipe, but within a few seconds that wasn't necessary. The stagehands were setting the "Under the Sea" ballet and the show was going on as usual.

La Verne stopped sobbing, but she was going into another number: the tragic queen, Mary of the Scots, and a little Joan of Arc thrown in for good measure.

"Thank God, Mother, I still have my voice."

"Yes, and you do still have your fatal beauty." I was too bored with her to spare her feelings. My voice was cold. "This is only a scratch. Anyway, you had it coming to you. If you don't stop tormenting Dolly, she really will get you one of these days."

"And if she doesn't, I will!" It was Gee Gee, tearing furiously into the room. The little balls on her Spanish hat were spinning like a windmill. I felt a breeze as she passed me.

"Gimme that." She grabbed the bottle of gin. Then she took off the guitar hanging from a ribbon around her neck. "It's tough enough doing *La Paloma* for those jerks out front without you and Dolly calling each other by your right names. Ruining my specialty because of a toilet!"

La Verne turned away to repair her tear-stained makeup, and suddenly Gee Gee started laughing.

"Gyppy, you'da died if you'd seen the Hermit crawling down from the fly gallery when the fight was on. He was in such a rush not to miss anything that he damn near broke his neck. He kept looking over his shoulder instead of looking at the rungs of that iron ladder and every now and then he'd miss."

Gee Gee flopped into a chair and put her feet on the shelf. "Then, when the 'Golden-Voiced Goddess' gets called a ..."

"Shh." I nudged Gee Gee and gave her the eye. La Verne was tensing herself, and it wouldn't have taken much for the fireworks to start all over again.

Gee Gee took the hint. "Well, anyway, when the names get called back and forth, he's already down onstage and in a flash he's on his way up to our dressing rooms! Him! Can you imagine? Not only that, but who do you think he runs into! Stachi! I tell you, Gyp, when the two of them got together it was a scream. Boy, did they start dishing us. They were both a little embarrassed to catch each other on our landing anyway. So real chummy like they get out to Stachi's corner in the stage entrance. Then they opened up. What they said about us!"

The very thought of the conversation made Gee Gee roar with laughter, but I couldn't see the funny side of it at all. I remembered Stachi's face when he stood on the landing. There was so much disgust in it that I felt, well, sort of naked.

Stachi and the Hermit were the only two old-timers in the theater. Everyone said they went with the lease and I guess it was true. Stachi had been there since the days of the Old Opera's grandeur. He was a singer and then something happened to his voice. He had taken smaller and smaller roles until he finally wound up as doorman.

The Hermit had been there almost as long. He had always been a stagehand but now he was too old to do any of the harder work, so he handled the flies. Some of the curtains worked automatically, but a lot of them were the old ones that operated on the sandbag principle. He handled those from the ceiling of the theater. It wasn't a hard job, but it was a lonesome one. He usually climbed up once a day and stayed there until the end of the night show.

Neither of them wasted much love on the burlesque actors. When they got together they talked of the past glory of the theater, and I guess they thought we were interlopers. We must have sounded like a band of wild Indians when we got started, so I could hardly blame them.

"They kept shaking their heads and clucking their bridge-work," Gee Gee said. She was impersonating the Hermit and had to stand up to make the act convincing. With her knees bent and her lips drawn tightly over her teeth, she walked around the room. "Yessir," she cackled, "it's a good thing Lily isn't here to see the class of people that are in her old dressing room."

Even La Verne had to laugh.

"The two of 'em keep shaking their heads at that dame's picture, you know. The one with a spear that Stachi's got hanging on the wall back of his chair. Well, the Hermit is doing a La Verne and talking to it like it was a person."

"My Gawd!" La Verne dropped her powder puff and turned to Gee Gee. First I thought she was mad again because Gee Gee said the Hermit was doing a La Verne, then I realized she was going elegant on us.

"That *dame* happens to be a picture of Lilli Lehmann in her Brünnehilde costume." If La Verne had been Brünnehilde herself she couldn't have been more indignant.

Gee Gee sniffed. "Well, she doesn't look so hot to me. And I'd sure hate to strip that regalia she's got on."

"She didn't strip. She sang." Our wounded Prima Donna looked at Gee Gee coldly. "There's other kinds of show business besides burlesque, you know."

The sarcasm was wasted on Gee Gee. "Sure, I know," she said, "there's movies and radio and…"

"And grand opera. Lilli Lehmann was a singer."

"Well, what was she doing in a burlesque theater, then?" Gee Gee said.

"It wasn't a burlesque theater then, you dope. It was an opera house."

Gee Gee was trying to figure that one out when the show girls came in, babbling as usual. They had just finished the ballet and were dressed in seaweed costumes. With the exception of Alice, the eight of them looked enough alike to be sisters. They were all blondes and all six-footers. H.I. Moss was very proud of them and they knew it, so they ran the strippers a close second for temperament.

"Did you see the old Gee that sends me the perfume?" one of them asked as she began undressing.

Alice Angel, the prettiest of the eight, pouted. When she wasn't pouting she was crying. She was that type. It didn't take much to make her do either, but she had a legitimate beef this time.

The perfume man had been hers for several weeks, and even though she didn't like the Djer Kiss, she did like the attention.

"He probably realithed I wathn't that thort of girl." Stepping out of her pearl costume, Alice hung it carefully on the back of her chair. She was the "Spirit of the Pearl" in the ballet and it was a coveted spot in the show.

"Anyway, I'm too buthy rehearthing to bother with twifelth." She spoke with airy unconcern. "Moth hath told me that ath thoon ath I get ready he'll let me do a thpethialty." She looked down her nose at Jean. "Tho there."

Jean wasn't interested. "What's this about a new toilet?" she asked.

We told her of the plans.

Gee Gee was balancing a mirror in one hand and an eyebrow tweezer in the other. "Yep. Everybody chips in a buck, she said

13

between pulls. Then she giggled. "Hey, Gyp, can you imagine that Lilli dame in the iron suit trying to..."

The picture was too much for her. She collapsed with laughter.

"When we get the new toilet, let's wrap the old one up like a Christmas present and give it to the Gruesome Twosome."

"Who'th that?" Alice asked, and Gee Gee paused a moment to get her breath.

"The Hermit and old man Stachi," she said, "They can press it in their memory book!"

TWO

DURING THE NIGHT SHOW, WHEN BIFF AND I WERE doing the "Pickle Persuader" bit in the second act, the stage manager waved frantically to me from the wings. He was clearly upset, so I knew there was trouble. I looked at the footlights for the red bulb to flash: that was our signal to cover up or clean up because a censor was in the lobby. If a strange cop, or anyone who even looked like a censor, came in, the ticket taker buzzed the electrician backstage, and the electrician used the red light to relay the warning to the actors.

But the light didn't flash. So I wasn't quite sure what was the matter.

Russell was playing straight for the scene and I saw him look out front. My eyes followed his. In the back of the theater, their buttons and badges shining in the dark, there were cops—at least twenty of them. It looked like a policemen's convention.

Then H.I. Moss padded swiftly down the aisle. There was no question about it. This was going to be more serious than the usual reprimand from the police.

Russell's voice shook a little, but he went on with the scene.

"Just wave this persuader under her nose and she'll give you anything you ask for."

"Anything?" With the police watching, Biff cut the habitual leer. "Would you sell it to me?"

"It's a very valuable article, m'boy," Russell said. "However, because you have an honest face, and because I like you, I will sell it. For one hundred dollars."

Biff shoved the money into Russell's hands. That was Russell's exit cue. And not a moment too soon, I thought. When he got to the wings he managed his last line.

"Remember, m'boy. Just wave it under her nose."

Biff held the pickle tenderly by the string that was tied around it. "Anything I ask for," he mumbled as he approached me, "anything." He was swinging the pickle.

"When the lights black out," he said under his breath, "try to get away through the coal chute. This is a raid."

I stared at him stupidly.

Biff went on in a loud voice, "Give me your money."

I bent over to get the money out of my pocket while Biff ogled my leg. "I don't know where the coal chute is," I whispered.

Biff pocketed the money. "Now give me a kiss."

I puckered up my lips. He barely breathed the words against my mouth.

"In the cellar next to the vacant room, through the hall."

Biff went through the business of counting the money and mechanically whispering in my ear. I couldn't put much heart into it, but I slapped his face, and that was the cue for the blackout where I made my exit. The orchestra was playing "Happy Days Are Here Again," which, under the circumstances, was the end of the show and meant that the audience was leaving.

"In the cellar, next to the unused dressing room," I whispered over and over again.

It was pitch-dark backstage. Someone, the electrician probably, had killed all the backstage lights. I thought maybe somebody did it to help the actors get out of the theater, but it made me feel panicky. I couldn't tell where I was going at all. I lost all sense of direction.

There were scuffling noises of people moving in the dark and then someone brushed against me. I didn't wait to find out who it was. I just kept on running. For all I knew I might be running into the arms of the nearest policeman. But it didn't matter.

Then my hands touched something curved and cold, the water cooler. Now I was all right. The cellar steps were to the left. I groped for the iron railing.

As my foot scraped the top step of the spiral staircase I felt a hand on my shoulder, then another on my throat. Suddenly two thumbs were pressed hard against my vocal cords. I dug my nails into the hands, but they only pressed tighter.

My mind suddenly blacked out, too. The hands loosened and I came to. I didn't even know it was I screaming.

The lights went on, all of them at once. A voice boomed in my ears.

"Where do you think you're going?"

The fingers now held my arm in a vise. I twisted around and sank my teeth into the hand. It had coarse red hair on it that caught in my teeth like shredded wheat. I tried to bite again, hair or no hair. As I lunged I looked down at a pair of thick-soled shoes, massive legs, and a *skirt*!

"Don't you bite me, you hussy," the policewoman bellowed, "or I'll bite you back."

"You don't have to strangle me."

I tried moving my neck around to see if it would still work. It worked all right, but I had to handle it carefully. I was mad clear through, so just for luck I gave those fat legs a good, swift kick.

The woman grabbed my other arm and started shaking me. I've been in a cyclone in Kansas, an earthquake in California, and once I was in an elevator that dropped four floors, but compared to her those things were kid stuff.

I wasn't the only one who was being rough-hustled. There was a cop struggling with Sandra, who was half naked. Another was fighting it out with Russell in the wings. Gee Gee was pounding

17

a copper on the head. If I hadn't been so mad I might have felt a little sorry for him.

"No use trying to get away," he shouted between thumps. "We have the place surrounded."

There was a shrill whistle and more blue uniforms piled over the footlights.

"Stop it! Don't fight!" It was Moss, climbing over the extended apron. "Don't fight! I'll fix everything."

The struggle ceased. Uniforms were straightened. Girls arranged their loosened kimonos. Then they were all crowding around Moss. There were a few muttered curses from the men and scattered nervous giggles from the girls.

My captor, the hairy-handed Amazon, shoved me ahead of her. "Get in line with the rest of the scum."

Moss was making a speech, trembling and wiping the sweat from his face with a limp handkerchief. His eyes, through the bifocal lenses, looked like Smith Brothers' cough drops.

"H.I. Moss has never in all the years he's been in the business let his actors down."

There was a round of subdued applause. Phil called, "That's right."

The little man held up a pudgy hand for quiet. "You will be out in an hour. I give you my word."

The applause was louder.

"And you are *not* riding in the wagon!" He waited a moment for the announcement to sink in. "I, H.I. Moss, out of my own pocket, have hired Cadillacs to take you to jail."

"Three cheers for Moss, our boss," yelled Mandy. The response was deafening.

Moss smiled, and accepted the tribute with the hint of a bow. "No artist that's working under the Moss banner rides in a pie wagon."

THE RIDE TO the police station began with some bravado. There were the usual stock jokes.

"I'm glad I got here early. The last time I took a ride I had to stand all the way..."

"This is the way I like to travel...for free..."

The cops in the car ahead of us had my sympathy. La Verne and Russell had already climbed in with Gee Gee when Dolly Baxter elbowed her way past those in front of her and jumped in beside them. Through the window I saw a tangle of arms. If Dolly was in form, Russell was getting the worst of it. I was a little pleased.

Biff was seated on the jump seat of our car. He had a bottle, and between gulps his voice rang out, "*If I had the wings of an angel, Over these...*"

Sandra Slade and Jannine, who were sharing the bottle, began harmonizing with him, "*. . .prison walls I would fly...*"

As we neared the station Biff leaned forward and poked one of the cops in the front seat on the shoulder. "You're a public servant, aren't you?"

The cop looked at him coldly.

"Yes, I am," he said.

Biff gave us a broad wink and said, "Well, then, get me a glass of water."

"What you hyenas need is a padded cell," said our uniformed escort.

The gray walls of the station sobered me at once. The steps leading to the entrance were almost blocked by news photographers and the curious. There were several cars in our safari and word must have spread that they were filled with burlesque actors. The policeman told us to get out and follow him while another cop brought up the rear. Jannine and Sandra climbed out of the car, smiling as the cameras clicked. Sandra raised her skirt as she started up the stairs; she turned and winked at one of the cameramen.

"That's one picture they'll use," she said to Jannine as they passed between the green lights.

I felt too sick to move. Everything had happened so quickly

that I hadn't realized I was actually on my way to jail. Biff held my arm. "Steady, Gypper," he said. "This is all in a day's work."

I had to brace myself to make the walk through the yelling crowd. The entrance was only a few feet away but it seemed like miles. A woman rushed up to me.

"I could have a fur coat, too, if I wanted to do what you do."

Another dragged her gaping child away. "Get away from that vile woman," she said, almost pulling the poor kid's arm out of joint.

A gray-haired man tossed a bunch of flowers at my feet. "*She walks in beauty, like the night,*" he quoted, and was roughly pushed aside.

Biff whispered, "Your public, Punkin." I tried to smile at him but I felt too much like Marie Antoinette being led to the guillotine to put much personality in it.

At the doorway Biff was told to wait and I was directed down a long hall. At the end was a huge oak door. Another policeman opened it and told me to enter.

I faced a theater audience! Instead of a stage there was a desk, but otherwise everything was the same. I even recognized most of the customers; the sailor who used to bring his dinner with him and sit through all four performances, Alice's perfume man, even the one that sent Dolly flowers on Mother's Day. They smiled encouragingly as I entered, and there was a scattered round of applause.

The sound of a gavel hitting the desk made me turn. The judge was a woman! And not a pretty prospect either. She was a little like the one that had arrested me, but instead of reddish hair, hers was black. She wore it pulled tightly behind her ears and she had a mole, with a hair growing from it, on her cheek. I heard Dolly gasp when she looked at her, and I couldn't blame her. The woman's angry eyes looked reprovingly at the audience. When they were silenced she nodded to a policeman and he took Sandra's arm. While he led her to the desk I felt my legs go weak.

I stared at the mole while the woman barked questions at Sandra.

"What's your name…age…American citizen? …" The woman was writing the answers on a card that looked like an application blank.

Suddenly I realized that I was standing before her. Automatically, I answered the questions. In a shallow wire basket to her right I saw a stack of the cards. Sandra's was on top. Hardly aware of what I was doing, I read it. There was a space that said "charge." After it, in broad penstrokes, was written "prostitution."

The full significance of that word slowly hit me. I stared at the card, not believing what was there. I watched her filling out the other spaces on my card. When she got to the charge blank I saw her write "Prost…"

"What are you putting down?" I heard myself shout.

"I'm booking you for prostitution, and don't speak unless you're asked to."

"Speak?" I screamed. "I'll tear this jail down, I'll…"

"Well, then," she said coldly, "what are you in for?"

"I'm an actress. A stripteaser."

"What's the difference?" said the matron and finished, "…itution."

La Verne was next in line and her screams added to mine made a healthy racket. There was some purpose to her noise. She demanded a telephone. One of the policemen led her to a pay booth at the end of the room. She turned and winked at me.

"Louie'll fix these tin-badge coppers," she said. "Let them put down what they want to. The more they put down the more he'll shove…"

The cop interrupted her. "Did you want to telephone?"

"…the more he'll shove down their throats," La Verne finished triumphantly.

The mention of threats reminded me of mine. While La Verne dialed her number I told the matron about the arresting officer choking me.

"If I hadn't screamed," I said, "she would have strangled me."

"Move along," the matron said indifferently. "Next."

A policeman approached the matron and whispered in her ear. She frowned at him, then she went through the cards and began scratching something out of each one with her pen. When she wrote on mine I saw that she put "Producing an obscene play" in place of "Prostitution." I'd won my point, but I didn't feel any better about it.

In the meantime, La Verne had reached Louie on the phone. She left the door of the booth open and I heard her say, "But, Sugar, I was sure you could fix it." Her scowl deepened as she waited. From her expression I had a good idea of what Sugar was saying and I knew it was nothing about fixing anything. Now, if it had been a nice, gory murder, Louie and his lawyers might have been some help, but a little thing like a raid was beneath their dignity.

" . . .But, baby, they were so mean to us." La Verne's silky voice wasn't fooling me and I doubt if it had any more effect on Louie.

I could visualize him on the other end of the phone. He was probably in his office at the back of the saloon. His feet, in their sharp-toed shoes, would be on the ornate desk, a cigar clenched in his yellow teeth and his mouth turned up in that horrible grin.

Louie was certainly no beauty boy. The grin alone made him hideous; when you add squinty eyes and black oily hair to the top of the face you get something you wouldn't want to run into in an alley, especially if it was broad daylight.

His last name, Grindero, might account for his nickname, "The Grin," but I think it dates back to the time he was in a street fight and someone tore his entire jaw loose. The doctor who fixed it must have been in a hurry—I'm sure some thug had a gun at his back when he operated—anyway, he sewed Louie's mouth up at the corners. Maybe he thought a perpetual smile would help the personality. Two thin scars pointed from Louie's mouth to the cheekbones. When he was angry the scars turned red. I thought they might have been red at that moment. No one likes to be called a clown-faced baboon, which was the least original description La Verne was using.

"If I stay in this clink overnight you'll be damned sorry," she shouted and slammed the receiver on the hook.

The night-court audience was having a wonderful time; between listening to La Verne and watching Dolly, it was a good show. Dolly was pulling her girdle down and her stockings up. She gave them a flash of leg before she went to the desk. La Verne sauntered out to the wooden railing where I was standing.

"Get a load of the makeup on Dolly," she whispered.

I hadn't noticed anything unusual about Dolly's appearance until La Verne called my attention to it. One look and I understood her amazement. Dolly not only had put on horn-rimmed glasses, but she had splashed lipstick from ear to ear! Her hair was pushed up under her hat and one eye was jumping, as though she had a tic.

Even her voice was different. When the matron asked her name she said, "Margaret Morgan."

La Verne nudged me. "She can't get away with that. They'll give her ten years for perjury." She smiled with a hint of satisfaction. "Ten years added to forty-some-odd will make it just dandy for her when she gets out."

A policeman was telling Biff that the men could leave. Biff was more surprised than pleased.

"Say, if you got any pull around here," he said confidentially to the cop, "I'll make it worth your while to see that the women aren't put in a cell with a lot of cokies."

"Put us in a cell!" His words made me forget about Dolly. I hadn't thought of what was coming later. It seemed bad enough to be standing in the courtroom having all those people stare at me with all my clothes on. But a *cell*!

And a cell it was! There might have been worse cells in the jail but ours certainly wasn't the bridal suite. The five women who were in ahead of us had taken most of the bed space, if you could call those unglorified boards beds.

There was an unpleasant odor in the small room that grew thicker and thicker. One of the women swayed in my direction. If I hadn't seen her move I'd swear she'd been dead for years.

"What are you in for?" the zombie asked.

I was in no mood for girlish confidences but Gee Gee spoke up, "Mopery."

"Ah, they can't put you in for that," said the woman with a beery smile. "Now take me f'rinstance…"

But Gee Gee had taken enough. One good whiff did it. She moved hastily away.

Two of the other women were playing pinochle on one of the cots. "Get one of your friends," said the thin-faced Negress who was playing, "and we'll play four-handed." She had sores on her face and neck; as she spoke she scratched her face with her cards.

"What about you, girlie?" the other woman said, beckoning to me. I tried to answer but could only shake my head. The stench and close air had me reeling.

I put my face as close to the bars as I could, and breathed deeply. Dolly stood next to me at the cell door with her hands clutching the bars. I hoped there might be a window open somewhere and if there was a breath of clean air I wanted to get it before it hit the room.

"Stinks, doesn't it?" Dolly spoke calmly, but I saw that her knuckles were white from their stranglehold on the bars. She was right about the odor; the corridor was almost as bad as the cell.

"How'd you like to spend ten days in a place like this?"

"Don't think about it," I said with more confidence than I felt. "Moss said he'd get us out in an hour and he usually keeps his word."

Dolly was silent. The only light came from a green-shaded globe at the far end of the hall. As it filtered through the cell the bars made long shadows on her face. A strand of pinkish hair had fallen from under her hat.

"I wish I'd had sense enough to give a false name, too," I said.

Dolly stared straight ahead. "Are you kiddin'?" she asked tonelessly.

"No, I mean…well, if you give a false name the newspapers…"

"You're a dope. Why don't you shut up," Dolly said.

I started to walk away from her but she put her hand on my arm. "Wait a minute, Gyp. I didn't mean to snap at ya but…dammit, I'm afraid."

That was obvious, but I still wasn't mollified.

"I think that dame at the desk recognized me," Dolly whispered. She looked quickly to see if La Verne was listening. The Prima Donna was talking to Gee Gee; Dolly went on: "She's the same one that sentenced me two years ago. Gave me ten days at hard labor. If she ever gets wise to who I am it's curtains…it's my third time up and they told me the last time to leave town and never come back. Leave town? Hell's bells, I gotta make a livin'. Where else can I go? I'm played out on Moss' circuit and I ain't even known in the West."

"She didn't look at you like she recognized you," I said.

"You don't know that dame," Dolly replied wearily. "She'd be dirty enough to string me along. Of all the guys on the police force I gotta run into her."

She was silent for a moment. I tried to say something but the words wouldn't come. That same feeling of pity I always had for Dolly seemed to choke me.

"Oh, it ain't the ten days I worry so much about," she said slowly. "It's Moss. If the cops get a conviction he'll lose his license sure as hell."

"What do you mean?" I asked quickly. "They can't do anything to him for what you do."

"Maybe not, ordinarily. But this new license commissioner has been waitin' for a crack at the Old Opera since he got in office.

Reform ticket or something. All he needs is a verdict of 'guilty' and he cancels the license. Why do you think Moss spends all that dough to get warnings when the censors are in the joint? Do you think he shells out to every cop on the beat because he wants 'em to have the finer things in life?"

"He must have slipped up on a payment," I said, "because we didn't get any warning this time."

Dolly wasn't listening to me. She looked at the bars in front of her.

"When they say hard labor they ain't kiddin'," she said. "They put me in the laundry. I stood over a tub scrubbin' heavy sheets and filthy rags for ten days. They gave me soap that was so damned strong it took all the skin off my hands. Even when they was bleedin', the matron wouldn't give me anything to put on 'em. Gawdawmighty, they were sore. My back was damn near broken from bendin' over and I got that neuritis that still bothers me from standin' in a puddle of stinkin' water from six to six."

She laughed, a mirthless laugh. "Dolly Baxter," she said. "Tub eight, American Family soap."

It was almost like a music cue; when she stopped talking I heard the sound of running water. Then Sandra's voice: "Look, ain't they considerate? We got a sink and everything."

I could just see her outline in the corner of the dark cell. She was taking off her dress and slip. When she got down to her undies, she took off her brassière and began rinsing it.

The card players stared at her with their mouths open.

"What in hell are ya doing?" one of them asked.

Sandra put on the dripping brassière, the water must have been cold because her teeth chattered and there were goose bumps on her legs and arms.

"Best thing in the world to keep your breasts from falling," she said. "Do it every night of my life."

A bundle of rags detached itself from the farthest corner. A tiny head emerged and stared at Sandra. It was like one of those heads the Indians prepare when they take all the bones out and fill the skull with clay; shrinking the head and making the skin look like tanned leather.

"There are devils in your body." The mouth snapped shut as though it were wired.

Sandra screamed and ran to the barred door.

The face spoke again: "I will drive the devils from your body. I will save you from a life of sin."

A policewoman peered into the cell. "Stop this noise." The rags collapsed and were still, then the policewoman laughed. "She'll be all right until morning." Her heavy footsteps echoed down the corridor while I got Sandra over to a cot where Gee Gee and Jannine were sitting. I threw my coat over her but she still shivered. We made room for La Verne and Dolly, and the six of us sat there, silent and miserable.

One of the other women spoke: "It'll go tough on me this time." She was a big blonde and she wore a red sweater that emphasized every line of her lumpy body. "Yep. They caught me with the stuff right on me. Third offense, too."

She sucked a tooth noisily and I wondered what she meant by "stuff." Dope, I decided.

"What did they get you dames on?" she asked.

La Verne spoke up. "They booked us on prostitution, but..."

"That's what they got Flossie on." The blonde tossed a thumb in the Negress' direction.

"Well, I know my rights," La Verne snapped. "They changed it or they woulda had a nice case on their hands...I'da sued 'em for false arrest or something."

"Yeah." The blonde found something in another tooth. "Who ya gonna sue? City Hall? Hell of a lotta good that'll do you. What *are* ya in for?"

"They pinched a theater I'm working in, a burlesque theater."

"You mean you're a burlesque dame?" Her voice was suddenly hostile. "These others, too?"

Dolly nodded.

27

The blonde moved away. "There's two things I hate," she said. "One's a baby killer, the other's a dame that strips down naked for a bunch of morons." She spat on the cement floor.

The Negress looked up from her cards. "It's bitches like you that are ruining my business."

Luckily, at this point the matron unlocked the door. "The six of you that came in last, walk out. One at a time."

We filed out without looking back. The blonde's angry voice followed us down the corridor right into the anteroom where Moss was waiting. The familiar smile was still there, his manner as courtly as ever.

"I said an hour, didn't I?"

He looked gravely at his thick gold watch. "Well, it's been exactly one hour and ten minutes. To celebrate ...I, H.I. Moss, invite you all to Moore's for a snack. Steaks and champagne."

At the door someone grabbed my arm. I felt a quick panic. It was the policewoman whose furry hand I had bitten. She gave me a searching look.

"I'm sorry I had to meet you under such circumstances," she said. "You know, if things had been different, we could have had a lot of fun together."

H.I. MOSS HAD reserved the entire second floor of Moore's restaurant for his celebration party. A long table was already set when we arrived. Ferns and carnations made a decorative centerpiece and gleaming champagne buckets separated every other chair. The waiters stood at attention as we made our boisterous entrance. We had picked up the men at the bar downstairs where they had been waiting. It was evident they hadn't been idly waiting.

"What in hell were *you* celebrating?" Dolly asked Russell Rogers. He had a death grip on a chair and it was the only thing that kept him from falling flat on his face.

"Wassh it to you?" he asked. Dolly didn't have time to answer him because La Verne had come between them and was smiling up into Russell's bleary eyes.

"We'll sit over here, Sugar," she said, leading him to a place near the head of the table.

"I hope she gets diabetes, with all that sugar," Gee Gee whispered to me. Russell leaned over and kissed the Prima Donna's ear.

Dolly turned her head away from them, then she pulled out a chair and sank into it. Moss had taken his place at the head of the table. "Everybody find seats and sit in them. I have a short announcement to make."

When the scuffling was over I found that I was sitting between Biff and Gee Gee. Mandy, the second comic, and Joey, his partner, were next. Farther down, Phil, the tenor, was helping Jannine with her coat. Sandra had put her blouse on inside out; she was still too dazed to realize it. Her mascara had run and she was rubbing her cheek with the wet end of a napkin.

Moss raised a hand and the commanding gesture had its effect. We all looked at him attentively.

"For me to apologize for what has happened," he said, "would be like apologizing because a mountain moved, making an avalanche." The attention he was getting seemed to please him; he let a smile cross his face.

"Nor do I expect apologies from any of you," he said. "I was watching the show from out front, not one actor did anything that would warrant such a . . .an ignoble act as that raid. Believe me, the stigma will be erased from your names."

There was a subdued round of applause, then Moss beckoned to a waiter and the champagne began to flow. Moss had remained standing and when the last glass had been filled he spoke.

"I drink a toast to my actors!" He drained his glass. The actors still looked at him; no one spoke and no one moved to drink. It was as though we waited for a royal command. Moss gazed with appreciation at his glass before he placed it carefully on the table.

He didn't seem to notice that none of us drank. With a half smile he took a cigar from his pocket and held a match to the end of it. Before speaking he let his eyes rest on each one of us.

"Some people must think that I'm *non compos mentis*; some people must think I'm a dope," he said slowly. "They must think the Old Opera is run by such a loony that he doesn't know what's what. I'm saying right now, and these four walls are my witness, not one thing goes on in any of my theaters that I don't know about. I know almost what you eat for breakfast. I know everything! For instance, number one." He held up his pudgy hand and turned down his thumb. "I know that there are inside forces that would like to see the Old Opera closed! Number two," he turned down another finger, "I know why! There is room for only one behind in the manager's chair and that behind is *mine*! Some people don't like that, they got ideas, big ideas. They want I should make a little room for them so they can move in. But they can't because I, H.I. Moss, am no dope. I own the controlling interest in the theater stock and what I say is the law."

He made a fist and pounded on the table with such force that his glasses slipped down on his nose. As he adjusted them he looked again at the silent actors. He waited just long enough for his next statement.

"Someone in *my* theater is responsible for the raid! Someone in *my* theater deliberately phoned in a complaint to the Purity League. Then they called the police. They deliberately kept the light from flashing in the footlights. I wasn't notified until it was too late to contact my friends in the station and settle the beef amicably. Yes: someone thinks they are smarter than H.I. Moss. How do I know these things, you ask? Because I got friends, that's why. I got friends that warn me of such schlemihls. This is my answer to such a dog."

He beckoned to a waiter. "Bring me the briefcase I left at the desk."

In a moment the waiter returned carrying a black leather case.

Moss took it from him and unhooked the catch, opened the two leather straps, and emptied the contents of the briefcase on the table. A sheaf of papers fell out, legal-looking papers, folded three times and clipped together at the ends. Moss picked up one of them and held it for La Verne to look at.

Her mouth fell open. "Why, it's a ..."

Moss interrupted her. "Yes, it's a share of stock for the Old Opera theater. My personal stock. To each and every one of my actors I give free and without cost one paid-in-full-share." He called to Mandy who walked to the head of the table. Moss patted him on the shoulder and handed him the paper. "This is my answer to the schlemihl who thinks he can close the backbone of the burlesque industry."

Mandy looked stupidly from the stock to Moss. Then he mumbled a self-conscious thanks and went back to his chair. It wasn't until he sat down and opened the paper that the realization of what Moss had done struck any of us. Phil leaned over Mandy's chair to read the small print on the paper. Moss had them printed especially. His slogans—*Gold in your pocket when there's silver in your hair*, and *Don't take a loss; share with Moss*—were in black letters across the top.

"These are the same ones we have been *buying*!" Phil said happily.

Moss beamed. "And why not? To me actors are like people; they work better when they work for themselves."

La Verne nudged Russell as Moss was talking. "Work for themselves, hell. Those damn stocks aren't worth a quarter if the theater really should get closed up. Now if he'd give us some of that old stock he's got it'd be different..."

Moss was bowing and accepting the thanks of the actors. I hoped he was too busy to hear La Verne. Biff heard her, though; he cocked an eyebrow at me.

"Our Prima Donna is looking a gift horse in the mouth again," he said.

When I laughed my throat ached. I looked in my compact mirror to see if there were any marks, and Biff asked me what was the matter.

"When that big-fisted female arrested me she damn near choked me to death," I said. Then I stopped short, it was the "big-fisted" line that made me remember; remember digging at the hand with my nails when it was around my throat. But those hands were *thin!* The policewoman's hands were thick and fat.

"Those stiff red hairs . . .they weren't on the hands that choked me. Biff! *It wasn't the policewoman that tried to strangle me!*"

Biff looked at me out of the corner of his eye, then he looked at the full champagne glass. "If just smellin' that stuff makes you drunk you better stick to your Seagram's no crown," he said. "Want me to think someone tried to kill ya?"

"Nooo ..." I admitted, "but I did feel the hands and they did press awful hard, then the lights going off and everything, Moss saying that it was an inside job and ..."

"It's too coincidental," Biff replied easily. "You keep reading them dime thrillers and you give yourself ideas. If someone grabbed you it's only because they were trying to find their way out, too. How could they see in the dark? And anyhow, who'd want to . . .oh, skip it, Punkin."

His smile made me feel a little better but I still thought that a neck was the last thing anyone would grab for unless they had a strangling intention.

Gee Gee was marching back to her chair. She clutched her share of stock in her hand as she nudged Biff.

"Hey, you're on," she whispered. "Don't keep Santa Claus waiting."

Biff pushed his chair back and sauntered to the head of the table. He was trying too hard to look unconcerned, like a kid getting a prize from a Sunday-school grab bag.

Mandy hissed at him as he went past, "Don't forget to say thank you to the nice man."

Biff ignored him, but the back of his neck was red. He grabbed the paper from Moss and made fast tracks back to his chair. Before he sat down he gulped his glass of champagne.

"That was an ordeal," he admitted. I wasn't sure if he meant accepting the gift or drinking the wine. It was probably a little of each because he made a face as he put down his glass.

"What's with the dialogue about champagne?" he said. "Tastes like citrate of magnesia to me."

Mandy had finished his drink, too. He poured the last few drops in his frizzy hair and began massaging it vigorously. "Anybody ever asks me if I drank champagne I can tell 'em I not only drank it but I bathed in it. And damned if bathing in it isn't better than drinking it."

Moss must have expected something like that because the next chorus of waiters brought bottles of Scotch and rye. He may not have been generous enough to please La Verne with the stocks but he certainly wasn't throwing a skimpy party; I got dizzy watching the bottles fly past me. He wasn't kidding about the steaks either; they were the biggest, most beautiful Porterhouses I'd ever seen.

One of the waiters put a plate in front of Moss, but Moss waved it away with a graceful hand. He turned his champagne glass around and put it to his nose; he closed his eyes when he breathed in the aroma.

A Bacchus in bifocals, I thought. He frowned and I had a sudden fear that I had spoken aloud. But Moss got to his feet again and let his eyes survey the table.

"Anybody that would try to break up this happy little family is worse than a schlemihl," he said.

As usual, Moss was right.

THREE

IT WAS SO CLOSE TO SHOW TIME WHEN THE PARTY broke up that Biff and I went right on to the theater. We took a double-decker bus to the end of Fifth Avenue and walked from there. Biff thought the air would do us good but I knew it was going to take more than a little air to make me feel like playing the matinee.

The night before had been too hectic for me; raids and champagne don't mix.

"Maybe an aspirin would help," Biff suggested.

We walked to the drugstore near the theater and Biff had coffee. I tried an aspirin, a bromo, then an Alka-Seltzer. By then I was feeling healthy enough to have coffee too.

During my second cup, I told Biff about Dolly's police record and what she had said about the license commissioner wanting an excuse to close the theater.

"Well," he replied vaguely, "that leaves her out. She certainly wasn't the one that tipped the cops."

It took me a moment to understand him, then I remembered Moss saying that the raid was an inside information thing.

"But does that mean that anyone can call the police and complain about a theater or something and bring about a raid?" I asked. It didn't sound right to me somehow. "At that rate I could complain about a revival meeting! That is if…"

"In burlesque, it's different," Biff explained. "First of all, it isn't the police so much as it is these self-appointed 'Purity Leagues.' They're beefing all the time to the cops. Naturally the cops can't ignore 'em. Not all the time anyway. So the cops call Moss and say that they're dropping in for a visit. Then we get our warning in the foots. By the time they get to the theater, there's nothing for them to see."

"What do they see anyway?" I exclaimed. "What's the difference between a pair of net pants that doesn't show from the front of the house and, well . . .no pants? I don't get it. Another thing. If someone in the theater *did* call the police they'd be jeopardizing their own jobs. Even the stock would be worthless, and now we're all stockholders."

"The old stock would still be good," Biff reminded me. "Say, for instance, that some big corporation is going to build a subway and they want to build it where the Old Opera is. Whoever owns the land is going to make himself a pretty buck or two. They aren't going to let a burlesque show stand in their way, you can bet on that. In our case the land is owned by stockholders. Moss has got a lot of shares but he wouldn't have to tip the cops. All he'd have to do is close down. In his lease it says the theater has got to stay open. He can close it for a month or so . . .alteration clause or something, but if it closes longer than that he's out. La Verne is a good example, too. She's got some of the old stock."

The counter boy put an order of scrambled eggs in front of Biff. While he ate them I thought about what he had told me.

"She wouldn't call the police unless she was out of the theater," I said. I was really talking to myself, Biff was too busy eating to listen. Lolita La Verne, the Golden-Voiced Goddess, in a police line-up. Not if she could help it, I thought.

"She couldn't have kept the footlights from flashing anyway," I said aloud.

Between mouthfuls Biff asked, "Why not? All she'd have to do is stand near the switchboard and cover the buzzer. She could lean an arm on it or something, maybe . . .Say . . ." Biff dropped his fork on the counter and pushed his plate away. He jumped up from the stool and made a dive for the door. "Wait here," he yelled to me. "I'll be right back."

In less than five minutes the door swung open and Biff came in, very pleased with himself. He ordered another pair of eggs before he told me what he had been doing.

"No one stood anywhere near the buzzer," he announced. "The thing is out of whack. Someone nipped the wire leading to the thing. Cut as clean as anything."

So Moss was right, I thought. It was an inside job. But who? Surely not La Verne. Not Dolly with her police record. Jannine? Gee Gee?

"Biff!" He was deep in thought. I had to call him twice to get his attention. "No corporation is going to let on that they're interested if they can help it, and they certainly wouldn't let a burlesque actor in on the deal."

"You're right, Punkin," Biff said. "Not only that, but I can't see any of those guys messing around with a buzzer backstage. That ain't the way they work. All they gotta do is squeeze. Do it all the time; they just squeeze the little guy out."

He finished his second breakfast silently. I drank my coffee and we went into the theater. We stopped at the switchboard and he showed me the warning buzzer.

"It looks like it was cut," I agreed, "but it could have been done accidentally."

Biff said, "Could be, if it makes you feel any better," and followed me upstairs.

The dressing room was close and stuffy so Biff opened the window for me. When the other women began drifting in he went to his own room.

The "good mornings" were brief. I guess they all felt as I did and that certainly was not good. Dolly was last in and the only one who was cheerful. She had three containers of beer under one arm, a stack of newspapers under the other.

"We're on the front page of every paper in town," she shouted happily as she kicked the door closed. La Verne hastily gulped a Bromo-Seltzer before trying to speak.

"I'm dying and that one comes galloping in with newspapers."

She wasn't alone in her dying act; the wet cloth on my head that was so cool a moment before now felt warm and heavy and the soothing effects of the coffee had worn off. "I'll never get through the matinee," I said. Gee Gee handed me a glass of something bubbly. I drank it but it didn't help. She mixed one for herself and made a little face when she downed it.

Sandra pulled her head out of the sink to gasp, "I've never been so sick in all my life."

I believed her. Her face was a pale green. She turned a bloodshot eye on Gee Gee.

"Do you think maybe we're poisoned?"

"Poisoned, hell," Gee Gee said. "You were just trying to drink old man Moss into bankruptcy."

Dolly pushed a container under my nose. "Here, kiddo, take a swig of this," she said. "It ain't like the champagne we drank last night, but it's on the cuff anyhow." I took just a sip. Dolly prattled on. "Louie sent it over, said he'd send more later. I was supposed to deliver it to her highness with the golden box, but . . ."

"That's right, you stinker," the Prima Donna mumbled. "Wait until I'm sick and try to get your dirty work in. Oh, the hell with it." She held out a weak hand and Dolly laughingly shoved a container in it.

Gee Gee and Jannine, sharing my container of beer, were deciding that a hangover was a small price to pay for the party the night before. While they talked I took another drink. It was so cold and tasted so good I took another before passing it on to Jannine. When she finished, she put her initials under the stain her lip rouge made and passed it back to me.

"Hey, wait a minute," Gee Gee yelled. "You two ain't married to that beer, you know. How's about me?" She waited until I put my initials under my rouge mark.

"I don't like taking things from Louie," she said as she tipped the container. "That guy never gives nothing for nothing." As she spoke she watched La Verne, watched her turn the two bracelets on her thin wrist until the largest diamonds flashed in the light.

La Verne handled them lovingly. With a half smile she said, "Oh, I don't know about that."

Gee Gee snorted. "Don't tell me he gave you those service stripes for saying no." Before La Verne could answer she added, "Two black eyes a week. A split lip, a busted nose. You paid for 'em, girlie."

Alice Angel, the featured show girl, lisped, "Yethir, I'll thettle for an old brooch that belonged to Mother." A look from La Verne squelched her, but only for a moment. "Maybe Louie thent uth the beer tho'th we'd tell him what ith like in jail." She really meant it.

"Sure, that's right, lame brain," Gee Gee replied tersely. "He's only having his mail forwarded to him from Alcatraz, but he wants to know what jail's like."

Alice pouted daintily. "Oh, look!" She was all glee again as she held the *Daily News* up for inspection. "They got uth on the thecond page. And look at all the pictureth. Hereth you, Thandra, going up the thepths."

Sandra threw the *Times* on the shelf. As she sauntered over to Alice she said, "This one don't even admit that we're a theater." She grabbed the paper from Alice.

"My Gawd, what a lousy picture. They coulda touched my chin up a little." She read a few lines. "Listen to this: '*Raid Rialto Burlesque, Broadway Burley Pinched On Quick Look By Vice Spy . . .but they arrived in limousines like high-priced Broadway actors. Gypsy Rose Lee, dazzling star of the troupe, was indignant. She said one detective who came to her dressing room was so worried lest she escape, he wouldn't leave the place while she changed from her beads to her minks.'*

"Beads!" I exclaimed. "I've never worn beads in the theater in my life."

Sandra stopped reading to say, "I suppose you've worn minks since you were born."

"Read that part about me again," Dolly said.

"*'I'm the home-type girl,' said Dolly Baxter, a rather coarse blonde.*"

"Not that part, dope," Dolly complained. "I mean the part where they say I came from Hollywood."

"Well, keep your pants on," Sandra said impatiently, "I'm getting to it." She continued. "*'I came on from Hollywood to make good in the hick town in a big way. I can understand now why they put the whole North American continent between Los Angeles and New York.'*"

"I think that's kinda cute," Dolly purred as she took the paper from Sandra and carefully cut out the item. While she pasted it to her makeup mirror with a gob of grease paint, Sandra read another headline:

"*Ada Onion Is No Rose to Purity Squad. 'I'm glancing with tears in my eyes,' the president of the Suppression of Vice Society cried chokingly over the phone yesterday. 'What's the matter?' he was asked. 'It smells to high heaven. Take it away. They call it Ada Onion from Bermuda, but I'd call it Gertie Garlic from Gehenna.'*"

"Gehenna?" Dolly said. "That's a new one on me. Where's that dictionary?" She tossed things around looking for it. It was buried under a *Science and Health* and several horoscope magazines. While Sandra read, Dolly thumbed through the pages.

"*'. . .It must be hot,' said the desk sergeant, and when called for volunteers the reserves stepped forward as one man. Pictures on pages 23–24.*"

"Geezer . . .Ge-gen-schein . . .Hey, here it is. Gehenna!" Dolly kept her finger on the paragraph in the dictionary.

"'Gehenna. Used as a dumping place for refuse. Hell. A place where prisoners are tortured.'" She looked up from the book, a crafty gleam in her eye. "Ya know," she said, "I think we got a case against these guys. They can't say we got a dump place here, and they gotta prove we torture people or we can sue them for libel or something."

"You and your suing all the time," La Verne sneered. "I got a life-size picture of you getting away with it, with your reputation."

Dolly slammed the book on the floor and pulled herself off the chair. She doubled her fist and waved it at La Verne. "Just one more crack, sister," she said, "and you get this right between the eyes!"

A loud banging on the door interrupted her. "Hey, are ya decent?" It sounded like Moey.

Alice pouted. "I wish he wouldn't thay that; it thoundth tho cheap." She wrapped herself in a gingham house coat, while the rest of us hastily covered up, and opened the door. Moey, the candy butcher, stood there with a bulky package braced on his knee.

"You sure took your time," he grumbled. "None of you has anything I haven't seen from out front a dozen times." He gave the awkward bundle a hoist and stumbled into the room. "Gimme a scissors, somebody," he said. "I gotta bargain for ya."

It wasn't until Moey walked into the light that I got a good look at him. His suit made my head ache all over again. Never in my life have I seen a suit like it. It had green and yellow threads running through the material, as though the purple wasn't enough! I couldn't look at the shirt, it made me too dizzy.

"My Gawd!" Gee Gee gasped. "Get a load of Beau Brummell!"

Moey smiled, then he eyed her suspiciously. "Is that good," he asked, "that Beau business?"

"On you it's good," Gee Gee said.

Her laughter put him in a better humor. He laughed with her, then said, "Somebody gimme a scissors or a knife or something. I got a bargain for ya."

Jannine handed him her manicure nippers to cut the thick cord. He pushed his green fedora back on his head and went to work with the scissors.

"Here, let me help you," Jannine cried.

He was cutting everything but the cord, including himself. "Get away," he said. "It ain't often I get a chance to make like Lady Bountiful, and anyway I ain't no cripple." The Lady Bountiful got me; headache or no headache I had to laugh.

He uncovered the package from the bottom. We saw the pale-blue enamel base, the bulging bowl.

"It's the toilet!" we exclaimed in chorus. "But where did you . . .?"

"Don't ask too many questions," Moey said meaningfully.

"It ain't hot, is it?" Gee Gee asked.

"Whadya mean hot?" Moey was indignant. "Who dya think'd go around copping a can?"

Gee Gee tried to mollify him. "I only meant, how come you got it so quick, and how come you got it anyway?"

"Well, it's like this." He opened the coat of his suit and twined his thumbs around the pink suspenders that had pictures of mermaids painted on them. "I got a pal in the business, see. And when Biff is in the saloon getting a quick one, he tells me how you dames are squawking about the old can and how everybody's chipping in to get a new one. So I think of this pal of mine, known him for..."

"Get to the blackout," Dolly said irritably.

"Like I said," Moey continued after a withering look in Dolly's direction, "I get in touch with this pal of mine that I've known for years. Him and me used to work together in the old days. When we got legitimate he took up plumbin'. Natcherly I think of him and whatdya know? He gives me it wholesale!"

Even Dolly had to admit that it was wonderful. Gee Gee threw her arms around the candy butcher and kissed him on the forehead. I couldn't get that close to the suit but I yelled my thanks.

"No one but you would think of getting it wholesale," I added admiringly.

Moey preened himself a bit. "Only suckers pay list prices," he said. "This little job sells for seven-fifty without the seat. My pal gives me it for four bucks and throws the seat in gratis. Not only that; I can save ya dough on the installation, too. A regular plumber would soak ya about ten skins, but my guy'll do it for half. He don't belong to no union."

"That's out!" Jannine jumped to her feet. She had just been elected secretary to the president of the Burlesque Artists' Association and she took her job seriously. Her eyes sparkled as she went into her speech.

"Plumbers got a union. We got a union. When we don't protect each other that's the end of the unions. Remember what we went through before we organized? Ten shows a day, no extra pay. Fired without even a day's notice. Seventeen dollars a week for the chorus girls? Forty hours a week rehearsal?"

Dolly said in a dispirited tone, "Hooray for the B.A.A."

Alice gave Jannine a baleful look. "Do we have to lithen to all that again?" she said.

"No you don't," Jannine answered. "But no yellow-bellied scab is walking in this room while I'm here!"

"So all right." Moey was getting annoyed. "Pay the ten bucks!" He went out, slamming the door behind him.

"Now look what you've done," Gee Gee said. "Now we gotta move this damn thing ourselves. You and your 'fellow workers tonight' dialogue."

"It's *unite*. Not *tonight*," Jannine replied with dignity. "And anyway, I'd rather move it myself than have a non-union odor in the room."

For all her big talk, Jannine was quite small. When the Columbia was *the* theater in New York, she was featured as 'The Darling of the Runways.' When you consider that the fire department made us take out the runways several years ago and that the Columbia had been torn down for over ten, it made Jannine a little old for the type of work she did. That week, for instance, she was doing "Won't Someone Please Adopt Me and My Baby?" She wore a short baby dress and carried a huge rag doll! When she stripped the dress, the audience got a flash of diapers pinned on with an oversized safety pin. If they were insistent enough she'd strip the diapers, too, but it took a lot of coaxing. The last few years she'd been finishing with the diapers on.

She looked funny, pushing and tugging away at the blue monument that stood in the middle of the room. We all got up to help her.

Gee Gee was panting a little from the exertion when she said, "You know what we oughtta do? We oughtta have a regular unveiling."

"Oh, yeth!" Alice clapped her hands gaily, "Like when they unveil thatueth of generalth and horsteth and thingth."

"We'll make it a party," Gee Gee announced, "very exclusive."

"Just us actors," Sandra added.

"And the stagehands," from Jannine.

"You gotta invite the candy butchers with Moey getting the throne," Dolly reminded us. She turned to me. "You get the waiters to bring the food." I nodded, and she told Sandra to do the invitations. Jannine was to get the plumber, of course.

"And on account of Louie being in the liquor business," she said to La Verne, "and you being so friendly with him, you get the beer and stuff."

We played a midnight performance on Saturdays and there was an hour and a half between the first and the last show, so we decided to have the party then. That was our regular party night anyway. The Saturday before, we had had spareribs. The actors had carried their food right on the stage with them because they were so afraid that by the time their scene was over the ribs would be gone.

The law since then was: "No spareribs in the theater." I thought a Chinese supper would be a good idea. The actors couldn't carry *that* onstage.

My menu planning was interrupted by the stage manager shouting, "Overture! The music's on." He threw open the door and stomped in. "I don't like to bother you dames, but there's a show going on," he said sarcastically.

As stage managers go, Sammy was about average, but that isn't saying very much for him. I've worked for a lot of them and I haven't found one yet that didn't think he owned the theater and everybody in it. Sammy was all right until he was annoyed. But he annoyed easy. He yelled at Dolly as she flew down the stairs. "You miss that opening and I swear I'll dock your salary."

Then he picked up the bedspread that Gee Gee was crocheting and began idly unraveling it as he read the newspaper clipping that was pasted on the wall.

"This damn raid'll hurt business," he said, shaking his head sadly. He put down the spread and felt behind the mirror for the bottle. With his thumb he flipped the patent top open and tilted the bottle to his lips. "Yep," he said, after clearing his throat, "soon as the jerkers think we're cleaning up the show, business takes a dive." He put the bottle back and without another word left the room.

A faint odor of "Tweed" went along with him.

"I guess he's sore because Moss didn't invite him to Moore's," Gee Gee said rather sympathetically. She hadn't seen the unraveling act or her tone wouldn't have been quite so soft.

"Well, if I'd known I was going to have a hangover like this," Sandra moaned, "he coulda gone in my place. I wish to Gawd he *did* have it."

Gee Gee put her fingers to her lips and tiptoed to the door. Sammy was quite an eavesdropper and she wanted to catch him in the act. This time he was too quick for her; by the time the door was flung open he was halfway downstairs.

44

FOUR

THE KITCHEN PORCH OF THE CHINESE RESTAURANT faced our dressing-room window. Before the big fight with La Verne and the waiters they used to send the food to us over the roof.

The fight occurred during an Indian-summer hot spell. The waiters used to stand out on their porch to cool themselves, and we kept our windows open for the same reason. They looked in. I always admitted that part, but I haven't seen a man yet that wouldn't look at a dressing room full of half-naked women when he had a chance. La Verne was the only one who made a scene about it. She stormed around calling them hopheads and yellow perils and threatened to have them deported.

One day I asked her why she didn't undress away from the window as the rest of us did.

"Why should I?" she screamed. "I guess I can dress and undress where I want to. It's my room, isn't it?"

"Sure," I said, "it's your room. But that's their porch too, and they're probably a damn sight warmer in their hot kitchen than you are in the theater." I should have known better than to appeal to La Verne. She had a heart, but it operated on the cash-register principle.

She wound up throwing a Coca-Cola bottle at one of them. It caught him on the side of the head and knocked him out. The other waiters called a cop and for a few days merry hell was popping. La Verne had to pay a ten-dollar bill for bandaging the Chinese waiter's head, but that didn't include a splint to patch up our beautiful friendship. They wouldn't deliver any more groceries across the roof unless I called them. How I rated I don't know, but every time I called "Hola ma," they answered me.

I waited until Friday night to order the food for the party. A small white-coated figure appeared on the porch and returned my greeting.

"I want twenty-five dinners for tomorrow night."

He went into the kitchen. I waited a moment. Then the screen door squeaked and he reappeared. He had a pencil and a pad of paper in one hand. The other held a small box. In a ray of light from the kitchen door I watched him as he crossed the roof.

"You want regular forty-five-cent dinner or special?"

"Special," I answered. "Ten orders chicken sub gum chow mein, six orders shrimp fried rice."

"Lot water chestnuts," he added. The pad of paper rested against the window sill and a delicate brown hand wrote the Chinese version of twelve egg rolls and ten orders of roast pork. "You want mixed fruit?" he asked.

"Yes, and tea and rice cakes. Everything."

He finished writing the order and put the pad and pencil in the pocket of his coat.

"Tomorrow night," I said. "Eleven-thirty sharp. OK?"

He nodded for an answer. Then I saw the box again. It was wrapped in loose foil and he was offering it to me. "Ginseng root," he said in carefully spoken English. "Grows only under the gallows where men have died. You eat it. Live forever."

Before I could tell him that it didn't sound like a good idea, he had forced the package into my hand and was gone.

"Hola ma," I called. "Hey, come back." The white coat gleamed like phosphorus. There was the sound of soft slippers crunching the gravel on the roof and the screendoor squeaked again as he disappeared into the kitchen.

With the package in my hand I went over to the shelf. I didn't want to open it in front of the girls, but I was too curious to wait until I got out of the theater. It was heavy and had been sealed with red wax. I held it up to my ear and shook it gently.

"What if it's a bomb," I thought. "Or what if poisonous air comes out when I open it?" I don't know how long I stood there turning the gift around in my hands, and the thoughts of sudden, horrible death around in my mind.

Gee Gee's petulant voice brought me back. "I asked you twice already," she said, "what's in the box?"

She raised an eyebrow and looked at me skeptically when I explained that it was a root that the waiter had given me and that it grew under the gallows where men had died.

"He said if I ate it I'd live forever."

She burst out laughing at that and turned to the girls. "Gypsy's got a new John." She took the package from my hand. "The Chinese waiter just gave her a weed that's guaranteed to make her live forever."

The girls gathered around her as she broke the seals. The first one was brittle and snapped off easily. The second she had to pry off with a nail file.

I suddenly wanted to get out of the room. My common sense told me that my fears about the box were stupid and childish, but I couldn't help it. I was frightened. "What if there is one flower in it?" I thought. "One flower that would disappear like dust when the air hit it." Then there would be a sickening sweet odor, bitter almonds maybe, and before we knew what had happened, we would be dead.

She had removed the lead foil and held up a tin box for the curious girls to examine. The tin box was also sealed. Great chunks of brick-red wax were on either side.

I wanted to stop her, but already she had begun to lift the top. There was no flower, no needle dipped in poison, no bomb; just a cotton-lined box with two long, dried roots embedded in the fluff. The roots were tied at the top with a piece of cord.

It was by this cord that La Verne lifted the gift from the cotton. She held it for a second and watched it sway back and forth. "Look! It's shaped like a man," she said.

Alice shivered. "Ugh. It'th dithguthting. Put it back in the box."

La Verne still stared at it, her green eyes wide and glistening. "Not so much like a man," she whispered. "More like the skeleton of one." With a cautious finger she touched the bleached, bone-like root. The pupils of her eyes dilated. She pushed the root and set it in motion again. Her heavy breathing was the only sound in the room.

She said, "A skeleton hanging from the gallows. Let me keep it, Gypsy. It fascinates me."

"Oh, cripes!" Dolly exclaimed. "Give her the damn-fool thing. I'm going to take a drink." She pushed a chair aside with an angry gesture.

The girls went back to their makeup places silently. Dolly finished her drink and pulled a step-ladder in front of the toilet door. She lifted a large box of laurel leaves and a hammer to the shelf that stood away from the ladder steps, then emptied a box of tacks in her apron pocket, took another quick drink, and began climbing the unsteady steps.

"Queer for roots," she mumbled, with a look at La Verne. "That's a new one."

La Verne didn't answer and for a few minutes only the sound of Dolly's hammering disturbed the quiet of our dressing room.

Suddenly Gee Gee nudged me. When I looked up, she indicated the door with a jerk of her head. Sandra caught it just as I did.

Framed in the doorway was a picture of dethroned royalty if I ever saw a Norma Shearer movie. Not that the woman who stood there looked like Norma Shearer; more like Nita Naldi maybe. She wore a black velvet Russian costume trimmed with caracul. The hat, a high Cossack affair, was fur, and she carried a huge caracul muff. She wore red leather boots with black tassels in front.

Not one of us opened our mouths. We just looked.

"Vere iss the star's room?" The accent was a cross between Russian and Dutch comic.

We were still speechless.

Dolly was the first one to get on with it. She teetered dangerously on the ladder. Her mouth was full of tacks and they made her speak indistinctly.

"There ain't a star's room," she said. Then, with a friendly smile: "There ain't a star, either. We're all getting forty per."

"How interesting," said the woman in the Russian getup. But she said it like you say, "How dull." She looked at Dolly with a half smile on her long, thin face. "And who are you?" Her dark red lips barely moved, but one side curled up a little.

Dolly wasn't sure if it was sarcasm or not. She spat the tacks out of her mouth one by one before answering. "I'm Dolly Baxter, Dynamite Dolly," she said. "And who are *you*?"

The woman threw back her head, her eyes half closed. "I'm the Princess Nirvena," she announced, "the star of this theater starting tomorrow." She let her eyes survey the crowded room. "Vere do I dress?"

She stood there waiting, as though we should all knock ourselves out helping her to a chair, or go into a deep curtsy.

Sandra suppressed a little giggle. "Well, that is the choice spot in the room." She tossed a thumb in the direction of a littered space next to the grimy sink. "It's so convenient, ya know."

The water stain had streaked the broken mirror. Some stockings were soaking in the sink, and a constant drip, drip was proof that very soon it would flood over.

The Princess ignored Sandra and the basin. She was looking at me, and at that moment I recognized her. She quickly averted her face, but it was too late.

"Didn't we work together in Toledo?" I asked innocently.

She stared at me as though I were some biped prehistoric marine mammal.

"I haff nevair been in—how you say—Too Ledo. Always I haff danced for royalty. Then the revolution and poof! It is gone. Now the Princess Nirvena throws pearls to swine." That was her exit line. Before we could answer she was gone. Nothing but a heavy scent of perfume to remind us that she had ever been there.

For a moment I thought I might have been mistaken. The blue-black hair, the dark skin, the thick-lidded eyes were different, but still...

Dolly snorted. "Royalty, my ass!" With one bang of the hammer another leaf was nailed to the top of the door. "She's a phony if I ever saw one."

The accent floated up to us from the stage. Gee Gee ran to the door to listen.

The Princess had found Sammy, the stage manager. "Do you tink that I would dress in sooch a place? I, the Princess?"

"That's the only room," Sammy said apologetically. "There's another room in the basement, but you wouldn't want to dress there. It's damp and..."

"I don't care vot it is," the Princess trilled. "I would rather dress in a pigsty than with those women." Her voice faded away.

Gee Gee turned away from the door. "I guess they're on their way to the rathole downstairs," she said, an unholy gleam in her eye.

I knew why the Princess wanted to dress alone and it had nothing to do with anyone in our room. Besides me, that is. It takes more than black hair dye, body stain, and an accent to fool Mother Lee.

"She kind of has pigs on the brain." Gee Gee's voice broke up in a laugh. "Throwing pearls to 'em and would rather dress with 'em."

Dolly mumbled a curse. "Broke my favorite nail." She examined the finger closely. "Way down below the quick, too." She waddled down the ladder and handed Alice the hammer. "Now you, angel pants," she said. "I'm pooped."

Alice took her place on the ladder and Dolly gave orders to follow out her design.

"It's supposed to be a bower, ya know."

Alice nodded knowingly and the steady bangs of the hammering kept the conversation down.

A little later Mrs. Pulsidski came in. She was the underwear woman who once a week made the rounds of the theaters. She made beautiful underwear but she was such a groaner that I usually had to get out of the room while she was there.

Gee Gee was trying on a blue satin nightgown.

"Believe me, Miss Graham, if I hadn't had so much sickness in my family, I couldn't sell it for less than seven dollars," Mrs. Pulsidski sobbed.

"I'll give you five bucks for it," Gee Gee said unsympathetically.

"I'm such a poor old woman. Not for my own daughter could I..."

I took a couple of cigarettes with me and left the room. The words "real Alençon lace" and "like a glove it fits" followed me downstairs.

I made myself comfortable on a pile of scenery under the steps and lit one of the cigarettes. I was dressed for my next scene, so I had enough time to relax.

Jake, the prop man, came over to join me.

"I've been looking all over for you," he said cheerfully. "The rest of the crew and I got some gags for the party." He looked around to see if anyone was listening. "I got the stuff hid in the prop room, for a surprise."

I would have liked to have been surprised, too, but when he motioned to me I pulled myself away from the comfortable bunk and followed him.

He shuffled toward the prop room, a large, drafty place to the left of the stage. Instead of stairs, a ramp led to the double door. Jake unlocked a huge padlock that was attached to a bar and socket. He opened the door enough for me to squeeze through.

"Don't want anybody to see the stuff until tomorrow," he said mysteriously.

With the exception of a small clearing for a card table and a few chairs, the room was filled to the ceiling with furniture and props that would be found only in a burlesque theater. A gazeeka box, loaves of papier-mâché bread strung together, dozens of bladders, all sizes, hanging from the ceiling, a chandelier made of wood with leather braces for the chorus girls to cling to, a park bench, a fireman's helmet, and the constantly used bedroom suite. The bed was made. It was being used in the show, as usual. A lavender rayon spread concealed the fact that instead of a mattress there were boards. A tired, droopy doll, wearing a tarnished silver gown, was draped on the pillow. At the foot were several carelessly wrapped packages.

"I walked me legs off getting some of this stuff," Jake said, "and wound up havin' to make most of it myself."

I gave him the "There isn't anything you can't make" dialogue and the wide-eyed admiration look. His thin chest bulged a little under the faded blue overalls.

"Take this, f'instance." His callused hand offered me a piece of board with two clamps on the side, a roller between. "Ya know what it is?"

I nodded yes. It was obviously a toilet-tissue holder.

"Well, get a load of this!" He inserted a roll of blue paper. With a dramatic gesture and all the timing of a good actor he tore off a strip of the tissue, then looked up, waiting for my reaction.

Music was coming from the roller! A tinkling music-box version of "Whistle While You Work."

"It's wonderful!" I gasped.

"Yeah? Well, that ain't all." He waved the piece of tissue under my nose. It was perfumed. "Heliotrope," he said proudly. "Now you see why I had to let you in on the secret. I gotta have help to get this stuff in the room so's nobody'll see 'em."

"Why not after the show tonight?" I suggested.

"The paint on a couple of things won't be dry for twenty-four hours," he said. There was a troubled wrinkle between his pale eyes.

I thought a second. "How's about the finale of the first act?"

He slapped a fist in his hand. "By golly, that's it!"

With all that settled, he began showing me the other surprises: a blue bath rug, a plunger painted to match with a rhinestone handle, a pair of oilcloth curtains.

"This is the most important of all," he said.

At the end of the room stood the floral tribute, a huge horse-shoe made of wax roses. A red ribbon with success spelled out in gold letters was draped from side to side. It was fastened to an easel and must have been over six feet high.

"I wanted to get something more symbolic," Jake said, "like when they open a barbershop, they make up a pair of scissors outta flowers. Only all my ideas were too corny."

"It couldn't be more beautiful." I assured him.

"Damn it all! Why don't you watch your cues?" Russell had thrown the prop room door open and was shouting to me. "You're on," he yelled.

I tossed my cigarette in a brass prop cuspidor and made a dash for the wings.

Biff was on the stage, ad libbing. "She told me she'd meet me here..." He saw me in the wings and scowled.

He was doing the drugstore scene. I had one line:

"I'd like ten cents' worth of moth balls." I fumbled in my purse for the money.

Biff gave me a double take, then a slow triple. "Who you kidding?" he said. "Moths have no..."

"Fresh!" I stamp my foot and exit.

"If it's fresh, I'll take some," he said as I left.

Before I got off, La Verne's high-pitched voice began screaming. She was way backstage, near the cellar stairs, but the noise almost shattered my eardrums.

"Why you no good, two-bit, broken-down bastard!"

I thought she and Dolly were at it again until she yelled, "I got enough on you to hang you. Understand? Hang you!"

Louie's voice answered her. "What you got on me don't count." There was a second's silence. Then: "The next time I see you hanging around another guy as long as I'm keeping you, I'll…"

"Keeping me?" La Verne hit a high C. "You got a hell of a nerve to say that to me when I'm doing four-a-day in a flea bag like this."

There was the sound of a quick slap, then a scuffling.

Louie's voice was low. It vibrated with fury. "You heard what I told ya. Well, don't forget it. This ain't nothing to what you'll get."

La Verne screamed again, this time in pain, not temper.

A couple of stagehands sauntered by. I peeked around the scenery and saw Sammy hotfooting it over.

"Stop the noise," he said, trying to separate them. "There's a show going on." The stagehands helped him pull Louie's hands off La Verne's throat.

Louie swung a left at her and Sammy got it. His eyes puffed up like a balloon.

"Poor guy," I thought. He was always on the receiving end of those fast ones.

He was afraid to blame Louie, so he turned on La Verne and booted her in the behind while the stagehands talked Louie into leaving quietly.

The blood trickled down La Verne's lip to her chin and she wiped her mouth with the back of her hand. She didn't seem to feel Sammy's knee when he booted her. Her eyes went from the blood on her hand to Louie's retreating figure.

"Dammit, I won't have all this racket during the show," Sammy shouted. He was ashamed of himself and tried to bluster his way out of it. Jake hurried over with his first-aid kit and pushed the stage manager aside. "Can't you see she's hurt?" he said.

Sammy mumbled an apology and turned to the group of

stagehands that had gathered. "Fine bunch of guys you are," he said. "Stand around and let a guy beat the stuffing outta a woman and not lift a finger to help her. Break it up now. We got a show to do here." Then he turned to La Verne. "I'm sorry. Forgot myself." When she didn't answer he shrugged his shoulders and went over to the switchboard.

I hadn't seen Russell standing in the wings until Sammy approached him. His face was like chalk and his mouth hung open. He was looking at La Verne.

Sammy said, "It's like working in an insane asylum, ain't it?"

Russell brushed past him without speaking. He stumbled toward the stairs and climbed them one at a time, slowly, like a blind man.

Jake was cheerfully patting iodine on La Verne's lip. "Don't know what we'd do without this little first-aid affair," he said.

La Verne's lip was swelling and the iodine must have stung because she pushed Jake away and followed Russell upstairs. At the landing she stopped and looked up to the men's dressing room, then she turned and went into her own room without speaking to him.

Was it the sight of the blood that made Russell so white, I wondered, or was it the first time he knew of La Verne and Louie being lovers?

Well, it was none of my business, but I did have to agree with Alice. No diamond bracelets are worth it. Like her, I'd settle for an old garnet brooch that belonged to Mother.

FIVE

I WAS SURPRISED TO SEE EVERYONE IN THE DRESSING room so early for the Saturday matinee. Then I remembered; the Princess opened today. On the itinerary I noticed that her specialty was in the middle of the first act, her second number opened the second act.

"Pretty good spots for a new woman, eh?" Jannine had been reading over my shoulder.

Gee Gee looked up from the bedspread she was crocheting. "She better not send her laundry out until after the midnight. When those guys get a load of that frozen puss of hers they aren't going to like it."

La Verne was vocalizing, trying to hit the notes without hurting her lip. It looked a little worse. The iodine stain drew one side of her mouth almost to the ear. She had tried to cover it with grease paint and that made it swell more. Alice kept asking what had happened to her.

"How in the world could you do that in your thleep?" she said wonderingly.

"Oh, nuts." La Verne dragged her Japanese kimono from a hanger. "I only said that to keep you quiet last night." She put her arms through flowing sleeves and pinned the robe on tightly. "As a matter of fact, I bumped into a fist. Now shut up, will ya?"

The chorus girls' chatter through the ventilator reminded us that the opening was over. La Verne had a number after Dolly's strip. They both began dressing hurriedly. The Prima Donna took off her kimono and pulled a plain black dress over her head and pinned on a floppy black hat with a red ostrich feather that hung down over her shoulder. She was doing "Love for Sale." It seemed a very appropriate song. The lip made her makeup complete. She vocalized the first eight bars, "*Love for sale, appetizing young love for sale...*"

Gee Gee had the courtesy to wait until she left the room before saying, "Young love. With that face!"

Alice sat with her knees up and her face cupped in her hands. "You know," she said, a puzzled look on her pretty bread-and-milk face, "I jutht can't thee how she coulda bumped into a fitht."

Biff kicked the door open. "Hi ya, Punkin. I got a container of coffee and a bag of buns for ya." He put them down on the nearest chair and made a dive for the stairs. "Gotta make with the jokes. See ya later."

Gee Gee shook her head. "I don't know which one of 'em is worse, so help me, I don't." She opened the container of coffee and the bag of sweet rolls. "La Verne's knocks her with fancy fists and diamonds and this guy knocks you out with cute words and cold coffee."

She was right. The coffee was cold. I dunked a roll and ate it. "Hot or cold, he's a cutie," I said between mouthfuls.

Dolly came in dripping sweat, La Verne almost following on her heels.

"Jesus are they tough today," Dolly complained.

"Oh, they were all right for me," the Prima Donna lied airily. "By the way, any of you seen Russell this morning?" Dolly's mouth got tight but she turned her head away with a tired gesture.

"Yeah, I seen him," Jannine answered offhandedly, "and was he loaded? Whee!"

"You mean he was drunk?" Dolly spun on her heel and faced Jannine. I thought for a minute she was going to strike her. Jannine did, too. She backed away quickly.

"Not exactly drunk," she stammered, "just kinda, well, hungover, maybe."

The orchestra picked up the last eight of "Dark Eyes" in four and forte. With a glance at the itinerary, Gee Gee shouted, "That's her!"

There was a mad rush for robes, kimonos, and house coats. In burlesque it's considered good form to wait until the second or third performance before catching a new act, but with the Princess it was different. We rushed downstairs, three abreast.

Dolly mumbled, "I've been playing this joint for seventeen weeks and they haven't given me a spot like this."

"She probably knows where the body's buried," Jannine said.

Even the dancers were in the wings, twenty deep. Gee Gee explained to one that ours was a professional interest. The kid nodded and let us move in her place.

The Princess was a smoothie all right. One peek convinced me of that. This wasn't her first stripping job, I decided. She had too many tricks that come only with experience, like dropping her shoulder straps and rolling a feather muff around her breasts. Not that it was original; Sandra had done it weeks ago. But I'll have to admit that she didn't get as much out of it.

There was a hum of appreciation drifting over the footlights. I looked through the peekhole at the rapt, sweating faces. Then she began slowly lifting the skirt of her evening gown with a dark-gloved hand, the other covering her breasts. A long, thin tongue licked the purple lips and the music built up to a crescendo. She flashed a rhinestone G-string, and with the same sensual, expressionless face she threw her torso into a bump that shook the balcony. The audience went mad. She dropped the skirt and waited for them to stop applauding.

Dolly whispered in my ear, "Get a load of those Bordens." I looked. The muff was over to the side and I thought that competition wasn't so tough after all. Just as I started relaxing—I never thought she'd have the nerve to take that brassière off—it

58

happened. She not only took off the brassière, but her G-string, too. I couldn't believe my eyes. There was nothing but a small strip of adhesive in front and a string of fringe in the back. How she kept that on I don't know. Glue maybe. The customers weren't thinking about that anyway. That strip was practically the end of the show.

She had darted behind the velvet curtain, and Phil, the tenor, was on doing a ballad. I gritted my teeth when I thought of the setup Moss had given her. To let her work that strong when we all had to wear full net pants. Right after the raid, too. And then to have Phil follow her in a pin spot with a ballad! I was so mad I shook, and I wasn't alone. Dolly's hot breath on the back of my neck was coming faster and faster. Gee Gee stormed her way past us on her way out front. It will serve Moss right if she does make a scene, I thought. How in the name of burlesque can anyone follow that?

I must have spoken aloud because Alice's coy voice asked, "Why didn't she wear full netth like everybody elthe?"

I like Alice, always have, but at that moment I could have strangled her in cold blood. "I'm—sure—I—don't—know," I said deliberately. Alice edged away.

Biff had also been watching from the wings. After my outburst he gave me a mischievous grin. "Why do you let it get ya?" he asked. "You don't work like that."

"No, I don't, but I have to follow it. How'd you like to have to follow a comic that spits in his pants for a laugh?" Sammy made a shushing gesture. "Oh, shush yourself!" I cried. Then Biff laughed. For a minute I didn't like him either, then I laughed, too. It was silly to get mad at a thing like a woman taking off her pants.

On my way upstairs I decided to keep my specialty so girlish that the audience would think I was a fugitive from a finishing school. Organdie ruffles, a big picture hat, or a parasol, maybe. A verse and a chorus of "Sweet Little Alice Blue Gown," and strip trailers like "Oh Promise Me" and "I Love You Truly."

Gee Gee was throwing things around the room again. A box of powder exploded on the wall. "Hot Springs!" she yelled. "I'll Hot Springs him." A jar of cold cream missed my head by inches.

Alice whispered, "Moth went away for a couple of weekth. Thatth why she'th tho mad."

Dolly was ransacking the old wardrobe trunk. A pile of gaily colored rags that were once costumes were heaped beside her. She finally found something that interested her, a piece of monkey fur about three inches square. With fiendish determination she glued it on in place of her G-string. As she stood before the mirror admiring her new "costume" I could visualize the cops walking down the aisles again.

Crash! An empty bottle hit the sink. Gee Gee paused to get her breath. "So help me," she vowed, "on the night show I'm going to take off a couple of layers of skin."

Alice and I tried to quiet her. "She can hear you through the pipe," Alice cautioned.

"And why give her the satisfaction?" I asked. "Moss will hear about the scene you're making and then he'll think we've been picking on her."

"Yeth. She'll have a beef and Moth will give her the betht of it."

From the ventilator came a soft laugh. "Moss vill giff me vot I want, no matter." I stuffed a towel in the vent before anyone could answer her.

The fight was all out of Gee Gee though. She began brushing her copper-colored hair, counting each stroke carefully. Suddenly her face lit up. "Let's shoot the wad and eat at Luchow's," she said. "I'm sick of that damned drugstore grub."

Her idea started a purse-fumbling contest. Dolly unsnapped the catch on her grouch bag and counted off two dollars. "A buck for dinner and a buck for drinks." She bit the inside of her mouth thinking. "Yep, that's for me," she decided finally.

With the exception of one show girl who was too stingy to

treat herself to a fancy feedbag and La Verne, who was too stingy period, a pre-party dinner was arranged.

Biff and Mandy joined us at Luchow's later. Biff had just won six dollars in a craps game so the first round of drinks was his treat. Gee Gee bought a round, then I had to go for one. Dolly loosened up for the whole two bucks and by then it was time for the theater again. An old German cuckoo clock went into its act; the bedraggled little bird poked its head out of the window eight times.

"My Gawd," Mandy yelled, "it's a half-hour and we ain't et yet." There was time for one quick round, though, so we all ordered another Martini each. They were served in big glasses with little sour onions instead of olives.

Dolly staggered a little when she went to get her coat. "Hic. Never seen it to fail," she said. "Every time I eat onions I get drunk."

Paying the check was an ordeal. The waiters had to collect an installment from each of us. Dolly tried to pretend she was too drunk to count, but Mandy held her while Gee Gee went through her pockets.

We never could decide why Luchow's didn't cater to us after that night. Dolly walking off with half the silverware in her purse might have accounted for it, but I always thought it was because Biff tried to take the hall tree with him. It would have been all right if there hadn't been so many coats and hats on it.

Siggy, the G-string man, was waiting in the stage entrance. His suitcase was opened on the trunk to show the new line of net pants and brassières. Over the lid the rhinestone gadgets were on display. He must have been waiting for a long time because there was a small mound of cigarette butts on the floor beside him. They were all smoked down to a quarter of an inch and the wet ends were pinched together.

Siggy used to get so enthused about making a sale that he'd forget he was smoking until the cigarette burned his lip. That was really how he got his nickname. If he had another name he'd probably forgotten it. The only thing he remembered was how much we owed him; he kept track of that in a little black book.

Jannine was the first to grab a rhinestone number that a couple of us had our eyes on.

"That there one is five bucks," Siggy said, with the usual cigarette hanging from his lower lip.

"Five bucks!" Jannine gasped. "Why I never paid over three since I been wearing them."

"Well, beads is gone up," he replied stiffly, "an' I got a living to make." He took the G-string from Jannine and held it up to his fat waist. "Anyway, this here one is plush lined. Plain, I can let you have one for four bucks."

The plush lining sold Jannine. With a giggle, she snatched the costume from Siggy and scurried upstairs. Siggy put her name in the black book with a note that she owed five dollars and turned to his other customers.

Gee Gee and I bought plain net pants and Sandra finally bought another brassière, not because she needed it, but because brassières were her hobby.

As Siggy wrote the items with a stubby, chewed pencil, he said, "Just seen Louie's waiters bringing in a barrel of beer." Gee Gee and I didn't answer. "And a case of rye, too," he said casually. "Must be gonna have a party, huh?" He wasn't quite as casual then.

Gee Gee looked at me and with a shrug of helplessness admitted that we did have something like it in mind. She turned to me and said, "I guess we'll have to invite him." Ungracious as the invitation was, I have never seen a G-string salesman move so fast. In one half-second the black book was in his pocket, the suitcase closed, and he was on his way upstairs.

"You'd think you never got a free beer in your life," Gee Gee yelled after him. "Anyhow, the party ain't until after the next show."

An expression of annoyance crossed Siggy's face, then he grinned.

"OK," he said brightly, "I'll wait." Swinging his suitcase in front of him he went back to the stage entrance and flopped down on the trunk. He pulled his feet up and braced himself comfortably before he began making a supply of rolled cigarettes.

"Hey, Gypola." Jannine stood on the landing with a Turkish towel wrapped around her. The towel wasn't quite large enough but it didn't seem to worry her any.

"I musta dropped my new G-string," she shouted. "Bring it up, will ya, and save me the trip?"

Gee Gee and I looked for it on the steps and we rummaged through the pile of scenery under them. The G-string didn't seem to be there either, but it was dark and we decided to wait for George, the electrician.

"He'll be back in a minute," I said, "and then he can give us some light."

"She's such a dope," Gee Gee explained. "She's probably got it on and with that dead fanny of hers she just don't feel it."

We didn't find the G-string and Jannine didn't have it on. Gee Gee still feels that if we'd looked hard enough we might have found it. She sort of blames herself for the murders. But as I tell her, if the murderer hadn't used that G-string it would have been another. After all, it may have been the only one that had a plush lining but it certainly wasn't the only one that had a string, and that's the part the murderer used.

SIX

DURING THE SHOW OUR DRESSING ROOM DID A lively business. Everyone and his brother dropped in to offer suggestions for the party. The fact that they also sampled the rye might account for the near stampede at intermission.

Mandy wanted to have us pull straws to see which one was to be queen. Biff thought things should be a little more dignified.

Joey, Mandy's partner, was still being a second comic. "I tell you," he said, shaking a finger in the air. "Break a bottle on it like they do on battleships and Winchell'll use it in his column."

"The freedom of the press ain't that free," Jannine said.

Jake ambled in a little later with some excuse about the sink leaking. It had been leaking for twenty-eight weeks that I knew of, but, of course, we didn't have a case of liquor every day. He righted a collar on the pipe and made like it was a job that called for fortification.

While he poured a healthy slug into a Dixie cup he winked at me. In a stage whisper that could be heard in the Eltinge uptown, he told me not to forget the surprises.

"What surprises?" Gee Gee asked.

Jake grinned. "You'll find out."

And she did. But not the sort of surprise Jake intended.

BEFORE I DID my scene with Biff at the end of the second act, it was settled that we would break the bottle, crown the queen, and still leave a little time for dignity. Russell passed by the room but wouldn't come in for a drink. He hardly glanced at La Verne when she called him.

"Give ya the old go by, eh?" Dolly was too pleased to conceal it. She was painting her toenails with bright red polish; little hunks of cotton between each toe made her feet fan-shaped. She managed to walk over to La Verne's side of the room.

"Why don't ya call him again," she taunted. "Maybe he didn't hear your golden voice."

La Verne brought a foot down on the newly polished toes. "Oh, excuse me, so sorry." La Verne's claws were sharpened. There was real malice in her smile as she looked up into Dolly's face.

Before Dolly could say any more than "Ouch!" Gee Gee grabbed her. Half playfully, half forcibly she led the fan-shaped feet back to the opposite side of the dressing room.

"No fights tonight," she said, pushing Dolly into a chair. "Little birdies in a nest." A drink of rye settled the discussion.

The laurel leaves over the door had decorated more peaceful spots than the strippers' dressing room that eventful night. The tension wasn't relieved any when Sammy barged in, making a noise like a stage manager.

He took a look at Dolly, then a glance at the half-empty bottle on the shelf. "I give you all fair warning," he said. He paused for a moment to build up for the following announcement: "Any man or woman that misses a cue *from now on*, and that goes for the finale, too, gets fired at once."

No one said a word. Dolly closed one eye to get a good view of the stage manager. Alice pouted a little and swung around in her chair, one of those, "well you didn't have to include me" pouts.

Gee Gee said in a cold voice, "Hear, hear."

"Don't hear, hear me." Sammy used a fist to pound on the shelf. The bottle went bouncing in the air and down again. "You're getting a little too smart for your pants anyway, Miss Graham," Sammy shouted and stomped out of the room.

Gee Gee waited until he was halfway upstairs to say, "What pants? Is he kidding?" She pulled the makeup towel out of the ventilator to listen in on what was happening upstairs in the men's dressing room.

Sure enough, Sammy was up there, but Mandy hadn't given him time to go into his routine. He was describing Joey's mother, catching the show. "Yeah, well she comes backstage and says, 'Oh, Joey, you was so funny! It was all I could do to keep from laughing.' " Sammy's voice tried to cut in, but Mandy stopped him. "That ain't all," he said, "there's a topper. Joey, he says to his mother, 'But I'm a comic man, Mom; you're supposed to laugh.' And she says, 'So all right then, let them laugh, just so you shouldn't make a fool outta yourself.' "

Mandy and Joey laughed, but alone. I didn't wait to hear if Sammy went into the spiel about missing cues.

BIFF STOPPED IN the wings and grabbed my arm. I thought he was going to tell me something about waiting for a laugh I'd muffed, so I began apologizing and explaining.

"No. It ain't that," he said quickly, "but now that you mention it, you have been stepping on that line since the first show."

"I told you when we rehearsed it that it wouldn't get a laugh and now you keep blaming..."

"Stop it, Punkin." There was something in his face that stopped me, little trouble lines around his eyes and a worried set to his face. He threw his comedy coat over my shoulders and kissed me on the nose absentmindedly.

"Come on. I'll buy you a quick one at the Dutchman's," he said with the same detached air.

"That's what I love about you. You're so romantic," I said with a dead pan. "Anyway, we haven't time to go to the Dutchman's, the finale is next. Let's run into Louie's. You can bend an arm there just as easy."

"Come on," he said with a trace of impatience, "I got my

66

reasons for not wanting to go to Louie's." With that he pulled me across the stage and through the alley door.

The Dutchman's was almost two blocks away but we must have made it in a minute flat. I was panting when we swung the double door open and made our way through the sawdust to a back booth.

"One Old Granddaddy for me," Biff yelled to the man behind the bar, "and a slug of the cheapest rye you got in the place for my illegitimate daughter." He handed me a cigarette and took one for himself. It seemed hours before he lit them. I was burning with curiosity and he knew it. Instead of telling me what was on his mind, he puffed deeply on the cigarette and let more wrinkles settle on his forehead.

"Hear you're having a powwow at the place tonight." The bartender had put the drinks in a little puddle of liquor left by a previous drink and was ready for his usual ten-minute conversation. He wiped his hands on a long white apron that made his front look three times larger than it was.

"If he doesn't go away and let me listen to Biff," I thought, "I'll..."

"Yep. Sure are," Biff said. "Drop in if you want to." The barkeeper waddled away after thanking Biff and thanking me.

"Look," I began, "I've been very patient with you. Now I want to know what's cooking."

"Drink up first. This is something you need a bracer for." He downed his Old Granddaddy in one gulp. I made mine in two. "There's going to be trouble tonight," he said without a change of expression. "It's Russell." He stared at the door that had just swung open. A bum stumbled in. Biff stood up and peered into the two adjoining booths.

"Thought maybe we were on the Erie," he explained.

"Who'd want to listen? And what about Russell?"

Biff looked like he was going to change his mind about telling me after all, then he leaned across the table and began to speak softly.

"The day before the raid I heard him talking to Dolly. I couldn't catch all the words but every now and then La Verne's name came up. Dolly was sore; she kept saying 'I don't believe it.' Then Russell says, 'You think I'd have anything to do with a dame that was mixed up with a guy like Louie?' Then he opens the collar of his shirt and says, 'Look, baby, if I can forgive and forget a thing like that you can forget any cracks I mighta made just because you got me sore.' I didn't see what he was talking about, but I did see Dolly's face. Her lip quivered like she was gonna cry and she said, 'Poor darling.' Then Russ puts his arm around her. 'Leave it to me, honey, and we won't have a thing to worry about as long as we live.'"

"Is that all?" I didn't even try to keep the disappointment from my voice. Biff ordered two more drinks and gave me a disgusted look while the red-faced waiter hurried over to the table.

"No, that ain't all," Biff said when he'd left. "Today I hear him talking to the Princess! He's playing a fancy game with three dames—the Princess, Dolly, and La Verne. What it is I don't know. He told the Princess he'd handle Louie. I got a good picture of Russell handling Louie, but that isn't what worries me. It's you I'm thinking about."

"Me?" I said.

"Yeah, you! I don't want you getting friendly with any of 'em. Something's up and it ain't healthy to know too much with guys like Louie around."

"But the Princess," I said, "what can she have to do with…" My eyes glanced at the clock above the bar.

"The finale!" I shouted.

Biff turned white. We jumped up from the benches, nearly upsetting the booths in our rush for the door. Biff yelled to charge the bill and we flew down the street. Sammy's exact words came to me as Biff almost dragged me through the alley. "Immediate dismissal . . .any man or woman that misses a cue . . .and that goes for the finale, too."

Biff lost one of his yard-long shoes and I waited for him to run back and pick it up.

Suddenly the orchestra went into action, loud, lusty, and lousy, "Happy Days Are Here Again." The finale was on and we'd missed it!

Biff didn't take time to put on his shoe. He tucked the toe of it in his pocket and yelled to me, "You take stage right, I'll take stage left." He hopped through the door on one foot. "Just run on waving your arms and singing . . .maybe we'll get away with it." With a grin he flew across the stage.

I was trying to be as quiet as possible, hoping that I could sneak by Sammy, when I collided with Stachi's swivel chair. It fell over with a crash like a kettledrum symphony with a cymbal finish, and I fell on top of it. The leather seat pillow helped to break my fall but I banged my head on the heavy leg. I was still dizzy from the crack on my head when I pushed the draperies aside and dashed through them. Biff had told me to wave my arms and sing. Well, I sang at the top of my lungs, but only a few bars. *I was the only one singing.* The orchestra had stopped and the musicians stared at me as I stood there petrified. It was the same feeling as when your brassière strap breaks before it's supposed to.

Biff's voice from the opposite side of the stage made me turn my head. He was singing too, and waving his arms like a windmill. Center stage, with their hands on their hips and their mouths half open in wonderment, stood Mandy and Joey.

Mandy was the first one to find words. "If you don't mind too kindly," he said with a little bow, "me and my partner would like very much to do 'Pick Up My Old Hat.'"

I don't know how I got off stage. Skulked, I guess, would be a good word for it. All I remember is making a beeline for the stairs. My only hope was to reach the dressing room before Sammy or someone would see me. I called myself several kinds of a fool for not remembering that the orchestra also used the finale music to bring scenes on. I stayed close to the wall on my way to the stairs. Most of the women were in their finale gowns. Gee Gee and Sandra were near the water cooler, but Alice, to my dismay, was in the wings. She'd be the one to tell Sammy, I thought.

The show girls were getting cokes from the candy butcher and Jannine was talking to George, the electrician, about her lights. I didn't wait to hear all of it, but she was complaining and George seemed bored. I tried to make myself little as I hurried up the stairs. The Princess was on her way down, and in my rush I nearly pushed her over the railing. I mumbled an apology, but as usual, she ignored me.

The show girls were being announced as I adjusted the last hooks on my wardrobe. Then I leaned down to look in Alice's mirror. I intended fixing my hair but something startled me. Not really a noise, a feeling. A feeling that someone was watching me.

As I glanced nervously around the room my eyes fell on the door to the new toilet. Someone had painted a thick glob of red paint across the lock and door jamb. It had sealed the door.

I looked at it for a moment, fascinated. Then I stretched my arm across the shelf and touched it. It was warm! My finger had put a dent in the thickest part, I pulled my hand back quickly and hurried downstairs. I felt like the one who always has to touch something that has a wet paint sign on it.

I was still breathless when the curtain closed in after the finale. Sammy rushed onstage before we had a chance to leave. "Curtain call," he barked. "Hold your places for a curtain call." The actors mumbled angrily but we waited for the speech that Sammy was warming up to.

"Where in hell is La Verne?" He started and ended his speech with those five words. No one answered him. His face set in grim lines. "When I said that anyone missing the finale would get their notice, I meant it." He paused for a moment. "And that goes for the Prima Donna, too, by Jesus." He looked at the actors standing in their places.

"Who seen her last?"

"Oh, nuts," Dolly complained. "We got a party on, Sammy. Anyhow we all saw her. She was getting into the finale costume when I left and everybody was in the room."

Sammy dismissed us after the women verified Dolly's remark. That is, he dismissed everyone but me. I was certain that he was going to call me down for the racket I'd made in the stage entrance so I had my excuse ready.

"I don't know what happened, Sammy. All of a sudden I got faint . . .my head was killing me and I just . . ."

"I don't care about that," Sammy said. "You made it and that's what counts. It's that damned Prima Donna that gets me sore. It's just like her to miss it on purpose so she could get Moss to hire her back after I'd fired her."

I thought he was finished so I started upstairs and he stopped me again.

"Wait a minute, Gyp," he put his hand on my arm and looked around furtively. First Biff with his secrets, now Sammy!

"Look, Sammy," I said, "if it's on the QT I don't want to know about it. I have so damn many secrets in my head now that I'm afraid to open my mouth for fear they'll fall out."

"It's no secret," he said, but I wasn't convinced. "It's about a letter."

"I don't want to know." I pulled my arm away and went up one step. "What kind of a letter?" I couldn't help asking.

I remembered the letter I had received a week before. It was a very formal business letter, I didn't pay any attention to it at the time, but it was about my theater stock. Thinking about Moss' speech I wondered.

"Well, I got this letter today," Sammy said. "It was from a broker and the idea behind it was, did I want to sell my stock in the Old Opera?"

I had received my letter a week ago, why had Sammy received his so much later? I tried to assume an uninterested air as I waited for him to go on.

"It was full of big words like interest and amortization and crap like that, but they offered me nearly fifty percent more than I paid for it. I . . .well, I wondered if you got a letter, too."

"No, I didn't," I said and went upstairs. I don't know why I lied about it. Perhaps because my letter hadn't mentioned profit, maybe because I was subconsciously being loyal to Moss, or maybe because Sammy's furtiveness annoyed me.

As I hurried upstairs and into the room I thought that Sammy was just the type to own a few measly shares in something and do more worrying about it than the president and the board of directors put together.

The party was in full swing; it didn't surprise me. When there's only an hour to have fun in, you don't waste time with preliminaries. Someone shoved a glass of beer in my hand and Biff shouted from across the room.

"Over here, Punkin. I saved a chair for you."

The room was so smoky, even with the window open, that I could hardly see him. He was sitting at my makeup shelf and the chair he saved for me was my own.

"What kept ya?" he asked as I sat down. "Sammy get you for messing up the scene?"

"No, it was something about a letter . . .a love note." I don't know why I added that, either. I do know that it would have saved an awful lot of trouble if I'd told him then what Sammy's questions really were.

The room was so noisy that I couldn't hear what Biff was saying. The quartet at the beer barrel were harmonizing, the victrola was going full blast. Siggy, with his cigarette hanging magically from his lower lip, was singing a solo. His black bag was beside him, in case he could make a sale, I guess. He was a little drunk.

Mandy and Joey were the bartenders. They wore a full makeup

for the occasion: white aprons, check shirts and big black mustaches. A stick filled to the top with pretzels was in Joey's hand.

The room was too full of smoke for me to find everyone. A group had gathered around Alice's victrola. Some baritone was singing "Water Boy" to beat hell. Between the corny quartet around the barrel and the victrola, conversation was impossible. Waiters from the restaurant climbed in and out of the windows like in an old two-reel comedy. I couldn't find the one that gave me the root, but then they all looked pretty much alike.

In the midst of all this Biff suddenly slammed his mug of beer on the shelf. "Say, we gotta get the Hermit." He started for the door. "Can't have a party without inviting him."

Gee Gee waved a hand, a "Go 'way" gesture. "He'll never come down from that perch of his," she said. "Not as long as we got another show to do. Once up, once down. That's his routine."

"I don't blame him," Jannine chimed in. "If I had to climb all those stairs and then scale that wall to get up there, I'd stay, too."

"He doesn't scale the wall, you dope," Gee Gee said. "He's got a ladder, sort of, iron rungs set in the bricks. I been up there, I know."

Biff had let them argue it out. He stood on the balcony and called the flyman. "Hey, Hermie. Hermie!"

There was no answer and Gee Gee continued, "Sure I been up there. It was a couple of months ago. I had a snootful and just to be sociable I went up to visit him."

She took a gulp of her beer and waited for Jannine to ask, "What did he say?"

"He didn't say nothing. Aside from being mean as hell. Sorta glowered at me and..."

"And what?" Jannine was getting interested. So was I, for that matter.

Gee Gee hesitated before answering, a puzzled look in her face. "I hope I just imagined it, but I thought when I yelled to him to help me get from the rungs to his platform"—she used her hands to describe a distance of a foot or so between the ladder and the flies—"he . . .well, dammit, I know I was drunk, but I'd swear he tried to push me."

"You must have been damn drunk," Jannine replied. "Why, if he pushed you and you really fell you'd smash your brains out."

"I had to grab the guy ropes . . ." Gee Gee's voice trailed off as she buried her face in the beer mug.

I joined Biff on the landing and added my voice to his. "Hey, up there!" The flies were in darkness and there was no answer. Biff yelled again. "Hey, are you all right up there?" A glimmer of light flashed.

"What do you want?" The Hermit's shadow loomed up and the ropes behind him made a phantomlike scene. The voice seemed to come from far away.

"Where in hell were you?" Biff shouted, and the voice answered, "I was taking a nap. What do you want?" He sounded angry.

Biff went on, "We got a party goin'. Come on down and have a drink."

The shadow stretched taller and taller but there was no answer.

"He won't come down," I told Biff. "Ask him if he wants us to send some beer up to him."

"If you want some beer send the elevator down," Biff shouted through his cupped hands. He went into the room to get the bottles and I waited for the elevator to descend. I knew it would, the Hermit didn't like us but he did like his nips.

"Biff's gone to get it," I shouted. Still no answer, but I heard the scraping sound of the elevator hitting against the brick wall.

The elevator was another invention of Jake's. It was a square box with four ropes that met in the center. They were fastened to a longer rope that worked from the flies on a pulley. When the flyman wanted hot coffee or the papers, he called downstage and asked one of the stagehands to put the things in the box and then he pulled it up.

I had watched the elevator operate a hundred times or more but that night there was something about it that fascinated me. As it passed the upstairs landing I saw something glitter. Then as the box descended through the darkness the shiny thing was gone. I wasn't sure, but I had an impression that a piece of bead fringe had been hanging from the rope. The kind of fringe Siggy used on his more expensive G-strings. At that moment Biff returned with the bottles of beer. After putting them in the box he gave the rope a tug and the Hermit slowly pulled up the elevator.

I hadn't really forgotten the fringe, I think I would have told Biff about seeing it if it hadn't been for Louie's voice coming from the foot of the steps. Biff went into the room and as I started to follow him Louie called to me.

"Didja get the beer and stuff?" he asked. I couldn't see him very well, just the outline of a short, bull-necked, thick-chested man. The outline was enough to make me feel repugnance. I knew he was waiting for me to ask him up but I couldn't.

"Yeah, we got it," I said and went into the room. I couldn't even say thanks. Invitation or no invitation, I heard his heavy steps on the stairs.

The noise of the room had subsided a bit. Moey was making a speech. In the same tone he used when he made his audience spiel he said, "Friends, we are gathered here tonight to pay homage not to a great man, not to a great woman, but to a great institution. Plumbing!" Loud cheers followed his speech.

Moey smiled proudly. After all, hadn't he got it wholesale? "Now this here friend of mine…" he began.

Dolly shushed him. "Get to the point," she said.

"Well," Moey went on, "in keeping with the informal spirit of this here unveiling, I suggest that we select a queen. I have here in my hand a handful of straws."

As he held them up for inspection, Jake moaned, "Me new broom!"

Moey gave him a reproving look. "We all make sacrifices," he said, "and as I was saying before the vulgar note of selfishness protruded itself, we select this queen in a way that's new. It's novel. It's exciting. We draw straws!"

He walked over to Sandra and with a little bow waited for her to draw a straw. It was a long one and she pouted. Alice and Jannine were next, then I pulled one.

"I vill be next." The Princess was half hidden by the smoke but the accent came through as clear as a bell. She approached Moey and condescendingly made a choice. I kept my fingers crossed that she'd win. "Princess Nirvena, Queen of the Can." It would have been wonderful.

But it was a long one, too. The Princess shrugged her shoulders and went back to her chair. She sat there as though she were inspecting the czar's summer stables on a very hot day.

It was a tossup between Dolly and Gee Gee until the straws were measured more carefully. I was glad when Gee Gee won. Dolly had been sulking all evening and with that bleary look in her eye she wouldn't have been convincing in the part.

Gee Gee's eyes sparkled when Moey put the cardboard crown on her head and the bottle of beer in her hand.

"When I count to ten," he said, "you break this on the door-knob, see?"

With the crown on her head and the bottle in her hand she reminded me of a beauty-contest winner made up to represent "Miss Columbia, the Gem of the Ocean." The horseshoe behind her and the laurel leaves framing the door were like the float.

"One, two, three," Moey counted slowly and Mandy knelt at her feet with his hat in front of him to catch the overflow when the bottle broke.

"Look at me," he said. "Hebe, the cupbearer!"

"Looks like you're doing the gladiator bit," Moey said. Then, "Seven, eight." Gee Gee suddenly got the giggles and Moey waited for her to stop. "Eight," he repeated, "nine, ten!"

Crash! the beer splashed in all directions, all over Mandy and the laurel leaves, even a little on Biff, who stood behind the horseshoe. Jake quickly took the broken bottle from Gee Gee so she could open the door.

She turned the knob and pulled. The door wouldn't budge. She pulled again and Jake jumped to help. He took a screw driver out of a pocket in his overalls and began chipping away at a spot of something on the door.

"What are you doing?" Gee Gee asked. Her big moment was spoiled and there was a trace of annoyance in her voice.

"On account of snoopers," Jake explained, "to keep 'em out until the unveiling, I sealed the door." Jake grinned with satisfaction as he worked.

So that's what had intrigued me so while I was changing for the finale, I thought, sealing wax. And I thought it was paint.

The wax chipped off easily enough and Jake stood aside for Gee Gee to try again. She turned the knob slowly. Just before she opened the door, the sound of music came from the closet. A tinkling sound of "Whistle While You Work." Her hand relaxed for a second, a puzzled look on her face. Then she threw open the door.

The cheers died in our throats. A sudden silence fell over the room. There in a huddle on the floor was La Verne! She was stark naked, her hair falling all over her face.

"Stop clowning," someone said. "Put your clothes on." It was Sammy, but his voice was weak and quivery. He knew she wasn't clowning. Her body was too white and too twisted. He set his jaw to keep it from shaking up and down. "Someone get Doc Mitchell," he said, "and help me get her outta here."

We all knew she was dead, even before they picked her up and carried her out to the light. The victrola was running down. The baritone was getting lower and lower.

No singer can hit such low notes, I thought. It was like a boot scraping on a wooden floor. He wasn't singing, I thought. He's scraping his boot on the floor and La Verne is dead and I am dizzy and sick.

"Look! Look!" Did I say it or did I just think I had spoken? "Around her neck." No one saw it. No one listened to me. "It's her G-string. It's choking her to death. No. It can't do that. It can't hurt her because she's already dead."

The victrola stopped suddenly.

SEVEN

WHEN I CAME TO, THE ROOM WAS FULL OF COPS. AT first I thought we had been pinched again. Then I remembered. I was lying on the floor. Jiggers, the cop, was kneeling beside me.

"Nice thing, a big horse like you fainting," he said.

My eyes burned and my face was wet. I saw the towel in his hand. "If you had to hit me in the face with a towel," I told him, "you could at least have found a clean one."

He looked apologetically at the cloth smeared with grease paint and threw it in a corner. "Jees, I'm sorry, Gyp." Then his expression changed. He was a minion of the law when he added quickly, "Come on. The Sergeant's asking a few questions and he wants to see you in particular."

There was a decidedly unfriendly ring to his voice. His eyes left me and went to the far end of the room. I saw then what he was looking at. Three men in plain clothes were silently spraying powder on the door of the toilet, a fourth flashed a picture of the doorknob. Then they took a thing that looked like a magnifying glass and peered through it at the door.

One man turned to Jiggers. "Until I can examine this at the laboratory," he said, "I'd say that they were identical." He nodded importantly to the man at his left who scratched his chin and nodded back at him. When they had nodded themselves dizzy, they turned to me, not saying anything, just glancing at me and then to Jiggers.

Suddenly I felt something sticky on my fingers and I knew what was on their minds. I put my hand up to my eyes. There was ink, black ink, on every finger! They were comparing my prints to those on the door. Suddenly it became funny to me. These silly men taking pictures of my fingerprints, Jiggers being so limb-of-the-law-like, and me on the floor with a dirty, wet face. The picture of La Verne's face was in my mind, too. The horrible face with the split lip and blue color. I laughed and laughed until Jiggers began shaking me.

"Stop it," he said. "Stop it, or I'll have to hit you." I stopped but my teeth were still chattering. He pulled me to my feet. My legs were weak as I followed him upstairs.

The men's dressing room smelled of dirty comedy clothes and sweat. It was full of people and in the stale smoke-filled air their faces were dim and blurred. I felt a warm hand grab mine. It was Biff's. He gave me one of those "I'll stick to you" looks and squeezed my hand tightly.

I saw Sandra. She was leaning on the messy shelf. She greeted me with a sickly smile before she turned her head away.

"Just like you said, Sergeant." Jiggers was still holding my arm as he spoke. "They tally all right."

The man he spoke to was seated at a table near the window. He had a lot of papers in front of him which he kept his eyes on as though something very important were written there. A broken glass and several pencils were pushed to one side. Without looking at me he asked me to sit down.

"Are you feeling well enough to answer a few questions, Miss ..." he consulted one of the papers, "Miss Lee?" His voice was soft and smooth. He reminded me a little of my grandfather; the same iron-gray hair and the same twinkling eyes.

"Yes, Sergeant," I replied, "I am. It was silly of me to faint. First time I ever did. I hope it didn't hold up the investigation."

"Not at all, not at all," he assured me.

What a darling he is, I thought, and so much like Grandpa.

"You see," I continued, "I had never seen a dead—that is, a corpse, before and..."

"And the sight unnerved you?"

"Yes. When I saw the G-string I . . .I . . ."

"You what, Miss Lee?" He leaned forward when he prompted me. His mouth seemed to harden a little.

"Well, I fainted, I guess. Maybe it was because the room was so close and stuffy. So many people, you know." Someone snickered when I said that, not a friendly snicker. It was the Princess. She sat just behind Gee Gee. "And of course I had been drinking a lot of beer," I added quickly for her benefit.

The Sergeant was silent for a moment. He was looking at my right hand. At the ink or at the tight little wad of Kleenex I had rolled? "You are very nervous, aren't you?" he finally said.

I dropped the Kleenex in my lap. His voice had suddenly become less soft. The blueness was leaving his eyes and they seemed to be turning away, icy gray. He wasn't at all like Grandpa, I decided.

"Not exactly nervous," I replied a little stiffly. "Only I do think the police could wait until I was conscious to take my fingerprints. There's some law about that, I believe."

The Sergeant raised one shaggy eyebrow. "Oh, a legal mind, eh?" He smiled with absolutely no humor. "Well, it just happens that at the time your prints were taken you appeared to be very much conscious. At least from the things you said we believed you to be, shall I say, aware?"

"That's right, Gypper," Gee Gee added. "You were talking to beat all hell." Her eyes were wide and glittery. She was trying to tell me something with them.

The Sergeant turned to her and shook his head. "Please wait until I speak, Miss Graham."

Gee Gee glared at him and by then I was angry, too. "Look, if all this dialogue is about my fingerprints on the sealing wax, you're out of your mind." The Sergeant made a clucking noise with his teeth that made me more angry. "I don't give a damn if I was conscious or not when they took 'em. As for them being the same as on the door, that's simple. I was conscious and I touched it."

"Why?"

"Why what?"

"Why did you touch the sealing wax?" His eyes were hard now and his voice was low and serious. "I'll tell *you*! Because you knew what was behind that door. You removed the original wax and replaced it with a seal of your own, a seal that you melted yourself from a package that was given to you by a Chinese waiter! You sneaked into that room after everyone had left. There was ample time for you to do what you did. You hated the La Verne girl and…"

"Stop it!" I yelled. All the time he had been talking it was like I was on a roller coaster. I had been going up and up, then the sinking feeling of falling, the car shooting out from under me. I stood up and after a second I felt better. Still standing, I began to tell him calmly what had happened from the time I went to the Dutchman's with Biff until the time I began dressing for the finale.

"I had a feeling someone was watching me," I said. "Then when I saw the splash of red paint—I mean wax—I, well, I touched it." I shrugged my shoulders and tried to find the words. The Sergeant waited, so I said, "That's when I found out it was warm."

"You admit that it was warm?"

"Certainly I admit it. What do you think I'm giving you— double talk? But I had nothing to do with changing it. And as for that other piece of wax, I haven't seen it since I saw it on the package the waiter gave me. And I didn't like La Verne, either! There are a lot of people I don't like. You for one. But that's no proof that I go around strangling them with a G-string."

The last words I gave out with a loud voice and turned to leave the room. A policeman stopped me.

The Sergeant had started to speak, the soft voice this time.

"Sit down, Miss Lee. I wasn't accusing you of murdering La Verne. I just mentioned that you hated her. And, of course, your prints were on the wax." He was being very charming, but I still remained standing. "We have our duty," he said. "We need your cooperation and I'm pretty sure you're going to give it to us."

I sat down, but not comfortably. I was on to him by then. That cooperation talk would have worked a few minutes ago, but not now.

"What makes you think she was strangled by a G-string?" He was doodling on a piece of paper, making little circles that overlapped each other. As he finished talking he put a dot in the center of one circle, then another.

"I saw it," I said slowly. "When the men picked her up and carried her into the dressing room, I saw the rhinestones glitter. The patch was hanging from her neck right below her ear."

There wasn't a sound from the others in the room. I looked around at them. Russell stood at the door with his eyes on the floor. Dolly and Jannine were sharing one chair. The Princess was smiling, too, but it was a sly twisted smile. She looked pleased about something, which meant bad news for someone.

I looked back at the Sergeant. His eyes were on me. From under the eyebrows he peered at me like a poodle. He had stopped drawing the circles and was tapping his pencil on the table.

"Stop looking at me that way," I said. "And stop that damned tapping. What's the matter with all of you?"

The tapping stopped.

"La Verne was strangled," the Sergeant said slowly. He began tapping again. "With a piece of dental floss." The tapping was slower. "There was no G-string and no rhinestone patch."

It took me a moment to understand what he had said. Then it hit me. No rhinestones, not a G-string, my fingerprints on the wax, and it was true that I hated La Verne! Biff's voice was the next thing I heard.

"I don't know what you're getting at, Sergeant," he said, "but it sounds like you're calling Miss Lee a liar." He stood next to the table and spoke emphatically. "You see, Punkin, I mean Miss Lee, and I were together all evening. Not for a second was she out of my sight."

"That's a God-damned lie!" someone shouted, and through the smoke I saw Russell come forward. "She was in the dressing room alone before the finale." His face was contorted.

"How do you know?" Biff snapped at him.

Russell paused and looked at the Sergeant, who asked in his softest voice, "Yes. How do you know Miss Lee was in the room alone?"

"Because I saw, I mean, that is..." He looked wildly around the room but there were no friendly faces to reassure him. Almost desperately he added, "Everyone was onstage for the finale and I saw her come in and go upstairs."

Biff waited for the Sergeant to speak. When he remained silent, Biff said slowly, and with a little smile, "Talking about God-damned liars, give yourself billing. You say everyone was onstage ready for the finale, that is, everyone but Punkin and—La Verne!" Russell winced when Biff continued, "You don't mention where *you* were. You also forgot to mention that you told us guys just an hour before they found her dead that you'd kill her rather than see her mixed up with a guy like Louie."

"And I wanted to kill her, the dirty double-crossing..." Russell's voice broke and he buried his face in his hands. "But I loved her. I didn't even know she was mixed up with him until I heard them fight. I wanted to marry her. I loved her too much to kill her."

Dolly opened her mouth to speak, but closed it quickly. Her lower lip trembled.

The Sergeant had been watching her, too. "Is there something you want to say, Miss Baxter?" he asked.

Dolly shook her head. "No. Nothing at all."

"Didn't you want to tell me that it was impossible for Russell Rogers to marry Lolita La Verne?" the Sergeant asked again.

Dolly kept on shaking her head. "No, no, no!" she cried hysterically.

"Impossible because he is already married?" Disregarding Dolly's frantic appeal, he added, "Married to you?"

If Jannine hadn't grabbed her, Dolly would have fallen. Sobs made her voice almost unintelligible as she cried on Jannine's shoulder. "We didn't want it known at first because Moss doesn't like to hire married couples. And I was playing here first. He was laying off. Then when they needed a new straight man I told them I had worked with him before and that he…"

She was crying too hard to go on, but with Jannine soothing her, in a moment she added, "When I saw her making a play for him I wanted to tell. Then he wouldn't let me. He told me he loved her, that he never loved me."

"And what did you tell me?" Russell's voice was deadly, his face ashen.

Dolly didn't answer, but began sobbing again.

Russell turned to the Sergeant. "Cry, cry, cry," he said derisively. "She wasn't crying the time she said she'd kill La Verne and me. No, there wasn't an audience then. And if you think I'm lying, look at this!" He tore his shirt open and unwound a woolen ascot tie that covered his neck. "Look at those marks!"

With his head thrown back the marks were visible; black-and-blue finger marks on his throat. Three deep red scars that might have been made by fingernails were under his ear.

"She did that. A week ago. The night I told her I was leaving her."

"It isn't true, it's all lies," Dolly screamed hysterically.

I almost believed her, but those marks on Russell's neck were definitely made by fingernails, and long ones at that. I looked at Dolly's brightly lacquered nails. They were long and they were strong. The one broken nail made her hand look unbalanced. I remembered when she had broken it, while she was nailing the laurel leaves to the door.

But had she broken it then? The thought hit me suddenly. Had she pretended that she broke it then to establish an alibi?

I pushed the thought out of my head. Why would she bother establishing an alibi for scratching up her own husband? No one in the world could blame a woman for losing her temper, especially if she was married to a man like Russell Rogers.

EIGHT

THE SERGEANT LISTENED CAREFULLY TO THE disclosures. Every now and then he wrote something on one of the papers in front of him.

"I want to speak to Louie Grindero," he said suddenly.

Aside from the scuffling noises of people turning around in their chairs the room was silent.

Jiggers left the door and went over to the Sergeant. He leaned over and whispered something. The Sergeant began writing quickly.

"Give that to Lieutenant Hanson," he said, as he handed Jiggers the folded piece of paper. Jiggers left the room pompously.

"Bet that's a dragnet for Louie," Biff said. The Sergeant glared at him and Biff settled down to an injured silence.

"Miss Graham?" Gee Gee sat very straight when the Sergeant called her. She was all attention as he spoke.

"When I questioned you earlier you said you were not in the dressing room alone at any time during the performance."

Gee Gee nodded her head quickly. "Yep. I mean nope I wasn't alone once."

The Sergeant consulted his papers again and Gee Gee smiled around the room like she was playing a comedy version of "Madame X."

"When is the last time you remember seeing the deceased?"

"The what?"

"The deceased, Lolita La Verne."

Gee Gee thought a second before answering. "Golly, I can't remember. What did I tell you when you asked me before?"

The Sergeant replied patiently, "You weren't sure, but you said you thought it was some time during the performance. You couldn't remember."

"Well, if I couldn't remember then, how in hell do you expect me to remember now? And anyhow, you know how it is, you get so used to seeing a person you get so you don't see 'em at all."

The Sergeant gave her the under-the-eyebrow poodle look. "No, Miss Graham, I don't know how it is. When I see a person, I see him. Now think carefully."

Gee Gee wrinkled her forehead and pulled tenderly on her ear for a while. Then she looked up with a quick smile. "After thinking carefully, I find that I don't remember a God-damned thing."

The Sergeant asked her to go to her own chair. "No, don't leave the room, please." Gee Gee reluctantly sat down instead of rushing out the door as she had been meaning to.

"Will you please sit here for a moment, Miss Slade?" He beckoned with a finger and spoke to Sandra. After she had seated herself he asked her the same questions.

She remembered plenty. "Well, I asked her to lend me a buck until the guy came back with the pay slip. They always pay off during the first night show or a little after, so it wasn't like I asked her to lend it for a long time, and I was simply dying for some coffee and I didn't have the money because I always send money home and by the time the end of the week comes around I'm flat. Of course I shoulda saved my breath, getting a buck outta her grouch bag was a major feat, but like I always say, nothing ventured not…"

"I see," the Sergeant said slowly. "You can't remember *just* when you saw La Verne last. Is that it?"

"Yeah. That's it," Sandra replied innocently. The Sergeant

was still patient. I don't know how he managed it but his voice remained the soft one that got me to say too much.

When he spoke to Dolly he was very kind. She had dried her eyes and answered most of the questions as negatively as the others had until he said, "You realize, of course, Miss Baxter—I beg your pardon—Mrs. Rogers, that you had a motive for killing Lolita La Verne?"

Dolly looked at him stupidly. She wasn't sure now if she could trust him. I sympathized with her. The Sergeant could make you feel pretty uncomfortable, and if you really were a murderer—well, there are other people I'd rather confide in.

"I didn't do it," she said.

"You *did* attack her with a nail file, though, didn't you?" When she nodded yes he added quickly, "And you *did* try to strangle your husband, didn't you?" She nodded yes again before she realized he had tricked her.

Jannine jumped up quickly. "You dirty stinker," she said. With a push she moved Dolly away and stood in her place.

"Since you started this mess that you call an investigation you've made one charge after another." She glared at the uniformed officer. "You've been scaring everybody half to death with your beady eye. First you pick on Gypper." She tossed a head in my direction. I would rather have handled my argument with him myself but Jannine was getting wound up. She threw a leg over the corner of the table and put her face close to the Sergeant's.

"Do you think that any of us would admit that we were the last one to see her alive? If Gyp had really changed the sealing wax, do you think she would leave a fingerprint right smack dab in the center of it? And anyway, they don't even bring up that kind of corny print business in dime magazines any more. Another thing—"

The Sergeant had opened his mouth to speak but she used a hand to quiet him, a hand and her voice that was getting louder every minute.

89

"Yes, another thing. We may have our fights and all that, but they are between us! There isn't anyone in this room that would tell on another if they thought it was going to hurt that person. We stick together, bejeesus!"

"Just a moment, please. Let me tell you…"

"You said enough to last you for a lifetime. I ain't finished yet. You and your know-it-all attitude. It's the social system of the upper classes that gives you guys the right to browbeat the workers! Well, you won't get away with it around here." She waited a moment to catch her breath. "What if I tell you that La Verne *was* strangled with a G-string? Well, she was! She always used dental floss instead of elastic. I know."

"You seem to know a lot." The Sergeant finally managed to get a word in.

"Damn right. And that's not half of it." Jannine smiled with satisfaction as she slid off the table. Her house coat opened in the movement and revealed a white leg, a thigh, and a glitter of bead fringe at her hip.

"Have any of your wise-o cops noticed that her bankbook's missing?" she asked.

The Sergeant looked down at her leg and quickly turned his head away.

"That peek will cost you a quarter," Jannine said as she sauntered back to her chair.

The Sergeant cleared his throat noisily and slid a finger under his collar. When he spoke there was a note of command in his voice.

"Sit down, Miss Jannine," he said.

Jannine sat. She wasn't quite as satisfied with herself when she faced him.

"I've been very patient with you people," the Sergeant said, "because I know that show people are generally excitable and this…murder has upset all of you. But this isn't a backstage feud or quarrel, this is a case of vile premeditated *murder*. Whether you liked the woman or not doesn't matter. What *does* matter is that we apprehend the murderer. To bring him to justice I must have your help."

He looked around the room. "Has anyone remembered anything that might be important?" he asked.

No one moved or spoke. Then the Princess stood up and faced the table.

"I haff joost remembered something," she said. "Through that pipe," with a long, dark-skinned finger she pointed to the ventilator. The Sergeant's eyes followed the imperious hand. "I haff heard voices, La Verne's and . . .somevone else's. The voices were angry. It wass joost before the last scene, that I know because I hear the music and I hurry to dress for the finale. I hear this La Verne say, 'You wouldn't dare,' and this other voice says, 'You think not?' Then I hear a not strange sound. In Russia during the Revolution, the *counter*revolution, when I am a very little girl, I hear such sounds, but only when someone is garroted."

"And this other voice—you recognized it?"

The Princess paused for a minute. She let her eyes fall on Dolly, who met them defiantly.

"I said," the Sergeant repeated, "did you recognize this other voice?"

"I'm not sure." She still stared at Dolly. "Maybe later I remember, eh?"

Dolly looked at her quickly, "Yeah, maybe you will," she snapped.

The Sergeant watched the little scene with no apparent interest. He seemed to be waiting for one of the other women to speak.

Alice broke the silence. "Aren't you going to athk me anything? You athked everybody but me and I think that'th mean."

The Sergeant glanced at her. The icy blue eyes softened. Alice did that to every man. As I watched her I thought that with a face like hers she could get away with murder, then I stopped thinking. This was no time for clichés, especially those with words like murder and death in them.

"When did you last see Lolita La Verne?" he asked.

"I gueth I wath the lath one to thee her alive," Alice replied innocently. The Sergeant looked up quickly. Alice giggled. "I mean bethideth the murderer, of courth. You thee, it wath like thith; when we all left for the finale she wath right behind me on the thetpth. And she thaid thomething funny—at leatht I thought it wath funny. It wath about that picture of her mother. She thaid that thome louth …" Alice put her fingers on her lips as though the word louse was the height of profanity; with a little blush she added, "That wath what she thaid anyway . . .thome bad perthon thtole her picture. I didn't anther her right away and she shouted in my ear, 'Where ith it?' I wathn't going to anther her until she thaid pleath, but she wath tho mad that I got frightened."

Alice shivered delicately and the Sergeant nodded his sympathy.

"I didn't want her to blame poor little me, tho I told her that no one thtole the picture because it wath right on her shelf, only it wath under the paperth. That wathn't the whole truth but I'm not a tattletale and I wouldn't tell her that Dolly hid the picture on purpothe to make her mad."

"Oh, nuts," Dolly jumped from her chair and took a step toward the door before the policeman stopped her. Alice cringed like a mistreated orphan.

"Thee?" She gazed appealingly at the Sergeant. "She's afraid I'll tell . . .the . . .other thing too." With that tear in her voice she had the entire police force knocking themselves out to protect her. The cops glowered at Dolly and showered love looks on Alice.

"You must tell everything," the Sergeant said softly. With a cold stare at poor, bedraggled Dolly he added, "No one is going to hurt you, Miss Angel."

Alice's lower lip trembled just enough to make a pretty picture. She said, "Well, La Verne didn't believe me when I thaid the picture wath there tho I went back to the room with her and showed her where it wath hidden. Then she *made* me tell who hid it. I honethly didn't want to but I wath afraid she wath going to hit me if I didn't tell. I *did* thay it wath jutht a joke, but when she got madder thtill, I left in a hurry. Then on the way downthtairth I thaw…"

Dolly shook the policeman's hand from her shoulder and stood up. "She saw me!" Dolly almost screamed it. "That's what she's leading up to. Sure I went back to the room. But I didn't say one word to La Verne, I didn't even see her." Dolly sighed deeply before going on. Her voice was more normal when she explained that she had gone back for a cigarette.

"Sammy called us too early for the finale," she said. "I didn't know it until I got downstairs, so I went back for my cigarettes. I got one and left."

"You didn't notice La Verne?" the Sergeant asked.

"I didn't *see* her," Dolly replied. "Words like notice I don't know from."

"Why didn't you mention this earlier?"

Dolly shrugged her shoulders. She did it well and at that moment it was a perfect gesture. She threw her next line away. "I guess it just slipped my mind."

The Sergeant looked at her from under his eyebrows. When he looked at me like that I almost confessed that I was the murderer, but he didn't upset Dolly.

"Anything else you want to know?" she asked.

"Not at the present." He turned to Sammy. "Would you see that I have a list of names and addresses?" he asked.

Sammy told him, with great importance, that he would "personally" see to it.

No one had dismissed us but there was a general movement toward the door. Joey and Russell left. The policeman didn't stop them, so I hoped that the meeting was over. Biff whispered to Dolly to "Buck up." I thought that she of all people concerned needed no encouragement. That was, until I looked at her. Her eyes followed Russell but I doubt that she really saw him. She seemed dazed, too dazed to know what was going on. The Princess swept past her without a glance. Then Sandra left.

"Come on, Doll," Biff said. "We'll go downstairs and get us a quick drink and…"

Dolly pushed his hand away angrily. "I don't want a drink," she said. "I can't go in that room again. Never." She was trembling.

It was heartless of me, but when Biff left her standing there, I followed him. I was on the verge of nervous shrieks myself and all I needed to go into my act was a word or two with Dolly.

From the landing, I saw that the rest of the company was on their way to the basement. I asked Biff what went on.

"They moved the party liquor down there," he explained. That was all I wanted to know; not that I'm a drunkard or anything close to it, but at that moment I would have given a lot for six straight ryes.

Biff must have read my mind. "I want a couple, too," he said. "But I gotta get something first."

The door to our dressing room was closed but not locked. I thought it strange that there were no cops guarding "the scene of the crime." Later I found out that the door to the toilet was locked and sealed. With their usual efficiency, the police picked the wrong door to bolt. Biff opened the iron door and entered the room. I wasn't much keener on going in than Dolly had been but I followed him.

They had moved La Verne, I thanked the Lord for that. Aside from a few used flash bulbs and the bolted closet door there was nothing to remind me of what had just happened. The window to the roof was still open, the faded chintz curtains blowing in a thin banner across the room. It was chilly and damp. I started over to close the window and saw that it was raining. A cold, misty rain. The window had jammed again and while I struggled with it Biff came over to me.

"Wait a minute," he said. He reopened it and threw a leg over the sill, then he dropped to the roof. He was looking for something. He flicked on his lighter and shielded the glow with his hands. It was so dark I could see nothing but the yellow wavering light, until he stooped down to pick up a glittering patch of rhinestones. Before he hurriedly concealed it in his pocket, I saw the plush lining and the string of dental floss. It was Jannine's G-string. The same one I had seen hanging from La Verne's neck!

"What in the name of Gawd are ya hanging out the window for, Gyp?" Dolly had evidently got over her nervousness about the dressing room. She looked a little drunk as she walked over to me and peered curiously at the window.

"Biff's out there," I said quickly. "He found Ja ..."

"It's all right." Biff was climbing back through the window. He flashed a warning glance at me. "Lost my handkerchief, jumped out to get it." He patted his hip pocket. "Got it right here."

"Well, cut out that flapping business," Dolly said. "You look like you're taking bows for a seal act." She pulled a bottle out of her apron pocket and began unwinding the top. "I'll make with the drinks, if you get the water."

"And where did you get that?" Biff asked, with a happy eye on the quart.

"It was the last bottle from the party," Dolly replied. "I didn't think one measly lil bottle would do 'em any good so ...well, here's to it."

The third time the bottle was going around, Gee Gee and Sandra came in. They had been to Louie's, they explained. Seems everyone had dropped in for a couple of quick ones when the party liquor gave out.

"Jiggers was there, too," Sandra said. "Only he was on business."

"What kind of business?" Biff asked.

"He was looking for Louie. Don't look." She had her coat and dress off before Biff could turn his head.

"Who's looking?" he said. "Did he find him?"

"Find who? Oh, Louie." Sandra reached for the bottle and wiped the top with the back of her hand before drinking. "Nope," she said, "and what's more I don't think they will," she added with importance.

"What makes you think that?" Dolly asked casually.

"Well, far be it from me to hamper justice." Sandra made a pious face. "Nobody bothered to tell the cops about the fight he had with La Verne. All they did was squawk about you and Russell, and Gyp. So I just told 'em about how he took a poke at her and what he said about giving her worse than that if she wasn't careful. Only I made it a little stronger and I said it loud enough for Moey to hear so he'd go and tell Louie. Sure enough, that's what he did."

"Louie's gone, bag and baggage," Gee Gee added helpfully. "Took his car too. Not that it'll help him. Jiggers said they got a radio thing out describing the car and what he looks like, what he was wearing and everything." She was taking her makeup off while she was talking. The cosmetic from her eyelashes she picked off carefully and put back in the little pan. She used so much she thought it wasteful not to remelt it for a second time.

"Say," Dolly exclaimed suddenly. "We got a midnight show. Why are ya taking off the war paint?"

"No midnight," Sandra said, pulling a beret on her head. "Sammy said he thought it would look too mercenary. With Moss outta town his word's law. Anyway, the place is crawling with newspaper guys. We got out through the coal chute."

Gee Gee giggled. "It'd've made ya die laughing. We got out right behind the crowds. Mandy helped us lift the manhole cover and he peeked around to see if anyone was looking. Everybody was hanging around the stage door, so when he told us the coast was clear we all crawled out and started mingling with the crowds. Mandy goes up to some goggle-eyed guy and says, 'What's cooking?' and the guy says, 'A dame just got bumped off in the burlesque joint.' Then Mandy goes, 'tch, tch, tch.' "

Gee Gee's imitation of Mandy going "tch, tch, tch" was almost as good as her imitation of the Hermit. Biff joined in the hysterical laughter.

Between guffaws Gee Gee added, "Mandy kept asking one guy after the other what happened and every time they told him he got that sanctimonious look on his kisser like when he's playing the preacher in the 'Peace on You, Too' scene. Once he said, 'The wages of sin is death,' and he shook his head real sadlike. I hadda roar."

"Well, I don't think it'th funny." Alice Angel stood in the door. Her eyes were a little red from weeping. They usually were, but she managed to look lovely in spite of that. Maybe because of it. When I cry, my face looks like a red balloon but on Alice tears were becoming, and she knew it.

"I don't know how you can joke about anything tho . . .thad," she sobbed. With a languid hand she brushed a tear from her cheek and turned her gaze on Biff.

"Make them thtop, pleathe," she asked appealingly.

Biff looked down at her. She did look helpless, I almost didn't blame him for smiling at her that special way.

"Where were you, and who made you cry?" he asked softly.

"Sergeant Harrigan wanted to athk me a few more quethtions," she said with a wan smile. "He wath very nithe to me but he made me thay thinth I didn't want to thay." She made wide eyes and puckered her lips.

"I don't know why he thingled me out but he thaid I wath the most obtherving woman in the theater." Dolly started to interrupt but Alice turned to her and smiled blandly.

"I only told the truth, Dolly," she said. "And if the truth hurtth you it ithn't my fault, ith it, Biff?" He got the smile then, a radiant one. I thought she was overdoing it, but Biff was as bad as the others. He melted right before my eyes.

Gee Gee broke up the act. "Well, I'll be damned!" She stood in front of La Verne's makeup shelf with her hands on her hips and her mouth half open. "The picture of La Verne's mother is gone!"

She turned back to the shelf and began moving things around looking for the photograph. She tilted the mirror forward and peered behind it, then she lifted a makeup towel and looked under that. There was something almost frantic in the way she searched. The bottle of gallstones glistened in the reflected light and Gee Gee pulled her hand away from it quickly. With the towel, she picked it up and tossed it into the wastebasket. Her eyes were frightened when she finally looked up.

"Do you think the . . .murderer took it?" she said.

Alice was the only one to speak. "I showed La Verne where it wath. I thaw her take it out from under the shelf paper where Dolly hid it."

"Shut up," Dolly said. "Nobody asked you."

Alice turned and faced Dolly, "I won't shut up." Her voice was as loud as Dolly's, her mouth was hard. "I think you took it. Tho there."

For a minute I thought we were going to have another fight on our hands, but Dolly turned her head away. "I don't care what you think," she said. There was a weariness to her face and voice. When she sat down her shoulders sagged.

Gee Gee smiled at her sympathetically. "It's my fault for getting so excited about it," she said. "The cops probably thought it was a clue, and they took it. I'll bet it's got a sign, Exhibit A on it right now."

When Dolly looked up I was shocked at the change in her face. She tried to smile and it was worse. The deep smudges under her eyes weren't from makeup and the yellow color of her skin was ghastly.

Gee Gee didn't stop babbling. "I hope the cops don't think every G-string in the theater is a clue, too. If they do we'll all be catching a hell of a lot of colds."

Dolly managed a little smile. I heard Biff laugh, so I turned to him. He was watching Dolly intently and the laugh was a prop if

I ever heard one. He said he would change his clothes and if we waited he would lift the manhole cover for us. When he passed Alice he put his arm around her.

"You're too pretty to get all mad like that," he said. Then he had the nerve to look at me and grin! I grinned back but it must have been rather terrifying because he left quickly. From the steps he called to me, "Punkin?"

I didn't answer, so he called again.

"If you feel hungry we'll go to the Peerless and put on the feedbag."

Alice was getting all my attention but I managed to yell, "OK"

She was going into a number that was pure summer stock. She couldn't help it if every man she knew fell madly in love with her. She didn't *want* men to feel that way about her, but she just couldn't help it. Her big blue eyes tried to tell me that she was sorry Biff felt like that. I let my big brown eyes tell her to stop kidding.

Meanwhile Gee Gee was finished dressing and I had to hurry to catch up with her. Dolly had pulled a hat over her face. I guess she thought it was easier than putting a full makeup on. Alice was combing her hair out. It hung in golden waves over her shoulders. I wasn't surprised when she said she wasn't going to leave with us. She tried to cover it up by explaining that she thought exiting through the coal chute was undignified and that "after all, we owe it to the preth to make an appearanthe." She was going to make an appearance, all right, dead-white makeup, a hint of blue eye shadow, and a pathetic mouth.

All she needed was an armful of lilies to make the picture complete. The crowd at the door would fall for it, though. I was certain of that. She'd give them one of those "I'm so small and you're so big and strong" looks and to a man they'd feel the urge to protect her. She rehearsed her character as she said good night to me.

"I wish I could be brave like you, Gyppy," she said with a little sob.

I didn't bother telling her that with what she had she didn't need bravery. On the way downstairs I rehearsed a little number myself. From now on I was going to be completely defenseless. Being a foot taller than most of the cops was going to hinder my style to a certain extent, but I made up my mind to wilt. And good.

NINE

GETTING OUT THROUGH THE COAL CHUTE WASN'T AS much fun as I had expected. I wanted cobwebs, eerie sounds, and maybe a skeleton or two.

The hall leading to it was dark enough and did smell a little dank, but that was no different from the regular stage exit. We had to walk single file because of the narrowness of the hall. Biff led the way and Gee Gee and he were giggling. Dolly was behind me and Sandra and Jannine followed so closely on my heels that every now and then they'd bump into me.

"This'd make a swell place to hide a body," Biff said with his usual misplaced humor. He added, "In fact, I wonder why I didn't think of it before."

When he said "body," Dolly grabbed me. She muttered, "The murderer, maybe he's hiding here." Her teeth were chattering and she held me so tightly that I almost had to wrench her fingers loose.

I wanted cobwebs and all that, but I didn't bargain for a woman who was pretending to be terrified. There was no doubt in my mind that it *was* pretense. She was no actress and the phonyness came through too strongly.

It must have impressed Biff the same way. He started shouting, "Bats! Bats!" in a loud voice.

Gee Gee faked a horrified scream and Sandra cried, "They'll get in your hair! Help! Help!"

Dolly stopped trembling and her voice was steady when she said, "Go to hell."

I heard Biff grunt from the exertion of lifting the manhole cover and our parade stopped. A streak of light, like a thin moon, was above us. Biff moved the cover over and pulled himself up through the opening.

He leaned over and grabbed Gee Gee's arms. I pushed from the rear and, after a struggle, she was out on the street. When Jannine climbed out she helped Biff by grabbing one of Sandra's arms and by then I had sensed enough to lean over and make a step out of my back. Sandra's heels pressed too firmly into the flesh for comfort, so I made Dolly take off her shoes when it was time for her to get out.

"They oughta get a ladder installed," Biff said. "Make it more convenient when we have our murders."

His remark brought on another fit of terror for Dolly. There was a difference of about forty pounds between her and the others, and even with the shoes off, my back was too tired for her to start that trembling act.

"I'm a stripteaser," I gasped, "not the under man for a balancing act. Make the jokes later, please."

By the time Biff grabbed my arms and got me out to the street I was weak. They all looked so funny staring down at me, and the idea of our being pulled out of a manhole started me laughing.

Biff was laughing and pointing. I thought he was laughing at me, but one look at the theater entrance showed me what he found amusing. Alice was making her exit and there wasn't a single man there to protect her or sympathize with her. The street was empty and the theater lights out; her scene was played to an empty house. When she saw us watching her, she waved sadly and with bowed head disappeared down the street.

Dolly didn't lose a second getting to the only light on the block. It came from Louie's bar on the corner. The three girls joined her. After the good nights were said Biff and I made for the subway.

"We make a fancy exit to avoid what crowds?" I remarked as we hurried along.

"You have to admit it was fun, Punkin. And if we'd gone through the regular stage door, we would have missed the perfect example of what not to do in case of murder."

"Alice?" I asked hopefully.

"And the terror of your friend Dolly." Biff emphasized the "your." He didn't give me a chance to remind him that she was as much his friend as she was mine. "She wouldn't be that frightened if she came face to face with a boa constrictor."

I had to agree with him. Dolly wasn't the type for trembling unless she wore a fringed skirt and had an audience of paying customers.

"She certainly wasn't nervous when the cops questioned her," I said. "The way she answered them you'd think she'd rehearsed it."

We walked along silently until Biff stopped at the corner. A bright street light made me remember how hurriedly I'd fixed my face, but Biff wasn't thinking of the way I looked.

"Did you get the crack Jannine made about La Verne's bankbook missing?" he asked. "The Sergeant let it slip right by him, and why didn't he ask Dolly where she sat in the dressing room? If she'da told him he woulda known that she couldn't get a cigarette without seeing La Verne. Not with them sitting that close together."

That was the cue for my helpless act. I should have clung to Biff and begged him not to get interested in those things, maybe cried a little on his shoulder. But like Dolly, I should have rehearsed it first; all I could manage was to remind him of what he had told me at the Dutchman's.

"You told me yourself it wasn't healthy to get mixed up with a guy like Louie and now you've got that 'butt in' look in your eye. That's what the police are around for ..."

Biff went "hurumph." It was another chance for me to get girly but I muffed it again. "You stick to your jokes," I said firmly, "and leave the deducing to the cops. After all, it isn't any of your business, and why do you pay taxes?"

Then I remembered the G-string on the roof. Biff must have known I was going to ask him about it! He tried a diversion. It couldn't have been the moon, because there wasn't one and a street light on Fourteenth Street isn't going to inspire a man to kiss a woman. The kiss wasn't one that a man would need inspiration for anyway.

It was a courtesy peck on the ear. After it, Biff held my arm tightly and hurried me down the street. While I tried to keep up with him, he said, "The trouble with cops is they don't understand actors."

BIFF WAS VERY clever about evading unasked questions. The subway was crowded and we had to stand until we got to Thirty-Fourth Street. I would have liked to have been a little closer to Biff, but we were separated by standees.

I wanted to tell him that I enjoyed being kissed by him even on Fourteenth Street, and I wanted to ask him so many questions. But you can't say, "Why didn't you tell me you knew where Jannine's G-string was?" when you're in a car full of people. I wanted to ask him why the G-string was on the roof, too. And who put it there? And most of all, why?

A man standing between Biff and me kept poking me in the eye with his newspaper. It reminded me of how the press would love our case.

STRIPPER STRANGLED.
BRUNETTE BEAUTY BUMPED OFF.

In my mind I wrote all the headlines. The pictures would probably be old ones, lots of leg showing, and the captions would all declare we were beauties. They would possibly mention my fingerprints being found on the wax and…

"Biff!" I shouted above the roar of the subway. "How did the police know my fingerprints were on the wax?"

The man with the paper glowered at me. "With lungs like yours, girlie," he said, "you oughta be hog calling."

The train stopped suddenly. We were at Thirty-Fourth Street. Biff reached an empty seat a split second before my friend with the paper.

"Look, chucklehead," Biff said to me, "the next time you get an idea, be a little more refined about blatting it out."

I squeezed in beside him. "But how could they tell?" I asked, quietly this time. "We saw Jake chip the wax off before Gee Gee opened the door. How could they tell the prints were mine from such little hunks?"

Biff smiled. "They got the hunk they wanted, Punkin. And anyway, when you fainted, one of the eagle-eyed boys saw the red on your finger. I tried to tell 'em it was rouge, that you put your lipstick on with that finger, but..."

"I do," I whispered.

"The colors were different; light-red lipstick, brick-red wax. Not only that, but they didn't fingerprint anyone else. They knew from the first that the prints were yours. You see, someone saw you touch the door."

"Who? They couldn't have." I shouted. Biff shushed me, so I lowered my voice. "The door was closed. No one could have seen me."

"Well, they didn't exactly see you touch the door, but they saw you wipe some red off your finger when you were leaving the room. Don't get sore and don't shout but it was—well, it was the Princess."

I didn't shout, but I did get sore. The idea of her telling the police a thing like that. She must have made it a pretty thick story, too, for them to suspect me as they did. I made up my mind to tell a few things about *her* the next time I saw the Sergeant.

"Where was *she* to see me so clearly?" I asked.

"She said she was downstairs and just happened to look up to the balcony as you came out." Biff raised one eyebrow. With a low whistle he added, "You see why I'm butting in, Punkin?"

I was going to say that I did and add a few little words of encouragement when the man with the paper interrupted me.

"Say, ain't you Gypsy Rose Lee?"

"Certainly not," I said. "Do I look like the sort of woman who would do a striptease?"

"Well, it'd be hard to tell with all them clothes you got on." He laughed gaily at his feeble joke and it was my turn to glower at him.

"Only you sure do look like the dame in this pitcher." He held the paper in such a way that I could see the large picture that Seymour took of me while I was playing the Rialto in Chicago. The caption was turned under a little at the corner. All I could read was *Lee, Material Witness*, and, in smaller print, *Searching for missing racketeer.*

I hadn't been far wrong in the headlines, I thought, when I heard Biff's stern voice.

"She ain't no dame, see?" He snatched the paper from the bewildered stranger's hand and went on. "She happens to be the mother of my future children, the bread-winner of my little family."

The man tried to step back but he was hemmed in by a wall of late night commuters. Biff stood up and menacingly grabbed the frightened man's coat lapel. For a moment I thought the poor guy was going to faint.

"Gee, Buddy," he mumbled, "I didn't mean nothing by it. I'm a family man myself. Why I'd be the last one in the world to make a crack about the little woman. I'm a…"

The train stopping at Forty-Second Street broke up the scene. Biff let go of the man and we elbowed our way to the platform. As the train pulled away I caught a glimpse of the stranger. He was too frightened to sit down. With a look of amazement on his face he still hung to the strap.

"Why do you make a scene like that?" I asked as we walked up the stairs. "You scared the poor guy half to death."

"I wanted to think," Biff said, "and the only way I can think good is to get my mind off what I'm thinking about. See?"

I said, "Yes, I see," and let the crowds carry me uptown.

The Peerless Bar and Grill was full of burlesque actors, as usual. Jannine was sitting with Stinky Smith, a comic from the Eltinge. She had the last edition of the evening *Mirror* propped up against a catsup bottle. Without looking up, she pulled out a chair for Biff, and I sat next to Stinky.

"Was business so bad," the comic asked Biff, "that you had to bop off La Verne for publicity?"

"The Eltinge ain't grossing enough for you to make cracks, unfunny man," Biff retorted. "And anyway, she wasn't bopped off. She was strangled."

"Bopped, strangled," Stinky shrugged his shoulders. "Kansa Schmansa, abe gasint!"

Jannine, munching on a piece of celery, interrupted the conversation. "Say, if I'd known all about Louie I woulda been scared to death of him." She read a little more before continuing. "It says here that in 1926 he was indicted for dope peddling."

"On the radio they said he was a white slaver, too," Stinky added.

"Yeah, they got that here. 'Louie Grindero, known as The Grin, served three years for white slavery. He was also accused of forgery and grand larceny.'" She looked up from the paper. "Jees. You never know, do you?" she said.

The waiter placed a limp menu on the table and nudged Biff. "Ya wanna eat?" he asked stoically.

"Yeah. Bring us a round of rye," Biff said. "Old Granddaddy and beer chasers." The waiter shuffled off and Biff kept looking at him. "I don't think he had anything to do with it," he said finally.

For a moment I thought he meant the waiter.

Jannine glanced up from the paper again. "If he didn't, why did he take it on the lam?" she asked.

"With a record like his," Biff answered, "I guess he thought they'd hang it on him. Anyway, he wasn't even there."

"You're drunk," Jannine accused. "He musta been there or how'd he know she was killed?"

Biff rubbed the side of his face. "I never thought of that," he admitted. Then he grinned. "I damn near forgot, Moey told him."

"But Louie *was* there." I had just remembered. The three faces that turned to me were skeptical.

"That's a fact," I said. "When the show broke I stopped to talk to Sammy and on the way upstairs I saw him. He asked me if the liquor and beer arrived OK and I told him yes. Then I heard him come upstairs."

"And not only that," Jannine went on with conviction, "he said he was going to kill her and he done it. That's all."

Gee Gee and Sandra made their entrance at that point. They were minus Dolly.

"Passed out," Sandra explained when we asked her.

The comic looked up at the clock. It was twelve-thirty. He turned to Jannine. "I'm damn near on. Hurry up if you want to catch any of the show."

He signed his check and the two of them left with hurried good nights.

Gee Gee sighed. "Kinda wish I'd gone with 'em. I haven't seen a burlesque in months." With a sudden inspiration she ran after them. "Hey! Wait for me!"

The waiter arrived with the drinks. It didn't surprise him that three of his customers had left. He put the liquor in the center of the table, picked up the check with Stinky's scrawled signature on it, and silently walked away.

Sandra was picking the polish off one of her fingernails when Biff said, "Wonder who it was that got her bankbook."

"Huh?" Sandra stopped picking to bite at a hangnail.

"Who was it that got La Verne's bankbook?" Biff repeated.

"Oh, that! That was Dolly."

Biff's hand, the one with the drink in it, started shaking. After trying to steady it he decided to drink the drink first and talk later. "Why in hell didn't you tell the Sergeant?" he managed to ask later.

"Same reason you didn't tell him about the G-string." Sandra replied quickly.

It was time for me to say something, so I mumbled, "What G-string?" I should have saved my breath.

Sandra ignored me completely and said, "You were a cute pair. Do you think Dolly's blind or something?"

Biff and I looked at each other.

"Sure she told me," Sandra sniffed. "Dropped your hand-kerchief! What did you think you were doing, a road show of 'Blossom Time?'"

"Look, Sandra, there's something fishy about that business. I ..." It was the first time I'd seen Biff at a loss for words. He touched his pocket as though to assure himself that the gadget was still there.

"The only thing fishy about it is you!" Sandra snapped. "You been withholding evidence, and what's more, I know why! Well, I saved your hide once by not talking, but don't depend on me doing it again. Dolly at least turned in the bankbook." She stood up and pulled her brown-and-white pony coat around herself. Then she picked up her gloves and started to walk out.

As she neared the door she turned and smiled at me. "As long as you're paying the check," she said, "and I know you are, you might as well ask your comic friend why he done it."

"Done—I mean, did what?"

"Why he threw La Verne's G-string out the window." Her heels clicking on the tile floor sounded like a Gene Krupa drum specialty. I watched her go around in the revolving door until she passed the large window. The neon sign, a red one advertising Schaefer's beer, made her face look like it was burning. Burning in hell, I thought, but that was wishful thinking.

"I did throw it out the window, Punkin," Biff's voice was low and faltering. "After I helped the guys carry La Verne out of the room I felt something heavy in my pocket; not exactly heavy, but like there was a pull on it, ya know. Well, I put my hand in the pocket and I feel this thing. I knew right away what it was. Just a minute before you had been screaming about the G-string. I looked at her neck and there's nothing there, nothing but a thin, blue line." He stopped talking and put his hands to his head.

"Let's have a drink first," I said. He shook his head.

"No. I gotta tell you, Punkin. It's been driving me crazy all evening. I knew someone had put that damn thing in my pocket while I was carrying her. I knew that it had been around her neck a second before because, well, because I saw it too. All the dames in the room had gathered around you. You were out cold but talking anyway, telling all about seeing the rhinestones and stuff. I thought they'd think you were delirious, but even so I wasn't going to let 'em find the thing in my pocket, so while the guys are messing around calling the doc and everything, I walk me over to the window and drop the gadget on the roof. I thought I'd get it later, but—well, you know I didn't have a chance."

"You could have told me," I said.

"I didn't want ya to lie, Punkin, because I love ya. And anyhow, you're a lousy liar."

"You aren't doing so well with that lying business yourself," I reminded him. "Dolly knows about it, Sandra knows about it; no telling how many others. You have to think up a pretty fancy excuse for the Sergeant. It sounds awfully bad."

"I'll just tell him the truth, I guess."

"It would be a good idea to beat Sandra to the punch. I have a hunch she's on the phone right now. Funny why she should be so vindictive all of a sudden, isn't it?"

Biff picked an ash out of his drink with a pinky.

"I said it's funny Sandra should get so mean."

"Yeah, I heard ya." He still fished around for the cigarette ash. "Maybe it's because she's jealous. You know we used to sort of go around together last season and ..."

"Another sister-in-law!" I gasped. I reached for my coat. "You oughta hold a yearly convention. You could call it 'The ex-Biff's Club' or something. Rent out the Yankee Stadium for a nice little family reunion. Well, don't invite me!"

He helped me into my coat and followed me to the door. "Wait a minute, Punkin. I got enough on my mind. And anyhow that was long before I ever met you."

"That," I said, "has nothing to do with it."

He crowded into the revolving door with me. "Look, honey."

"Don't honey me," I snapped. "First it was Sugar Bun Kelly, then Joyce Janice. Now it's Sandra." I counted them off on my fingers as we walked around in the door. "I think it's revolting," I added.

"Revolving, you mean," Biff laughed. "This is the third time we've been around. Watch me grab the gold ring."

We were back in the restaurant again. Biff put his hand out and the waiter pushed the check into it.

"Pay it or put your X on it," he said. "I can't wait all night while you two play merry-go-round."

Biff held the door while I reluctantly re-entered the saloon-café. We sat at the counter and ordered a nightcap.

"Can I help it, Gyp, if all the dames fall for me? Honest, it sometimes embarrasses me the way they follow me around and ..."

"And you call me a bad liar," I said. "Here you are breaking yourself up."

"Liar. Liar. What does that remind me of? Oh, yes!" Biff snapped his fingers as though the thought had suddenly hit him. "What am I going to tell the Sergeant?"

"Well, don't look at me," I said. "I'm only here for the low notes."

111

"You aren't still mad?" he asked. "A broad with your girl—I mean a girl with your broad mind mad about a..."

"Stop it," I snapped, "I'm thinking. Who was close to you when you picked up La Verne?"

"Let's see now. There was Mandy, and Sammy, and Phil. I knew you weren't mad, Punkin."

"Stick to the script."

"Siggy and Russell..."

"Did you see Louie at any time during the party?" I asked.

"No," Biff said slowly. "Of course he might have been there. The room was so full of people I don't remember everybody."

I tried to reconstruct the scene in my mind. Gee Gee stood at the door. Jake must have been close by, because he had just helped her open the door. Moey was there and Mandy was directly in front, holding out his hat. Alice and some of the women were around the victrola.

Where was Sammy? I couldn't remember. Neither could Biff when I asked him.

"No. He could have put it in my pocket, though," Biff commented. "After he called for someone to get the doctor."

"Who went for him?" I asked.

Biff thought a moment before answering. "I think Moey, but I'm not sure. If he did, then he could have told Louie about it like Sandra said. That is, if Louie wasn't there." Biff gulped his nightcap.

"I must have looked like a damn fool fainting like that," I said while he was drinking.

"I thought it was cute," he said soothingly. "It was a womanly thing to do and I liked it; made me feel protective and strong-like."

"Protective. Yeah, I know. With all the practice you've had you..."

"Don't start that again," Biff said quickly. "Come on. Drink up. You gotta get some sleep."

He walked me to the hotel, kissed me good night, and promised to call the Sergeant as soon as he got up.

"Try to make it before noon," I yelled to him as he sauntered down the street. He waved back at me and continued walking. He didn't look as if he had a care in the world, let alone the G-string of a murdered woman in his coat pocket. The hotel lobby was dark. My mailbox was empty so I decided not to awaken the night clerk or the elevator boy. They were both sleeping in the large leather chairs. The clerk's mouth was open and he was snoring softly. I had only two flights of stairs and I didn't feel like answering a lot of questions.

I paused at the first landing and wondered how the papers could have a story about the murder so quickly. The radio I could understand. I fished around in my purse for the heavy key. As I approached the door to my room I saw a thin strip of light. I turned the knob and the door opened. It was unlocked!

"Hello, Gypper." Dolly was sprawled on my bed. A bottle of rye on my night table was half empty; an ash tray was spilling over on the bedspread.

"I been waitin' for hours and hours."

She was very drunk. Her shoes were kicked off, one on the bed, the other across the room. A garter belt hung grotesquely over the upright phone.

"There was something I hadda tell ya, Gypper." She tried to sit up and fell over. I pushed her over on the bed so she wouldn't fall off. "S'ank you, Gypper, you're a pal. Thass what you are, a pal." She scowled a little when I took the bottle away from her. "Thass no way to act when I got something important to tell you." She started to cry.

I said, "Nuts!" and began undressing. She would pick a night like this to get drunk, I thought. Take up the whole bed and get the room smelling like a brewery. I pulled my dress over my head.

"It was about the Princess, too." Dolly yawned. "And now you made me forget what it was."

By the time I got my head out from under the dress she had passed out. I was on the verge of tears when I picked up the phone. The sleepy voice of the night clerk answered.

"Yes, Miss Lee?"

"I said I want another room," I shouted. "And the next time you let anybody in my room when I'm not here I'll..."

Click. He had hung up. In my temper I threw the garter belt across the room. It landed on the sink and it looked so funny I had to laugh. I was still laughing when the clerk came up with another key. He saw Dolly lying across the bed.

"I didn't let her in, Miss Lee," he said pompously. "She must have passed me while I was checking the mail or—"

"Or while you were pounding the hay," I said.

I collected my toothbrush and cleansing cream and followed him down the hall to a room a few doors away. He opened the window, checked the towels, fussed around the desk, turned down the bed, and, after one glimpse at my face, hastily retreated. I fell into bed and slept like a log until twelve-thirty.

TEN

THE INSISTENT RING OF THE PHONE AWAKENED ME.

"Good morning, Punkin." It was a very cheerful Biff. "I been trying to get you for a half-hour. The dope at the desk didn't know you'd changed your room."

"It's a long story, honey." I yawned a little. "Did you call Harrigan?" I asked.

"Didn't have to; they were all waiting for me when I got to the hotel."

I was wide awake by then and Biff said: "You were right about Sandra beating me to the punch. Uh . . .uh-huh . . .Yeah."

"Who are you talking to besides me?" I demanded. "And where are you?"

"I'm talking to a couple of cops and I'm in jail."

"Jail? Oh, honey, what are they doing to you? Why did they put you in jail? They can't do that, can they?" I was out of bed while I spoke, looking around for my clothes that were in the other room.

"Take it easy, Punkin. I'm all right. They just wanted to ask me some questions and it was so late when they finally decided that I was just an innocent spectator that I slept here."

It was a moment before I spoke again. Time to sit back on the bed and collect myself.

"You mean to tell me you slept in a jail because you were too lazy to go home?"

"No cracks about this here jail." The even more cheerful voice of Biff came through the receiver. "It's a damn sight better than that riding academy you call a hotel."

I was going to hang up when he lowered his voice.

"Look, the cops just left. They found Louie's car last night."

"*What?*"

"I said they found Louie's car. Looks like he never got away after all. It was around the corner from the theater. Bye now, Punkin. My escort just showed up. See you at the theater."

I jiggled the receiver, but there was no answer.

The phone rang again. It was Dolly, all apologetic.

"Gyp, I feel like a heel," she said.

"That's OK. I mean it's OK about you sleeping in my room, not about you feeling like a heel."

"I found the coffee and stuff," she said mournfully. "It'll be ready in a minute."

I told her the cups and saucers were in the bottom bureau drawer and that the can of milk was on the window sill.

"Please hurry, Gyp."

She sounded ill so I made it as quickly as possible. I could smell the coffee as I walked down the hall. It was perking away merrily as I entered the room. Dolly was collapsed in the only good chair. She turned a haggard face to me.

"I feel like I been through a keyhole," she said. Then she glanced at the bottle on the dresser and made a wry face. "I'm through drinking for good," she vowed.

I poured the coffee and cut the day-old honey bun in half. Then I stretched out on the bed with my breakfast balanced on my lap. I was going to tell her about Louie's car being found. Then I thought it might be better if she told me what was on her mind first.

"What were you going to tell me last night?" I asked nonchalantly as I dunked the bun in the coffee.

She stopped blowing on her coffee and her eyes narrowed. "Huh?"

116

"Something about the Princess," I said. "You told me it was important."

"I musta been drunker than I thought I was. Hell, you know as much about her as I do." She looked at her watch. "Hey! We're late." She gulped her coffee and began dressing.

"You told me that you had been waiting for hours," I insisted. "Was it . . .?"

"Maybe it was, and maybe it wasn't. And maybe I changed my mind about telling you, too." She slashed at her mouth with a lipstick, folded the upper lip over the lower one. She looked at me from the mirror and her face softened. "The less you know in a case like this," she said, "the better off you are."

So she wants to play, I thought. Well, let her find out about the car herself. Just to give her something else to think about, I said: "Sandra shot her mouth off to the cops last night."

Dolly didn't ask me what Sandra had said but she turned quickly and said, "That's what I wanted to tell you about." She began talking faster. "I don't know why I told her about Biff being out on the roof, but when you and him started lying to me I guess I just got sore."

"I know exactly how you felt," I said. "I hate to have people lie to me, too."

Dolly searched my face for sarcasm and I smiled sweetly.

"We do have to hurry," I said, still smiling.

After our silent subway trip the deserted theater didn't help any. For a matinee there are usually a few customers hanging around the box office, but, as Sammy had reminded me, our burlesque patrons didn't like the idea of raids and then a murder in their favorite theater. I took a quick look inside. Aside from a few people down front, the house was empty.

Walking down the alley, I made a mental note to ask Moss to transfer me to another job. Dolly was probably thinking the same thing.

Stachi helped us open the heavy door. He nodded a cool good

morning to me and ignored Dolly completely. Sure enough, on the call board was the week-to-week notice signed by H.I. Moss.

"This is to notify all stagehands, musicians, performers, and chorus that the Old Opera will close a week from Saturday unless you are notified otherwise."

It didn't surprise me.

The sight of Jake and three of the stagehands sitting on the floor with a sheet spread out in front of them gave me a jolt, though. The four of them were sitting crosslegged, each at a corner of the sheet. Piled high in the center were the white ostrich fans the dancers used in the ballet. They were soaking wet, the most bedraggled-looking fans I ever saw. The stagehands were trying to curl them.

"In all the excitement last night Minnie had her kittens," Jake said sadly. "She's resting comfortably now and the babies are all right, but ..." He expertly drew a dull knife across a bunch of feathers and watched them curl tightly. "But, well, dammit all, this is the first time I haven't been around to console her."

"Console her hell!" George, the electrician, said. "Once she had 'em in my toolbox. Then she had 'em in Moss' file case. Now she has to have 'em on feathers, by Gawd!" He took a vicious jab at the plumes with his knife while the other stagehands laughed.

"Miaow. Miaow." In a box next to him was Minnie with her new family.

George leaned over and gently took off the cover. "Good old Minnie," he said softly. "Poor old girl. Don't you fret now. Uncle George sent to Luchow's for liver for ya. Squeechy, weetchy." He poked at the kittens with a calloused hand.

"Hey, don't touch 'em," Jake warned. "They ain't supposed to be handled."

"Who's handling them?" George snapped. "Guess I know as much about it as you do. Squeechy, weetchy."

Dolly and I made a path through the feathers. The orchestra was tuning up in the basement. There was the babble of voices coming from the dancers' room; the usual noises of a theater a few minutes before curtain time. Dolly pushed ahead of me on the stairs. She was taking off her hat and coat as she hurried. The black satin dress showed every line of her plump body and her back wobbled from side to side. I decided that from the rear she looked a little like a duck.

"Think I'll move my makeup stuff to La Verne's place," she muttered. "Never did like dressing so close to that damn window."

Sandra yelled a hearty greeting as we entered the room; not a word about tipping off the cops or an apology for being so nasty the night before. Just a gay, girly good morning. I wanted to clunk her but gave her the glad hello instead. I was in no mood for arguments and, anyway, I was late.

While Gee Gee was helping me get into my first costume, I saw the new itinerary over the sink. I noticed that Alice was doing a strip in La Verne's place. She was rehearsing a lyric and fumbling with a zipper on a pale-green satin skirt.

"If you want to thee a little more of me ..." Zip ..."Clap your handth like thith."

I suggested that she talk the song instead of trying to sing it.

"I'm tho nervouth. I'll probably forget the wordth anyway," she giggled.

She was too excited to hear Jannine say, "As long as you don't forget to take off the dress, you'll be all right."

"If you want to thee my thigh, don't thigh. Clap your handth!" Alice was out of the skirt by then. Her face was glowing. "Jutht think, Gyp, here I am doing a thtrip!" The magnitude of it nearly threw her. "And in a featured thpot, too!"

It was too much for me. With Dolly cooing over the new dressing shelf and Alice gurgling about her specialty, I was beginning to get a little ill. Gee Gee took one look at me and guessed what the trouble was.

"I don't blame Dolly," she said. "If some dame was breaking up my home I'd be singing hallelujah if she got herself strangled."

"Well, I think she's overdoing it," I replied.

Gee Gee was dabbing rouge on her cheeks with an old rabbit's foot. The bright tangerine was bad with her hair, but I wasn't thinking of that.

"I'll be a darn sight more comfortable when they catch him," I said.

Gee Gee turned around in her chair and leaned her arms on the back. "You know, Gyppy, I don't give a damn if they catch him or not." She was silent for a moment; her eyebrows were drawn together in a frown. "I guess it's awful, but I felt worse when my chameleon died than I do now. Honest."

One of the show girls took a pair of silver shoes from La Verne's shoe bag. "She owed me a buck," was her comment. We watched her while she tried them on.

"That's what I mean," Gee Gee said. "Nobody cares. It's like opening a window and letting clean air in. Look at Dolly, for instance."

She and Jannine were leaving the room. They had their arms around each other. Dolly laughed softly at something Jannine said.

"You can't go by that," I told Gee Gee. "You should have seen her this morning. She certainly wasn't laughing then. She's like a—like your chameleon. One minute she's suspecting everybody of the worst; the next minute she's all sunshine and light. Like when we were leaving the theater last night, and even when we were arrested. First she's scared to death the matron will recognize her. Then when her right name is all over the papers she's delighted."

"Maybe someone told her the case was dismissed," Gee Gee said casually.

"Dismissed?" No one had told me that. I must have sounded surprised.

Gee Gee looked at me strangely. "Sure. It was thrown out before it ever got in," she said.

"But they told Dolly she couldn't work in the city. She was really afraid the matron would recognize her."

Gee Gee laughed. "As Moss would say, do you think you're working for a loony? He's got pull, honey. How do you think we keep right on working after what's happened? The cops were all for closing the theater, until he started his ball rolling."

We were talking so softly I didn't think anyone could overhear us. Sandra's voice really startled me.

"We won't be working for long if the business stays like it is today."

Gee Gee glanced at her. "Bad, huh?" she asked.

"Not good," Sandra replied. She pulled up a chair and joined us. Gee Gee offered her a cigarette and she took it, but she kept an eye on me.

I knew she wanted to apologize for last night but I certainly wasn't going to make it easy for her.

She puffed on her cigarette and put her feet on the shelf. "I had half a bun on last night," she said idly, flicking her cigarette.

I just looked at her. Gee Gee picked an imaginary something from a tooth.

"Sure. You don't think I would have told the cops about Biff finding the G-string on the roof if I was sober, do you?"

She was talking a little too fast. I knew she was uncomfortable and I didn't feel at all sorry for her.

"It's just that I got sore, that's all. At Biff, I mean."

I let her suffer for a minute or two. Then I got up and left the room. Gee Gee could handle it from there, I thought. On the way downstairs I heard Sandra still protesting. I hoped my pal would keep the beady eye on her until she learned her lesson.

Russell was sitting on a prop tree stump under the stairs. When I passed him, he tried to smile.

The effect was ghastly. He looked as though he hadn't slept for a week. His eyes were red-rimmed and swollen, a cigarette dangled from his nicotine-stained fingers.

I was going to say something to cheer him, but it suddenly struck me that he was acting. That look of dejection, the sad, slow smile; it was all part of a very bad performance.

"Don't go, Gyp." He put a trembling hand on my arm. "Please sit down and talk to me. I'm going out of my mind, I tell you. This thing has knocked me out."

I sat down, but if he expected sympathy he was going to be a very disappointed actor.

"What's the matter?" I asked him. "Got a hangover?" I gave him the same look I'd given Sandra, but he ignored it. He was going to finish his act if it killed him.

He flicked ashes into the cuff of his trousers and stared across the stage. "Like a candle..."

He decided to switch it, so he started over again. "In the prime of her life, she's snuffed out like a candle."

If he wanted corn I decided to give it to him. "Yes," I agreed, "and she had so much to live for." My sigh matched his, only I managed a convulsive sob for a finish.

I might have known he'd try to top me, but when he hung his head and started to moan, it was almost too much.

"Look, Russell." I put my hand on his shoulder. "Let's stop kidding. I know how you feel about it. We're all shocked but none of us feel that it's an awful loss. People die all the time, good people. There's no sense to pretending that her death is..."

Russell threw my hand off his shoulder. "Don't touch me!" he cried. "You're cold, heartless. You'd never know how I feel." He buried his face in his hands and sobbed.

For a moment I believed him. I almost felt that I was heartless and cold. Then he looked up and I saw that his eyes were dry. He'd played his scene and it was as though the curtain had closed in.

I was prepared for anything. Anything, that is, but his next words.

"I'll bet she left a lot of dough. Besides making a good salary,

Louie gave her plenty, and you know how she was with a nickel."

I was too staggered to answer. Dolly as a chameleon was strictly small time in comparison to Russell.

"It puts me in a hell of a spot." Russell's voice had lost the note of respect it held when he spoke of La Verne's assets. He was plainly worried. "She was putting up the money for my play, you know."

"No, I didn't know," I said as I jumped up, "and what's more, I don't want to know. If your play is anything like you, it'll stink." There was a lot more I wanted to say but Biff's voice called me.

He was standing in the wings with a heavy-jowled man whom I'd never seen before. On the way over to them I shouted, "Keep me away from that Rogers guy. He gives me a song and dance about his broken heart, and before I snap my fingers he's told me the story of his downfall. La Verne's dough is..."

Biff put his arm around me. "I want you to meet Mike Brannen," he said quickly. "Homicide Squad. A good guy to know."

The man put a hand out and I offered mine. While he pumped it, Biff told him what a good-natured kid I was.

"Always clowning," he said.

I gave the policeman a frozen grin and pulled my hand away. I wasn't sure that I liked the way Biff was explaining me to the long arm of the law and I definitely didn't like his prop laugh that followed. It was about as subtle as H.I. Moss asking an act to take a salary cut.

"What's all the comedy build-up?" I asked. My hand felt as if it had been pounded into round steak, and I was still annoyed with Russell.

Biff kicked me with his eyes. Then, when he saw the cop was too busy watching Alice's strip number to pay any attention to us, he winked. I still didn't get it.

The policeman was holding a green satin skirt in his red hand. It was Alice's. I knew that if she had that off it was just about the end of her number. She finished with the music and just before dashing out for her bows she tossed Mike Brannen a chiffon hanky.

"You're a baby doll to catch my thingth," she cooed.

The cop turned red and she rushed back onstage.

"Ohhhh, boyth, you don't want me to *take* that off?"

The few customers we had convinced her that they most certainly did.

Alice still pouted and simpered, "If I *take* that off, I'll catch cold."

I didn't have to watch her to know when it came off. Mike Brannen's face was a dead giveaway. After a good look, he gulped, "She's beautiful, ain't she? She's got a face like an angel."

Alice may have looked like an angel, but he wasn't looking at her face. He must have misunderstood my grunt, because he added quickly, "Oh, I think you're pretty, too."

I told him to save it, that I wasn't having any, and Biff roared.

"See? What did I tell you about her? Always kiddin'!"

The policeman didn't hear him. He was too busy wrapping Alice in her satin skirt. I stood it as long as I could, but when he got to the part about how much he enjoyed her dancing, I had to get away.

I walked toward the prop room. The props were all out on the ramp and after moving the bladders from the park bench I sat down. Biff joined me there.

"For a smart dame, you can be the dumbest I ever knew," he said with no attempt to hide his disgust.

"And you can be the most aggravating," I said. "All night long you hang around with cops. That isn't enough. You have to drag them to the theater with you. And speaking of dumbests, that's no mental giant over there, you know."

We were behind the props and Biff had to lean over to see that Brannen couldn't overhear me. "He doesn't have to be bright. He's a cop," Biff said. "As for me sticking around with 'em. Well, you won't be sorry when I tell you what's up."

He lit a cigarette for me and one for himself. "First of all, they found something interesting in connection with La Verne's bankbook. On the day she was murdered she drew out ten thousand bucks!"

He waited a moment for that to sink in. "And they can't find the dough!"

"Russell's play! I'll bet she got the money for him." I was sure of it.

"Yeah, that's what the cops figure. But they think Louie's got the dough. He only got a couple hundred from the saloon and without the car that wouldn't get him to Jersey City. Not only that, but the cops found the picture frame.

"No, not the picture." He must have felt me jump, because he added that very fast. "Just the frame. It's an old-fashioned kinda picture frame. In the back there used to be velvet or something, only the velvet's gone now. It leaves a space big enough to carry a basket lunch, almost. Well, they pick around this back part and whadda you know? There's a piece of paper that looks like it's been torn off a..."

Biff heard the faint noise just as I did. It was someone tiptoeing past us. Biff held my arm and I held my breath. I had that same tight feeling in my throat that I get when I play hide-and-go-seek backstage.

Then I knew who it was!

My sense of smell, that was going to bring me close to becoming a well-dressed corpse, told me that Sammy, the stage manager, was up to his old tricks. The odor of "Tweed" was unmistakable.

It was a dirty trick, but I felt that someone had to break him of that ugly habit of listening to other people's conversations. In a loud whisper I said, "I heard that Moss is firing Sammy."

Biff picked it up. "Yeah, that's what I heard."

The sound of someone tiptoeing faded away. I had to work awfully hard to keep from laughing out loud.

Jake was the next one to disturb us. He apologized, but he

needed the bench for the park scene. I was on next so I hurried upstairs to dress.

While I was dressing I realized that I hadn't asked where Dolly had found the bankbook. I hadn't found out what the paper was either. All I knew was that Russell was worrying plenty about ten thousand dollars.

ELEVEN

I CAN'T SAY THAT I GAVE MY USUAL STERLING performance that afternoon. The first act seemed to run for hours. My number went badly. I couldn't find the pins and when I finally did, eight bars too late, I stuck myself. The audience was very unreceptive. They didn't even have the courtesy to yell, "Take it off!"

I was glad when intermission came.

Alice and Brannen, the cop, were sitting under the stairs with their heads close together, like they'd known each other for years.

"Gypper!" I turned when Alice called me. "Thith nithe man jutht ordered thome beer for uth."

One glance at his face convinced me that the "us" was the wrong word. He wasn't too happy when I sat down next to them on the trunk.

"A little beer will thathte tho good," Alice cooed. "Not that I drink..." She let her voice trail off.

"Neither do I," I added, "but on a warm day, well, you know..." I let my voice trail off, too.

Moey's spiel began, and instead of listening to Alice sigh and the cop breathe heavily, I listened to him.

"Friends, through the courtesy of the California Confection Company from Los Angeles, California, I have here a little article. Spicy, daring, intimate. Now friends, you're not children. A woid

127

to the wise is sufficient. You're here to have a good time and this here little book is just what you've been looking for."

I hoped it wasn't the same little book that he was selling last week. One pinch in a week is enough.

Alice giggled. "Oh, Mr. Brannen, you do thay the funnietht thingth."

I hadn't heard what was said, but I had my own ideas of how funny it was. "Now, friends," Moey's voice was getting louder. "This here little book looks like an ordinary book. But let me assure you that it is not! It is anything but ordinary. All you do is hold one of these pages up to the light or hold a lighted match behind one of these pages, and you will see men and women in many intimate poses. Yes, friends, in-ti-mate poses!"

"Oh, pleathe, Mr. Brannen!"

I looked quickly at the cop to see if he was getting ideas from Moey's spiel. Everything was all right, though.

"Pleathe don't talk about the murder," Alice whimpered. "It'th too gruethome. And anyway, if all the polithemen are as thmart as you, they'll catch that Louie right away."

"Well, they're not *all* as smart as me," Office Brannen admitted.

"You're too modest," I said, not too low. All I could think of was, this is what we pay taxes for.

The cop looked at me strangely for a second. Then he laughed. "Biff told me what a regular clown you are," he said.

I started counting. If, when I got to ten, the beer hadn't arrived, I decided I'd skip it. Nothing was worth the mental anguish of sitting through such dialogue.

" . . .For ten cents, one tenth of a dollar, you receive this daring book *and* three and one-half ounces of genuwine, delicious California Confection Bom Boms. I assure you that once you have examined this little book, you will not part with it for a ten-dollar bill."

"And do you alwayth carry a gun, Mr. Brannen?"

"Nearly always. Now my idea is that he tried to ditch the car and beat it out of the country. Through Canada, maybe."

"Seven. Eight. Nine."

The stage door opened and the call boy came in. It was the first time I ever thought he looked like Santa Claus.

Our host gallantly opened the containers. "For you," he said, handing one to me. "And for you." His chin scraped the floor when he bowed to Alice.

She fluttered her eyelashes and sipped daintily.

The call boy waited for the formalities. Then he turned on his heel. "I usually get a dime for doing errands," he said distinctly, but the cop was too busy telling Alice about how he captured a desperado single handed.

Alice swallowed the beer and the story. They didn't miss me when I walked away.

I stood in the wings and listened to Moey.

He was breaking in a new bit of business. "Stop the sale!" he shouted, and his assistants, who were milling through the audience, stopped and looked at him.

"I heard what that man in the third row said," Moey sounded as though his feelings had been hurt. Then a vindictive note crept in. "He said that these prizes will not be given away this afternoon. That is a fabrication. In fact, it is a lie!"

I looked through the peephole. Moey was standing on the top step that led to the stage. He held up a hand and dramatically beckoned to a boy in the back of the theater. The boy walked down the aisle and handed Moey several large boxes. One of these Moey opened and held up to the audience.

"This here gift. Yes, I said *gift*, will pos-i-tive-ly be given away today. You can see that it is a valuable gift, a gift that any girl would be proud to own. One hundred and nineteen pieces of genuwine ivory praline, complete with satin-lined box!"

The audience smoked and, for the most part, ignored him completely. A man in the first row studied a racing form.

I couldn't see the customer who had "fabricated," but then I didn't waste too much time looking for him.

"And because the California Confection Company is anxious for the general public to try their superior Bom Boms, I am giving away free, and without charge, this pair of genuwine French Mignon opera glasses. Use them today, tomorrow, in fact, every day! See what you came to see!"

The man with the racing form became interested.

"Now, friends, my confederates will go through you."

One man laughed with Moey.

"I mean will pass through you. I thank you."

Moey walked up on the stage and through the wings to where I was standing. His kinky hair was standing on end. Streams of sweat poured down his face. "How'd you like the 'stop the sale' gag?" he asked, seeing me.

I told him I liked it fine and he took the container out of my hand. After a healthy gulp he went over to the peephole to check on the sales. He still clutched the beer, but that isn't why I followed him.

I'd just remembered Gee Gee telling me how he was the one that tipped Louie.

I asked him casually if he knew Louie.

"Know him?" he said. "He's a relative of mine; cousin or something. I don't keep up with that family racket much." His beady eyes were following the salesmen. If a candy butcher could clip Moey for a dime, he certainly had it coming to him.

"Do you think Louie killed her?" I asked.

He took another drink before answering me. "If he done it, I'm a monkey's uncle. You wanna know who I think done it?"

I said yes.

"Well, I think one of the Chinese waiters is the guy. Who else would strangle a dame, huh? Don't all them Chinese strangle? And wasn't they there? Damn right!"

From upstage I could hear Alice romancing her cop. The musicians were getting noisily into the pit. There was a dank odor of

130

marijuana coming from the basement. That would be Benny, the trumpet player, I thought.

"It's the East Indians that strangle," I said. "You got the Chinese mixed up."

All Moey heard was "Chinese." "Damn right they done it. And I allus trusted the Chinese, too." He started away after that, beer and all.

"Hey! Gimme back my beer!" I yelled to him. He took one more gulp before returning it.

Just then I saw Sammy hotfooting it across the stage. He was completely out of breath, and with a wilder gleam in his eyes than usual, he asked me where the Princess Nirvena was.

"Me?" I pointed to myself as if he had asked me if I had spread the bubonic plague.

"Her number's after the opening and she isn't in. And I don't know where she's stopping. And—oh! Beer! Thank Gawd!" He killed the quart and shoved the empty container back in my hand. "Not only that, but Moss is out front; flew in from Hot Springs because of…"

His long legs took him upstairs in three leaps. Moey and I followed in a few more. By then we were at the landing. Sammy didn't knock, but burst into the room. There was a scramble for kimonos and robes again.

"It's like dressing in a goldfish bowl," Gee Gee complained, and then added, "if I may coin a phrase."

Sammy glared at her. "The Princess is missing!" he shouted, "and I gotta worry about knocking on doors yet." He looked wild-eyed around the room. "Don't any of you know where she's living?" he asked desperately.

No one knew and no one cared, for that matter, but Jannine did suggest that perhaps her ladyship had got tired of throwing pearls to swine and had high-tailed it off with Louie.

"You're nuts!" Sammy said, slamming the door behind him.

As soon as we were sure he had left, we all looked at each other and laughed.

"It's too good to be true," Gee Gee said.

Dolly added, "To get rid of both of 'em in twenty-four hours! Damn right it's too good to be true." A crafty gleam came into her eye. "If she was murdered," she said slowly, "it would be pretty tough on the cops to try and pin it on any of us."

Jannine stopped with one hand on the door. "What makes you think she was murdered?" she asked.

Dolly didn't answer. She was busy brushing her hair. At least she looked busy.

"And even if she was, how come the cops couldn't pin it on any of us?" Jannine had walked over to Dolly and thrust her face so close that the brush nearly clipped her chin.

I wouldn't have liked it if someone had pushed herself on me like that, but Dolly answered with a half laugh and kept right on with her hair.

"None of us knows where she lives, do we? And we all left together last night, didn't we? And the joint was full of cops watching every one of us, wasn't they?" She finished her brushing with a flourish and thumped the brush on the shelf. "Well, then, how could any of us do it?"

The crafty gleam was gone. One of triumph had taken its place.

Jannine sniffed and left the room. At the door she turned. "You got it all figured out good," she said. Then, as an afterthought: "*I* wouldn't get so far out on the limb for a guy like Russell!"

TWELVE

THERE WAS NO PRINCESS FOR THE FIRST MATINEE.
We struggled along beautifully without her. Louie was still missing
and that was a different matter altogether. Someone really wanted
him: the police.

Biff said it was because they needed a fourth at their pinochle
game, but Alice settled that once and for all.

"I don't think he knowth how to play pinochle," was her topper.

As soon as the curtain was down Sammy called a rehearsal. The
chorus went through its routines on the stage and we rehearsed
the scenes in the ladies' lounge, out front. It was a large, airy room
with comfortable wicker furniture. Long mirrors covered the
walls and the windows were draped with satin damask that was
probably left over from the heyday of the Old Opera.

Sammy told me I was doing the bride in the wedding finale so
I started worrying about my wardrobe again. I had promised to
make a strip costume for Gee Gee; I had two to make for myself,
and now a wedding dress!

"And we're doing the 'Gazeeka Box,' " Sammy added. "You
done the third woman before so I got you down for it."

Well, I didn't have to worry about that costume; three yards of
chiffon and a rhinestone clip would do.

Biff and Mandy were rehearsing "Slowly I Turn." I watched
them through the mirror and in the reflection it looked like
there were six Biffs. At first I thought how nice it would be. Then

133

I remembered the cops and decided that one Biff was plenty.

"Look, Punkin." One of the six approached me. "I got a new twist on the 'Gazeeka Box.' When Phil does the 'Ala gazam, ala gazam' with the first woman, we go right into the 'Pickle Persuader' bit!"

A new twist! I looked at him coldly, but he continued.

"They want a full stage scene in the spot and we just did the old version of the 'Gazeeka Box,' so…" He grinned when I took it up from there.

"So you're rewriting it?"

"Yeah." Still grinning. It was a waste of time trying to be subtle with Biff.

Phil joined us and we talked the scene through. It was one of Moss' favorite scenes. He liked the prop, the "Gazeeka Box"; said it reminded him of a sarcophagus. I had to look that one up. It turned out to be a mummy's coffin. Cheerful thought!

But I had to agree with Moss on one thing. When Jake painted the box and lined it with red satin, it was a nice background for a girl. The old version was one of those "She's been dead for two thousand years" things. Then the comic looks at the first woman and she winks at him.

He says, "For a dame that's been dead for two thousand years, she knows class when she sees it."

Of course, every comic has his own version of the scene. Biff's idea of combining the "Pickle Persuader" wasn't bad, but I was too annoyed to give him the usual encouragement.

"What are ya going to use for a blackout?" I asked in a cold voice.

"Oh, you get the seltzer water in the pants."

Just like that he tells me! *I* get the seltzer water in the pants! That's what I mean when I say one of Biff is enough.

I could tell by the too-innocent look on his face that he expected me to blow up, so I didn't give him the pleasure. With my usual dignity, I told him to get another naked woman.

"And what's more, funny man, I'm not working *any* of your scenes from now on!"

It was an exit line so I played it right down. Fastening my kimono with a dramatic gesture, I brushed past him and made tracks for the door. It isn't often I get a chance to clinch an argument. This was no exception.

I no sooner had my hand on the knob than the door opened, not slowly, but with force. It staggered me first, then hit me on the nose. Or was it the other way around? It doesn't matter. My big moment was shot to pieces. Biff started to laugh. Then he saw who was on the other side of the door.

A vision in deep purple with gold braidlike epaulets on the military coat, and purple boots to match! Slinky Stinky, otherwise known as Princess Nirvena, had come back to the Old Opera.

Without a glance at any of us she approached Sammy. "I haff just spoken to Mr. Moss."

The "Mr." was definitely sarcasm, but Sammy took it calmly, the kind of calm before the storm. "Slow burn" is what the actors call it.

"Yes?" he waited for her to go on.

She did, after gazing at herself in the mirror for a full minute.

"Yes. And in the next show my specialty will be joost before the finale of the first act."

This was a choice bit of news. The next-to-closing spot was mine. I should have made a scene right then, but I thought she was lying.

Dolly, sitting in the far corner of the room, took care of it for me. "Where does Gypper's number go, then?" she asked.

Sammy was coming out of his trance. "I can always depend on you, can't I?" The "can't I" was a full tone higher than his normal voice.

"Well, you don't have to scream at me," Dolly said peevishly. "I wanted to know because it affects my changes."

Sammy threw the scripts on the shabby carpet before he

realized what he was doing. They scattered all over the room and he sank to his knees to gather them up.

"Gyp does her audience number there and it runs longer than..." Dolly was afraid to go on. I didn't blame her. Sammy had turned an unhealthy blue.

"Damn your changes! Damn show business! Damn Moss!"

I thought he looked a little funny down on his hands and knees like that but Dolly was insulted. She got up to leave and Sammy screamed again.

"When the day comes that a stripteaser tells me how to run a theater, that's the day I open a hot-dog stand." He pounded on the floor with both fists.

"You run a theater!" Dolly sneered. "Stage manager hell!"

With that she really left. The door slammed louder than Sammy's screams. I'd seen him angry before but not like that. For a minute I thought we'd have to pour water on him.

During the excitement, the Princess had draped herself over one of the wicker chairs. She carelessly flicked her cigarette ashes on the carpet.

With a satisfied smile on her exotic face she said, "She has quite a temper, that Baxter person." She wet her lower lip with a long, thin tongue. "The sort of tempers murderers have; is that not so?"

Biff whistled softly; then he made a grimace. "You ought to see her when she's really sore."

The Princess left shortly after the fireworks were over. We went on with the rehearsal. I don't know how I remembered what went on but I'd done the scenes so often I guess I could have walked through them in my sleep.

It rained all day and all night. The downstairs room was flooded and before the matinee of the new show the Princess moved in with us. She took the place near the window, not by choice, but because we had arranged it that every other space was taken.

There were a few opening remarks to make her feel at home,

like "funny what comes out of the ground after a rain," and "They use water to flood rats out, too."

She had the thickest skin of any woman I ever knew. And I did know her. I was getting warmed up to tell just how much I knew when it happened!

With all the nonchalance in the world, she let her robe drop to the floor. Everyone in the room stared at her until their eyes popped. The long, stringy breasts she had flashed the day before were standing straight out! They were the most voluptuous breasts I'd even seen. Sandra, with all the ice and cocoa butter, could never hope for such a result.

The Princess knew she was causing a sensation. She paraded around, showing off. Then she stared at her image in the cracked mirror. She was humming the first eight bars of "Bublitchka" as she admired herself.

Gee Gee, stretched out on the army cot, looked up from her crossword-puzzle book, and watched the show intently. After a while she asked, "Hey, Gyp, what's a four-letter word for paraffin?"

I saw the Princess pale but the reason hadn't struck me yet.

"Lard," I suggested.

The Princess stopped humming. She turned a furious look at Gee Gee. "Vot are you insinuating?" she demanded.

Gee Gee glanced at the brown breasts with the rosebud nipples. "Nothing." she said innocently, "nothing at all. Only I knew a guy once that had paraffin pumped in his face because it sagged so. Looked good, too—for a while."

The Princess covered her breasts with a robe. She hurried so that she put the wrong arm in the wrong sleeve.

Gee Gee went on unsympathetically. "Yep, sure looked swell. Until one night he stood near an open fireplace and damn if the stuff didn't melt!" Gee Gee laughed gaily. "You shoulda seen him. His face fell down right over his collar!"

The Princess unconsciously put her hands to her breasts and Gee Gee went back to her crossword puzzle with a contented sigh.

I knew then why the Princess had missed a performance.

The second matinee had been as rough as second matinees usually are, perhaps a little worse. Two of the show girls were out; the scenery fouled twice; the Gazeeka Box still wasn't finished and we played the scene in front of a palace set; Russell got tight and blew half his lines, and I walked out. Union or no union, I packed my makeup and quit.

This time I really meant it. They had switched my number to the second act. The Princess not only had my featured spot, but she came on last in the finale.

Moss caught me in the alley. I wasn't going to stop. My bag was packed, and as far as I was concerned the Eltinge had a new stripteaser. But there was something compelling in his manner when he opened the door that led to his office, the office just off the stage-entrance side of the alley.

It was really a cubbyhole, with room for a desk and two chairs, and even so it was crowded. Although Moss had an office uptown, complete with switchboard and oil paintings, he preferred transacting his business in this little room. "Because I got my start in burlesque here," he explained.

On the walls were framed program and newspaper clippings from a show called *Whirlwind of 1921*. Moss had invested thousands in the show and it ran for three performances. He said he kept the clippings around as a reminder to mind his own business—burlesque.

I didn't pay any attention to office or clippings then, though. I was mad, I was packed, I was through. But I followed him into the room.

He leaned back in his swivel chair and gave me a quizzical look. "Now, what's all this I hear about you giving your two weeks' notice?"

"No two weeks' notice. Sue me," I said, refusing the chair he offered. "I'm not taking second billing to anyone, especially a broken-down dame like that Princess!"

He didn't answer me and for a moment I felt uncomfortable. He *could* sue me, but I hadn't thought of it until I told him to go ahead and do it! I was uncomfortable standing, too. I felt so tall and my bag was getting heavy. But I knew if I sat down I was lost. Once I got settled he could talk me into anything. It had happened before.

Moss had taken off his glasses. He wiped them carefully with a little pink cloth. There was something graceful in his movements and without his glasses he had a sort of esthetic appearance. But he looked so tired, more than just tired—worried.

I suddenly thought of all the good things he had done for me. I remembered Toledo and how broke I had been, the meal ticket with one punch left. He had kept his word with me; I was a star. I didn't have diamonds in my hair, but I did have an annuity. I, well, I sat down.

"I don't suppose I'd mind so much if she wasn't such a gloater," I said.

Moss put on his glasses and stared at the tidy desk top. His legs weren't long enough to touch the floor when he sat back in his chair and they dangled like a kid's. A kid sitting in a swing, I thought.

Then the Princess came to my mind and I was in a fury again. "She's running the whole theater! Misses a show and nobody had the nerve to even ask her where she's been! Walks around the place as if she owns it, looks down her nose at us. I tell you I can't stand it! If I hung around her much longer, I'd wind up maiming her. I didn't give her a chance to gloat today, though, believe me. I got out of that dressing room so fast that anybody standing next to me would get pneumonia from the draft. And what's more, I'm not going back!"

I had to bite my lip to keep from crying. That always happens to me when I try to stand up for my rights. I miss all the important things in my argument and knock myself out bringing up stupid issues like the Princess looking down her nose at me. Who cares?

Moss sat quietly and let me wear myself out. He was used to listening to complaints and his silent system was usually successful.

I changed my tune completely. "I don't want to leave, Mr. Moss," I said in a very businesslike manner. "All I want is for things to go along smoothly. I want my same spots in the show. I don't want to have her follow me in the finale. If the rest of us women can make their entrance on "Happy Days," so can she. Sixteen bars of "Beautiful Lady" for her finale entrance indeed! And as far as her stripping is concerned, I don't care if she takes her teeth out for a finish. I just don't want to follow her. *And* I won't dress in the same room with her!"

With that off my chest, I sat back and waited. I didn't feel that I had been unreasonable, but Moss still didn't speak.

"Oh, you don't know how awful she is," I blurted out. Then suddenly I remembered, and when I remembered I realized why Moss didn't speak.

"I . . .I'm sorry, Mr. Moss. I..."

"You recognized her, huh?" he asked quietly, and I nodded. "It was so long ago and she's changed so much. She was pretty then, wasn't she?"

It hadn't been so long ago. Two years isn't long, and I couldn't say I thought she had been pretty either. She was a blonde then and everyone knew Moss was in love with her. Not like he loved his wife and two grown boys, but a nice kind of love anyway. Certainly more than she deserved. I'd worked with her in Toledo. She was in the chorus and after a while she quit. Moss rented an apartment for her, I heard.

"She went to South America, you know." Moss' voice sounded hollow. He adjusted his glasses and fumbled with some papers on his desk.

"Now she's back," I said.

"Yes, she's back," he said wearily. "Letters, canceled checks, and copies of hotel registers. She's ..." He looked up at me and a slow smile crossed his face. "She's stage-struck."

I didn't understand him. "Stage-struck?" I repeated.

"She wants to get out of burlesque and she wants me to produce a show for her. I told her to wait, and she's waiting." He crossed his hands on his fat stomach and dropped his head.

I could understand her wanting to get out of burlesque, but a show! What could she do? She couldn't even talk, and with that weird shape of hers they wouldn't want her in the back of a road-show chorus. I told Moss what I thought.

"She doesn't want to be in any chorus. She wants I should star her! I gotta tell her tomorrow or she's going to my..."

"Your wife?" I helped him finish.

He nodded slowly and mashed his cold cigar in an ashtray. His eyes stared at the framed clippings. There was deep loathing in them. I didn't know if he was thinking of his Broadway failure or if he was thinking of the Princess.

I got up. "I'll tell Sammy I'm staying," I said and left the room, closing the door quietly behind me.

THIRTEEN

THE PRINCESS NIRVENA'S BODY WAS FOUND THAT night. She had been strangled with a piece of dental floss. Under her right ear the rhinestones of a G-string glittered!

Jake found her. He had pulled the Gazeeka Box out of its place in the prop room and was hurrying to get it finished so we could use it for the rest of the week. He said later that he thought it was a little heavier than usual but, because it had rollers on the bottom, it wasn't very noticeable.

He had painted one side of it a bright red and had started on the front panel. He said at first he thought the paint had run; there was a stream of red pouring out of the bottom where the door was. When he opened the door of the box, the body fell out. The blood came from an arm wound. It was a deep gash running from the shoulder to the elbow.

I didn't see the body. In fact, I didn't know she was dead until the police asked me to go upstairs to the men's dressing room.

The Sergeant sat at the same table. The room still smelled of sweat and comedy clothes. The questions were the same. It was as though we had rehearsed it; La Verne's death and now the Princess'!

La Verne's was a dress rehearsal, I thought; this is the real performance.

The banter of the first investigation was missing. Gee Gee wasn't playing "Madame X" and Jannine wasn't telling the Sergeant how to run the show. Their faces were tense and no one looked at each other. The police hadn't given us time to take off our makeup. The cosmetic smeared on Dolly's cheek and Mandy's putty nose was dented in the middle.

The Sergeant spoke to Biff. "You say that the property man called you when he discovered the body."

Biff nodded.

"Why did he call *you*?"

"Maybe because I was just, sort of, walking by," Biff replied. "You see the finale was just over and the others had gone upstairs. I was going in to tell Jake to hurry with the Gazeeka Box because the scene was stinking up the theater without it. You can't play a scene like that without your props.

"Anyway, I get going on my way. I was about ten, fifteen feet away from the prop room. I hear him. He doesn't call me at first, you see. He sort of gasps. 'Migawd,' he says. Then he sees me and he tells me to hurry. He's standing there with his paintbrush in his hand and it's dripping red paint.

"I think he's hurt himself until I see it ain't paint that's got him; it's terror. The guy was petrified. He couldn't say a thing, just stood there with his mouth and eyes wide open. Then I saw her sprawled out in a puddle of blood."

Biff stopped talking. The only sound for a moment was a loud ticking. I suddenly realized it was a watch. He held it in his hand and looked at it.

"If it's right about her being killed around five-thirty, six o'clock, that means she's been dead about six hours," Biff said.

The Sergeant glanced at him. "How did you know about the medical report?" he asked.

Biff smiled. "I made it my business to find out," he said innocently. I noticed that Jiggers looked embarrassed.

Then: "I don't know much about dead bodies and stuff like that, but that blood, doesn't it congeal or something?"

The Sergeant didn't answer him. He was looking at Jiggers.

Biff, unaware of the byplay, went on. "I tell you why I got so curious. All this blood and everything; well, I figured it was sort of dammed up at the bottom of the box. When Jake moves the thing he maybe opens the door—just a crack, ya know. So, while he calls the cops—I mean the police—I take a look at the body. The hand is flopped over to the side with the palm up. Naturally I see the cut. It was a long one, right near the thumb. Only it's dry. It ain't new and sticky like the cut on the arm."

The Sergeant looked intently at one of the papers on the table. "We have a report on that mark. It is a jagged tear, but it occurred a day or two ago; nothing to do with the case at all. What else did you 'look at' while you were alone with the body?"

The sarcasm was wasted on Biff. He scratched his ear and thought hard.

"I noticed the G-string, of course." He added quickly, "but I didn't touch it. I didn't touch anything."

"Isn't it unusual for one of the featured performers to miss his act?" The Sergeant had spoken to Sammy, who had been leaning against the door.

He jumped when he realized the Sergeant had asked him the question. "Huh? I mean what?"

"How is it that no one missed the Princess during the show?"

"She'd missed one before and, to be absolutely frank with you, I was damned glad she was out." Sammy spoke bitterly. "She caused more trouble. Not that I care, ya know, only, well, of course everyone missed her. I just told 'em all that she was resting."

"A good, long rest," Jannine mumbled, almost to herself.

The Sergeant asked her what she had said.

"I said she was going to get a good, long rest," Jannine snapped. "And, by God, I want one, too. What's the idea of holding us all here? If she was killed at dinnertime, how could any of us have done it? We all eat, and we all eat together. Gyp and Biff and Dolly ate with me. They know I didn't leave the restaurant;

I know they didn't leave. Ask the others who they ate with and stop wasting time! Not that I want you to hurry on my account. Hell no. Far as I'm concerned you can fiddle around until we're all murdered."

No one tried to stop her as she flounced out of the room. At the door, she turned.

"Only *I* won't be here to get it," she said. "You've waited for your double feature, but if you think I'm going to be the encore, you're nuts."

The Sergeant let her leave. I guess he thought he'd give her time to cool off.

After a pause, Jake cleared his throat. "I'd like to say something," he said hesitatingly. "It's about the Gazeeka Box."

"Yes, that interests me," the Sergeant said. "Very ingenious place to hide a body. The property room is cool; it would have taken some time for decomposition to take effect. The body might have remained concealed until..."

"Until it was opened onstage!" Russell gasped.

"No, I had to reline it," Jake said. He was fingering a hammer that hung from a hook on his overalls. There was red paint on the handle.

Or was it blood? I shuddered as the thought occurred to me.

"But that isn't what I wanted to say." Jake faltered before he went on. "What I mean is, I was in the prop room all through the show. A lot of stuff wasn't ready for the show today and everybody was gripin'. They couldn't've put no body in that box or I woulda seen 'em doing it."

"The body wasn't placed in the box during the performance," the Sergeant said patiently. "The Princess wasn't murdered until five-thirty or six. The show was over at five-twelve."

Jake nodded helplessly. "Yeah. Yeah, that's what I mean. You said six to eight. Well, when the show was over, everybody went to eat. I didn't go out until later, but I only went to the corner. I got me some coffee, and, well, dammit, nobody coulda put her in the box at no time! When I left the room, I locked it!" His puzzled face broke into a frown.

The Sergeant leaned forward. "Wasn't that unusual?"

Jake nodded. "Had to keep it locked. Someone was stealing all my props. Only a week ago, when we wuz doing the restaurant bit, I lost all my dishes that we use in the scene. A certain comic—I won't mention no names—walked out of here with a bundle so big he could hardly carry it. Well, sir, I get to thinking about that bundle, see? So the next night I gets me a glimpse of the same comic. This time the bundle's bigger, and me with no dishes for the scene. So I goes up to the comic and I says: 'What you got in that package?' He turns white as a ghost. 'Laundry,' he says. Laundry! Why that guy never had more than one shirt at a time in his life!"

Mandy, who had been staring at nothing in the corner of the room, jumped up.

"That's a lie!" he shouted.

"What's a lie?" Jake demanded. "That you stole my dishes or that you got only one shirt?"

Mandy lapsed into an injured silence. I knew that he hadn't really stolen the dishes. They always got broken during the scene and he just took the broken ones and mended them. Then, when the new ones arrived, he switched them.

Jake was like an old woman about his silly props, anyway. That was the first time he had actually accused Mandy of stealing them, though, and he was mad all over again.

"When that bundle went crashing to the floor it didn't sound like no laundry," he added belligerently.

"And that is why the prop room is kept locked?" the Sergeant asked.

"That, and other instances damn similar," Jake said.

The Sergeant waited a moment, then said, "You take your job very seriously, don't you?"

Jake thumped a fist on the rickety table. "Damn right I do.

There ain't nothing I wouldn't do for H.I. Moss. He did me a turn once and I won't never forget it."

The Sergeant asked what the "turn" was and Jake told him about the time Moss let him have five hundred dollars. Seems Jake's wife was sick, had to go to Arizona and, without Jake even asking for it, the money was in his pay envelope.

"It's things like that you can't never repay," Jake added simply.

"Sometimes a person can find a way," the Sergeant said.

Jake looked at him quickly. His thin, wiry body trembled. "Whaddya mean by that?"

"I mean that if you knew a certain person was blackmailing this benefactor, you would find it easy to, shall I say, dispose of the blackmailer? Justification, you would say to yourself, but it would still be murder!"

Jake jumped back as though he'd been shot. "I didn't do it!" he cried. "I told her to get out but I didn't kill her. At first I didn't recognize her; when I did I told her I knew who she was and she said 'So what?' Then she told me he begged her to come back. I knew it was a lie; those rich clothes and her airs and all. I accused her of blackmail and she laughed at me."

"Where were you at six?" the Sergeant snapped.

"I wuz eating. Brought my dinner with me in a lunch box."

"With whom?"

"I wuz—alone." Jake's shoulders slumped and he let his head fall forward. "But I didn't kill her," he mumbled.

I believed him. Jake a murderer? Never!

The Sergeant was of a different mind. He fired questions at the prop man until it's a wonder Jake didn't admit it just to get rid of him.

He stuck to his story, though. He ate his lunch-box dinner immediately after the show and then he went to the corner drugstore and had a cup of coffee. After that he came back to the theater.

"You went directly to the prop room?" the Sergeant asked.

147

"Yes—that is—yes, I did."

I couldn't stand it any longer. It would have been better if the police had actually third-degreed him.

"Look, I know I'm butting in, but I can't help it."

The Sergeant looked at me quizzically.

"Even if you think Jake had a motive to kill the Princess, that doesn't explain La Verne's death. You said yourself that it looked like one murderer."

The Sergeant asked one of the policemen to give him a box. It was a lunch box, the ordinary kind with a rounded top, made out of green tin. The Sergeant placed it on the table.

"Is this yours?" he asked Jake.

"Wait a minute! Don't answer that!" Gee Gee suddenly shouted. "It's another trick." Then to the Sergeant: "All those boxes look alike. How could he tell if it was his or not?"

"I think he will identify it," was all the Sergeant said. And he was right.

"I know it from that dent in the side," Jake added tonelessly. Gee Gee groaned.

The Sergeant was taking something from the box, a square of cardboard, like a playing card. I wasn't close enough to the table to get a good look at it, but Sandra spoke up.

"That's La Verne's picture of her…" Then she realized what she had said and stopped short.

"Yes, it's the missing picture. It was found in this box that Jake identifies as his."

"I found it! Honest to Gawd. I found it!" Jake tried to snatch the picture from the Sergeant's hand. "It was on the steps the night they found La Verne dead. When I went up to put the wax on the door, that's when I found it. I was going to turn it in, but then I heard all the stink about it being stolen and I got scared. You can't arrest me for having a picture I found on the steps!"

He turned to Biff. "They can't, can they?"

Biff patted him on the shoulder, but before he could speak the Sergeant said:

"We weren't thinking of arresting you—yet. We just want the whole, unvarnished truth. Now, let's see…" He went through the papers again.

His papers were beginning to remind me of Russell's briefcase. I think they were just props he used to make himself feel important. He found one piece that seemed to interest him.

After staring at it, he said, "Was the picture the only thing you found on the steps?"

"Yeah."

"You didn't see a frame? Or, perhaps, a piece of paper folded like a contract?"

"Nope."

The Sergeant was about to dismiss him; at least he looked as though there was nothing else on his mind when Jake suddenly said, "Stachi can tell ya. Him and the Hermit was sitting right in the stage entrance. They musta seen me."

"The Hermit" the Sergeant said. "Who is that?"

"He's the guy that handles the flies. They call him the Hermit 'cause he's sorta cooped up like. Him and Stachi are sitting there talking when I . . .No, by golly! The Hermit wasn't there. I got it mixed up with the time the two girls had the fight."

Jake scratched his ear and then he rubbed his thin face with a paint-smeared hand. "I guess I'm going nuts or something," he said apologetically. "I didn't see 'em that time at all."

"You might have seen me."

At first I didn't know where the voice came from. Then I saw Stachi. He was standing in the doorway.

"I was sitting in my chair, dozing." As he spoke, he walked into the room. It wasn't until he got into the light that I got a good look at him.

The veins on his forehead were swollen and blue. His maroon sweater was unraveled at the elbow. Around his neck he wore

149

a soiled piece of flannel with a safety pin holding it on. There was an odor of carbolic acid about him that reminded me of a hospital.

"He passed me at the door," he said. "I was dozing, as I told you, but I saw him go upstairs for a moment. When he came down, I saw him stoop and pick up something." He shrugged. "It might have been the picture."

Tiny beads of perspiration made Stachi's face glisten. As he spoke he seemed to sway on his feet.

"You're ill," I said. "Let me get you something, an aspirin or something." I had half risen and Stachi took a step backward.

"No," he said, "I'm all right." He turned to leave and the Sergeant spoke for the first time.

"Just a moment," he said kindly. "You say you were dozing. Could anyone have passed you at the door while you were asleep? Coming in or going out, I mean?"

Stachi turned and faced him. He hesitated a bit before answering. "I said I was dozing, not asleep. My job is to stay there, so I didn't leave the door all evening."

"Then you would have known if someone passed you?"

"Certainly. There was no one."

When he left, one of the policemen put out a hand to stop him, but the Sergeant shook his head. "I'll talk to him later," he said, and the policeman relaxed.

It was Alice's policeman! I hadn't recognized him in his uniform. He glanced rather sheepishly around the room. Then his eyes met hers and he smiled.

Alice tried to smile back, but gave up in a flood of tears. She had torn a wispy hanky to shreds and she dabbed at her eyes with the rag.

If a cop was ever torn between love and duty, it was Mike Brannen at that moment. He looked from the Sergeant to Alice. Love won.

"There, there, angel flower. Don't cry." He walked over to her and handed her a handkerchief the size of a bed sheet. With an apologetic look at the Sergeant, he patted her blond head.

Alice sniffed a coy thank you and tossed a half-defiant, half-triumphant look around the room.

"He's hooked good," Gee Gee mumbled. Alice managed to smile, a serene smile.

FOURTEEN

"HEY! I GOT A C.O.D. PACKAGE FOR GYPSY ROSE LEE!"
The loud voice of the call boy penetrated the dressing room. "It's from Dazian's," he added, as though that made everything all right.

"My material for next week's wardrobe," I explained. "I'll be just a moment. May I go?"

The Sergeant told me to hurry back.

As I came downstairs the call boy was goggle-eyed with curiosity. He was peering into the room.

"Did they find the body in here?" he asked breathlessly.

"No, but I don't want to talk about it." When I saw the disappointment on his face I added, "She was in the Gazeeka Box."

He gave me the package and a slip to sign. "Gazeeka Box, eh. Was she . . .?"

"That's all," I said sternly.

He started to grumble. "All the guys in the drugstore keep askin' me questions and I don't know nothin'. And me here all the time, too. It's unfair discrimination, that's what." He was still complaining as he left me.

The heavy package rested on a chair. Knowing that the materials were wrapped in the butcher's paper gave me a sense of reality. I had four costumes to make for the new show. Tomorrow I'll start work on them, I thought. Then I wondered, wondered if I'd be alive to wear them. Alive to make them, for that matter.

It was a grisly thought but I couldn't help it. The entire theater held a sense of doom. I knew somehow that we hadn't seen the end of the murders.

A scuffling noise on the stairs reminded me that I had been told to hurry. A strange cop was halfway down when I met him.

"The Sergeant wants to…" He stopped. His eyes caught sight of someone climbing down the rungs on the brick wall. He drew his gun and shouted, "Stop! Stop where you are!"

I tried to grab his arm and tell him it was only the Hermit, but he was yelling so loud he didn't hear me.

Hermie was so startled he lost his footing. One leg hung from under the bar; the other shook weakly. He looked like a toy dangling on a Christmas tree.

"It's all right, Hermie!" I yelled and ran downstairs to help him.

He had steadied himself by the time I crossed to backstage and was slowly descending. The policeman, still pointing his gun, waited until he reached the bottom rung. In the semidarkness Hermie's blanched face turned to me.

"Thanks. I was scared for a minute." Then to the policeman: "Ain't a man got a right to go home without having his innards frightened out of him?"

"When there's two murders in a joint in two days, nobody's got a right to nothing." He took Hermie's arm and led him toward the stairs.

I started to follow them when I saw the light. It was in the flies and it flashed once and then went off!

"Wait," I said. "Look up there. A light just went on and off." I pointed and they both looked up.

There was nothing but darkness; the light had gone.

"It may go again," I said.

The cop looked at me skeptically. Hermie shook his head.

"Couldn't be no light. I put 'em out," he said. "Always careful about that."

Was it my imagination, or did he seem particularly anxious

for us to leave? He walked on ahead. The policeman hesitated a moment, then followed him.

"It looked like a flashlight," I insisted.

"Look, lady," the cop said slowly. "We got a lot of trouble. We got a murderer, maybe two of 'em to find. So all right! It was a flashlight. Now come along. We been gone long enough."

While he was talking I remembered something, something I saw the night La Verne was murdered. I brushed the Hermit and the cop aside and flew upstairs. When I arrived in the room I was too out of breath to speak.

The Sergeant asked me to sit down but I couldn't. I was too excited.

"The night La Verne was murdered, I…"

Everybody was staring at me. Biff had rushed to the sink and was bringing me a glass of water. His hand shook so that the glass was empty when he thrust it at me and suddenly I felt that what I had to say wasn't important enough for all the attention.

"Well, it probably wasn't much," I said falteringly. "Only when Biff and I went out on the landing to call the Hermit to the party—that was the night La Verne was found—Hermie said he didn't want to come all the way down, but he would take some beer. So Biff went back to the room to get it…"

"That's right," Biff agreed. "I got two bottles for him."

"It was when Biff was in the room that I saw the elevator coming down and when it hit the side of the wall I saw something flash."

The Sergeant looked at the policeman who held Hermie.

"I thought at the time it was a piece of fringe."

I was getting only half the Sergeant's attention. The policeman looked at him knowingly. "Just now she seen lights, so she says. I didn't see nothing," he said.

"I did see a light. And the night La Verne was murdered I saw a piece of the G-string that she was strangled with!" I hadn't meant to go quite that far but the disbelief on the cop's face was too

154

irritating. "That's what was hanging on the elevator," I said with assurance.

I don't think anyone would have believed me if it hadn't been for the flyman breaking down.

"I don't know a thing about it, honest I don't." Then he collapsed in the cop's arms. "He told me if I let on he was up there he'd blow my brains out. He had a gun and I knew he'd do it. But I was going to tell tonight; I couldn't stand it any longer. He's still up there. That's what the light was."

The Sergeant waited for the Hermit to go on, but the poor guy was scared to death. Just kept mumbling, "He's got a gun, a gun."

"Who has a gun?" the policeman asked.

Hermie looked at him blankly. "I don't know. I never seen him before." He was still crying in terror when the Sergeant ordered his men to bring the man down.

"Wait!" Hermie suddenly pulled himself together. "There's two ways to get up there. If half the police cover this side of the stage and the others use the opposite rungs we can trap him."

Biff and the two comics, Mandy and Joey, followed the cops. I watched them from the balcony.

Hermie was explaining how there was a catwalk that extended from one side of the stage to the other. "It's purty narrow," he said. "We only use it when we got scenery repairs and there ain't nothing to hang on to, so you better let me go in the lead."

"For a guy that was paralyzed with fear a minute ago, he certainly is making like a hero now," Gee Gee whispered in my ear. She was standing behind me on the balcony. "Did he say who it was?" she asked and I said no. But I had a darn good idea.

I had to lean over the rail to see Biff. He was on his way up. He was going to climb the rungs to the flies.

"Biff!" I screamed. "Don't go! He has a gun and…"

"Listen!" Gee Gee's long nails dug in the flesh of my arm.

A voice was coming from the ceiling of the theater. "You ain't gonna fry me! I ain't gonna take no hot squat!"

The voice was Louie's!

Then the Sergeant spoke. "We got you covered, so come down quietly."

Across the stage, the police were cautiously scaling the wall. They were using one hand to hang on with; the other held a gun.

One cop called to Louie. "Throw down your gun and surrender!"

Louie's answer was a bullet. It was the first time I'd ever heard a pistol shot. It didn't bang; it sort of whizzed. Then there was a crack.

"Must have hit the brick wall," Gee Gee muttered.

"It's horrible," Dolly said through clenched teeth. "They got him cornered like a rat."

It was true. Police were on both ladders.

"I'll plug every head that passes the landing," Louie shouted.

There was another shot. Someone cursed and groaned. Then silence.

The Sergeant whispered to the men and suddenly the lights went out. They were going to climb up in darkness. Gee Gee's fingers dug deeper and deeper into my arm as we heard the grating sound of brass buttons scraping against the brick wall.

Crack! Crack! The shots were coming from the catwalk. Louie was firing blindly from the narrow bridge. Again he fired and a crash of shattered glass followed.

"He musta hit one of the bunch lights," Dolly whispered.

Crack! Then there was a click, click, click.

"His gun's empty." The Sergeant's voice boomed out, "Lights on. Lights on."

Every light backstage went on: the borders, the foots, the bunches, all the reds and blues, and even the trucks. The stage was illuminated for a ballet. On both sides of the wall, blue uniforms moved steadily upward like flies. They closed in on a lone man who cringed with knees bent and a look of hopelessness on his grinning face. He moved his head from side to side, watching and waiting for the first man to step on the catwalk.

From the other side of the stage a figure cautiously made its way toward him. It was the Hermit.

Louie clicked his useless gun, and with a curse he threw it at the flyman's head. He missed and the gun went clattering to the stage below.

The Hermit closed in, and from the opposite side a policeman approached.

Louie looked from one to the other.

"You'll never get me!" he shouted and then leaped straight ahead.

Gee Gee screamed as the sound of ripping scenery filled the air, then the squash of a body hitting the stage. Dolly fainted. If Gee Gee hadn't held her she would have rolled down the stairs.

The lights bathed the broken body that was sprawled in the middle of the stage. Some impulse forced me downstairs. The police were approaching slowly with their guns drawn.

It wasn't necessary. Louie, clutching a shred of the gold flitter backdrop in his stubby hand, was dead.

FIFTEEN

"'THE TEN THOUSAND DOLLARS WERE NOT FOUND on the body of the dead racketeer.'" Biff stopped reading the morning paper and looked at me. "Want to hear more, Punkin?"

The voice of the call boy from the far end of the drugstore counter came to me.

"Sure I wuz there. He damn near fell right on me!" The attention he was getting from his wide-eyed listeners didn't add any more to my appetite than the two eggs that were staring at me from the thick plate.

I pushed my breakfast aside and asked Biff to read the finish of the story.

"Aside from some loose change, there was less than three hundred dollars in his wallet. The bartender claims he gave Grindero the bills. George Johnson tells his story exclusively for the *Journal* on page ten..."

"Is that the bartender's name?" I asked.

Biff turned to page ten and found the story. "Well, I'll be damned! Know who it is?"

"I could tell better if I had the paper," I said peevishly.

"It's the Hermit. And just because you haven't had enough sleep, you don't have to be in such a bad humor."

"I'm sorry honey, but ..." I couldn't go on. The smell of dishwater, Coca-Cola syrup, egg salad, and ice cream wafting from behind the counter was making me ill.

Biff tossed some change on the counter. "Come on, Punkin, let's walk around the block."

He turned around on the leather stool and gave me a hand. The paper, with its glaring headlines, *Stripper Strangler Falls to Death*, he tossed into the basket on the corner as we walked toward the park.

We passed Louie's saloon. A Negro was sweeping the pretzels, cigarette butts, and dirt of the night before into a dustpan. He grinned at Biff and said good morning.

Biff didn't ask, "What's good about it?" and I was glad.

"Wonder who gets the saloon with Louie gone?" he said.

It was very much the thing Russell had said when La Verne was found, but it was said so differently. I thought for a second, not only of what Biff had asked, but why I wasn't annoyed at him for thinking like Russell. He knew he wasn't going to get the saloon.

"Moey, maybe. He told me he was a relative; cousin or something," I replied.

We passed the pool parlor and the barbershop. Then the surroundings changed abruptly. Large apartment houses with trees growing in cement boxes in front of them were side by side. The handsomely dressed doormen stood at attention. Everything smelled very expensive.

"When I get rich, I'm going to live in one of those places," I said.

"Yeah, and I'll be one of the doormen," Biff laughed.

Then we looked more carefully at their uniforms to find the one that was the most flattering. Biff liked a bottle-green number. "The bottle part of it is what appeals to me," he confessed, but I held out for a maroon with brass buttons.

The park in front of us looked so green. The rain had washed the leaves on the trees and they were shining as if they'd been sprayed with brilliantine.

We stared through the bars of the high fence at the children playing. They were all starched and combed and all had governesses watching them.

"For rich kids, they look sorta anemic, don't they?" Biff asked.

"When I was her age," I pointed to one who was about seven, "I'd been in show business for years."

The only comment Biff could think of was that *I* didn't look anemic. Then he looked at the benches. "Wouldn't you think they'd have a couple of them outside? It's things like that start revolutions. Makes me want to sit down just lookin' at 'em."

We were silent for a few minutes. It was the first feeling I'd had of peace for days. I felt as if I wanted to wallow in it. I took off my hat and let the breeze muss my hair.

"I'm glad you feel better, Punkin."

"Are you?"

It was a silly thing to say. Biff thought so, too. He said, "Yes, I am," and we both laughed.

We both stopped laughing at the same time. It was as though a cloud had passed overhead. I felt chilly.

"Biff?"

"What, hon?"

"Were you thinking about Louie?"

"Not so much about him as other things," Biff admitted. "He couldn't have put that damned G-string in my pocket, for instance. And how did he get the Princess in the Gazeeka Box? What did he want to kill her for, anyway? Why did he want to kill La Verne, for that matter? I can't get a clear picture of him sneaking up on a dame and strangling her with a G-string. If it was a gun, maybe yes, but strangling! And he didn't have the dough, so who got it? He didn't have time to stash it any place."

We sat down on the curbstone and Biff lit two cigarettes. He gave me one and we smoked for a little while. The feeling of peace was gone. I didn't think I'd ever feel peaceful again.

It had to be Louie, it had to be Louie, I said to myself.

"Who else could it be?" I asked.

The clock on the Edison Building gonged twelve times.

Without answering me, Biff rose. He helped me up. He brushed off the back of my dress and we started back to the theater.

We passed one of the more pretentious apartment houses, but we weren't playing our game this trip.

"This is where the Princess lived when she was in the chorus of the People's Theater. She had the penthouse, someone told me." I was just making idle conversation, but Biff stopped short.

"What's the matter? Got a stitch from walking so fast?" I asked.

Biff threw his cigarette away. "No, I just thought of something. When you asked me a minute ago who else would kill the Princess, I couldn't think of anyone. But, who do you think is going to be the happiest over her death?"

"I give up. It looks like a toss-up to me."

"Have you thought about the guy she was blackmailing?"

He had asked me the one question I wouldn't even ask myself!

"But he was in Hot Springs when La Verne was killed," I said. "And the cops said that one guy murdered both of them."

"He *said* he was in Hot Springs. Who saw him? Nobody. All we know is that *Sammy said* he called him from there. Sammy is a guy that's working for him don't forget. He didn't check into a hotel. He didn't even take a train. Have you ever heard of him driving a car that far?"

I hadn't but I wasn't going to admit it. "Moss would no more kill a woman than I would."

"There you go, jumping to conclusions. I didn't say he killed 'em. I just said that he'd be damned glad to have one of 'em damn dead.

"One of them is right," I said quickly. "If you can show me one reason why he'd kill La Verne, I'll put in with you."

Biff stood perfectly still on the corner of Sixteenth Street and Irving Place. If someone had walked up and handed him a million dollars, he couldn't have looked more surprised, more pleased.

"You're absolutely right, Punkin," he said. "He certainly didn't have a reason for killing La Verne."

161

I knew better than to remind him that I had just said that. When Biff gets that look in his eye it means he's thinking. When he's thinking, it's a waste of time to talk to him.

He started walking and he took such big steps that I couldn't have talked if I'd wanted to. I had all I could do to keep up with him. I waited to speak until we got to the drugstore. I was breathing a little heavily when we went in to have our coffee.

Jake was sitting at the counter. He was dunking a doughnut, but it didn't look to me as though he had his heart in it. It was absent-minded dunking.

Russell and the two comics, Mandy and Joey, were at the counter, too. We said good morning to them and they moved down one stool to make room for us.

"Good morning," I said to Jake. He jumped a foot. "I didn't mean to startle you," I apologized, but Jake went back to his sloppy dunking without a word.

Mandy, out of the corner of his mouth, told me that Dolly was just in and had asked Jake to put a bolt on the dressing-room door. "Meaner'n hell about it," Mandy added in a whisper. "Said there was altogether too much stuff missing from the place. Then she tells him that she'd get the lock—like, if he got it, there wouldn't be no reason for the bolt."

The counter boy was putting the coffee in a container for me when Stachi came in. With him was the oldest-looking man I've ever seen. I hardly expected a word of greeting from him, so I wasn't disappointed when he brushed past me. But the old man interested me.

He pounded on the counter with his cane. When the boy saw whom it was, he dropped my coffee container to wait on him first. Ordinarily I'd be annoyed at such bad service, but this was rather amusing. The old man's beady eyes peered at the menu behind the counter.

"What's that say, boy?" he asked. His voice was pitched as high as a woman's and if he couldn't read that menu himself, I'll play four weeks of stock for Minsky. Those beady little eyes weren't missing anything. He let the boy go straight through the menu. Then he ordered a ham sandwich to go out.

The boy fixed it for him. Extra ham, I noticed. When the old man left, Stachi left with him.

No one else in the drugstore seemed to think they were an unusual pair. Biff was matching pennies with the boys and they didn't look up from their game.

"Who's the old guy, whom you made with the fancy service for?" I asked the waiter.

He was looking ruefully at the nickel in his palm. "Him? Oh, that's old man Daryimple. Richest guy in the whole world, I guess. Lives across the street." With a toss of his head he indicated the most expensive-looking residence in the neighborhood. "He's in here real often. Stingy as all get-out. Tips me a nickel."

He held the nickel up and looked at it again. What the old man tipped didn't interest me; what he was doing with Stachi did.

"The three of 'em play cards nearly every night," the boy said when I asked him. "The other guy works in your joint, too. He's a stagehand or somethin'. Even when I deliver sandwiches to the old guy's house, he don't gimme more'n a nickel." He put the coffee in the paper bag and handed it to me.

"Maybe he really isn't rich," I said.

"Isn't rich! He owns damn near all the town. All down there is his." The boy made a gesture that took in more than half of the city. "And all down there is his." That gesture took in what was left. "And still he only tips me a nickel."

All that talk about tipping put me in a spot. I gave the kid a quarter so he wouldn't talk about *me* and left.

I waved at Biff from the door and he yelled, "See you in there, Punkin, soon's I clean these guys out."

He flipped a penny on the floor. Then he moaned. Biff's cleaning up in gambling games usually meant that he was the one who had to borrow a nickel for the car fare home.

Three old men playing cards every night. One of them the richest man in the world, one a doorman, and the other a stage-hand in a burlesque theater. The only stagehand whom I could fit into that puzzle was our new hero, the Hermit.

Oh, well, I thought as I kicked the stage door open, that's what I like about burlesque; something doing every minute.

An odor of theater hit me. Some actors like the smell, but to me it's plain bad, like any other unclean odor.

It was dark backstage at the moment. It won't be so bad when the lights are on and people are around, I thought, but I knew if I saw the spot where Louie had fallen, it would have made me too weak to go on for the matinee.

On the way upstairs I made a fervent wish that there wouldn't be a bloodstain.

When I walked in, I heard Gee Gee saying, "Bad luck and deaths run in threes." She turned to me and asked if that wasn't right. "About threes, I mean."

It sounded like a buildup for a little fortune telling and I wasn't in the mood.

"I'm not superstitious," I lied.

"Just careful?" Dolly asked. She was beading her eyes, so I couldn't see her face, but there was a funny note in her voice.

Gee Gee didn't pay any attention to her. If it wasn't tea leaves on her mind, I was sure it was cards. I was right.

"Gyppy, tell my fortune." She shoved the cards under my nose. "Not a big fortune; just the circle."

"Later, honey. I'm not anxious to find out what's happening around this mansion of mirth anyway, and…"

"That's why I want you to tell it, Gyp." She was absolutely serious. "I gotta hunch about something and…" She lowered her voice and looked around the room to see if anyone was listening.

They were all intent on their makeup with the exception of Alice. She was laboriously writing. The well-chewed pencil scratched the paper as Gee Gee spoke.

"I don't think Louie was the murderer."

I raised an eyebrow because she expected it, but, after listening to Biff, I wasn't as surprised as I might have been.

"Who do you think?" I asked.

"The Chinese waiter, that's who."

I thought she was kidding. When I realized she meant it, I had to tell her I thought she was crazy.

"Crazy, eh? Well, whose sealing wax was it on the door? Who was in and out of the room all night? Who hated her like poison?" As far as Gee Gee was concerned, the waiter was as close to the electric chair as he could be without getting singed. She had a look in her eye that told me she'd be delighted to pull the switch.

"A guy isn't going to kill a dame just because she heaves a pop bottle at him, you know."

Gee Gee gave me a knowing look.

"And what about the Princess?" I asked "Why and how did he kill her?"

The knowing look vanished. "Oh, Gyp, you always spoil everything," she said petulantly. "I go work up a case and you gotta stick a pin in the balloon."

She put her elbows on the shelf and cupped her face in her hands. I was frightened to death that she was thinking. I was right again.

"Maybe the Princess was Chinese." She closed her eyes a little, visualizing a picture that would probably have something to do with the death of a thousand-and-one cuts. Gee Gee's pictures are always good ones, if you have a strong stomach.

"Or maybe the Chinese is one of these Russian Chinese. She could have been kidnapped and he could…"

"Honey, I hate to stick another pin in another balloon, but the Princess was a Pollack. Her right name was Rose Yabilowshsky or something."

Gee Gee glared at me. But that name was too much for her. While she tried to think of an answer a new country was heard from.

"Doeth thith thound legal-like?" Alice had finished writing and she held the paper out for someone to read. No one reached for it so she read it aloud herself: "Dear Mr. Moth: Thith will therve ath my two weekth notithe. If you could let me go thooner I would be deeply grateful. Alithe Angel."

She waited for a moment for a comment before asking, "Maybe that 'deeply grateful' ith too much, huh?"

"No, it's all right," I said. "But why are you giving in your notice now that you have a strip spot and everything?"

She blushed and tried to change the subject, but I was insistent.

"Well, I'm—that ith, he—I'm going to get married and he doethn't want me to ...Oh, I don't want to hurt anyone'th feelingth or anything, but he doethn't think thripteathing ith nithe for a married woman."

Dolly tucked her crocheting in a pillowcase and pinned the top carefully. "I don't blame him," she said with finality.

"I do," Jannine said. "It isn't modesty or anything else, but damned selfishness. Like a lot of guys want the most beautiful paintings in the world and when they get 'em they won't let anybody look at 'em. They hang 'em in some old hallway."

"I don't think that Alice's new husband will hang her in any hall..." I put my hand to my mouth, but it was too late.

Alice was in tears already.

I tried to console her, but Dolly really did it. "Is it that beet-faced cop?" she asked.

Alice was so mad she stopped sniffling. "He'th not beet-fathed," she said dramatically. "And he'th not a cop; he'th a politheman."

Jannine groaned. "My Gawd! One of my fellow workers marrying a Cossack!"

SIXTEEN

INSTEAD OF GOING OUT TO DINNER AFTER THE matinee, I had two hamburgers sent in. By the time I got around to eating them they were cold, but in my wardrobe-making days I always ate cold hamburgers, so the two sort of went together.

As soon as everybody had left the room, Jake wheeled in Sarah Jane. She was my dressmaker's dummy and I kept her in the prop room when she wasn't needed. Jake helped me spread newspapers on the floor and attached the sewing machine for me. While I pinned the blue velvet on the model, he kept up a steady flow of conversation.

"Yes siree. Takes a thing like these murders to find out who your real friends are."

I was too busy to pay much attention to him but it did seem to me that there must be an easier way to test fidelity.

"Take that Dolly Baxter, now," he said in an aggrieved tone. "Nice as I've been to her, she didn't bat an eye when them police was arresting me."

"There wasn't much she could do," I replied.

"Maybe not, but that wantin' a bolt and makin' a remark she'd get the keys—that hurt me right to the quick, nice as I've been to her."

He waited at the door a minute. He was so quiet I thought he'd left. Then he spoke again.

"Ya know something? I don't think Louie was the guy that did the killings at all."

I was so startled I stuck myself without realizing it. "Who do you think did, then?" I asked without looking at him. I was on my knees in front of Sarah Jane, and through her cage-like bottom I could see Jake's feet. The shoe with the cutout for his bunion traced a design on the floor.

"Well, I got to thinking about it," he said. "First of all, nobody yet has explained how he got the Princess in the Gazeeka Box, and it seems to me if Louie had been hanging around after killing La Verne, he'da been pretty dumb. And dumb he ain't! Wasn't, I mean. Nope, I think that once he got in that car of his, he'da kept going. That is, if he killed her.

"What I think happened was he heard that radio alarm in his car and he came back to find the real murderer. What's more, I think he found him. Maybe he didn't have a strong enough case against him and at the last minute he knew how tough it'd be for him to convince the coppers, so he hid out. He never meant to kill himself, the way he did or any way. He was just trying to get away."

"Yes, I know that," I mumbled. While he had been talking I had pinned the hem of the skirt together. My mind wasn't on my sewing, but then to have someone else say that they doubted Louie was the murderer was enough to make anyone pin up the wrong seams.

"I tell you, Gyp Lee, when people go around makin' up excuses like crazy, you can bet your bottom nickel they got something to hide. I won't mention no names, but there's a certain woman in this theater that's lied plenty. First she lied about not being married to a man. I won't name him either. Then she lied about not seeing La Verne the night she was murdered, and then she lied about the Princess. Said she didn't know where the Princess lived. Hurumph. She knew all right, all right."

"Jake!" I stopped him. "You don't know what you're saying."

"Oh, don't I?" He seemed to be torn between telling the facts as he knew them and keeping his mouth shut, but the chance to prove his point was too great a temptation.

"*I* knew she knew where the Princess lived because I followed her one night. She was following Russell, and Russell was arm-in-arming with the Princess. It was the night Lolita La Verne was killed, and first she went into Louie's for a drink with the two girls. She was pretending to be drunk. As soon as she sees Russell, she acts like she passes out. Then the two girls leave the saloon, leave her sitting there in a booth. Soon as they get past the corner, she straightens up and high-tails it after Russell. He met the Princess at the Dutchman's and they walked down the street together, Dolly behind him, and me behind her. Then they got in a cab and she gets in one, too. Me, I get in one, too."

"Wait a minute," I stopped him again. "What were you doing following the Princess?"

"I? Well, I was hoping to get something on her so I could get her to leave Moss alone. I heard her talking to Russell about him and I thought maybe if I caught the two of 'em together, I could…"

Jake shook his head and with a thin hand he rubbed his eyes, using the third finger and his thumb to press the corners tightly.

"I dunno what I was goin' to do," he said wearily. "Anyway, in this cab I follow the others and they stop a few feet apart at the Lincoln Hotel. The Princess and Russell get out. Dolly waits until they get in the lobby. I watch from outside and Russell goes right over to the elevators while the Princess gets the key at the desk. Then she joins him and they get in the elevator.

"Dolly scoots over to the bar in the lobby and gets a seat facing the elevators and orders a drink. She don't take an eye off the elevators, though, and she sits there for the better part of an hour. By then I decide there ain't nothing I can do but go. So I do."

"So that's what she was going to tell me the night she passed out in my room," I said.

"Huh?" Jake cocked his head. He didn't understand me and I was just as pleased. "Don't get me wrong, though," he said. "I didn't mean that she's the one that did the killings. I only mean that she's pertecting the guy that did, pertecting him because she loves him."

He didn't give me a chance to answer. As he finished speaking he turned on his heel and left the room. I sat motionless until I heard the stage door slam. Then I jumped up quickly and closed my door. The latch was still broken, so I propped a chair under the knob—not because I was frightened or anything. I just felt better to have the door closed when I was alone in the theater. I was glad to see that the window was bolted, too.

It took me a few minutes to undo the mistakes I had made as I listened to Jake, so I worked fast. Sarah Jane creaked at every pin thrust. She wasn't the newest dressmaker's model. In fact, she dated back to the hobble-skirt era. Making a dress on her for Gee Gee took a lot of imagination. Where a head should be, she had a gold knob like a doorknob, and she was covered with black stocking material. Her bosom, and, believe me, that was what it was, went from her neck to her waist. But I was used to her; we got along beautifully together.

"I think I'll give you two panels for a skirt; one in front and one in back. Then you can strip a petticoat from under them." With my mouth full of pins, I explained how the bolero top would work.

"You strip the brassière from under, too. Then you wear red shoes and a rose in your hair and you're on."

I patted her straw-filled bottom affectionately and unpinned the costume. After making chalk marks for my seams, I began sewing.

The whir of the machine increased. It was a nice, restful sound; the needle traveling over the material making little piercing noises. Like wallpaper, somehow, plain white, then a little design. Plain white, then a little design. Plain white, then a little design.

"Everybody's got a different idea who the murderer is, Sarah Jane. Who do you think did them?"

The sound of my own voice startled me. I took my foot off the

170

pedal and the machine stopped. Then I realized how silly it was.

"I'm getting as bad as La Verne and the Hermit," I thought, "talking to a dressmaker's dummy." I stretched my back and looked around the room.

Sarah looked a little naked with her old stocking body bulging out in the wrong places, so I tossed a wardrobe sheet over her. Then she looked like a corpse, so I took it off quickly. Thinking of corpses wasn't such a good idea considering that at that same time yesterday the Princess was being murdered. I wanted to think of anything else, but somehow my mind kept going back to death and murder.

"Well, Sarah," I said nervously, "one sure thing, they can't strangle you."

She groaned a little for an answer and I reached for a cigarette. I managed to get it to my mouth, but lighting it was something else again. I had to decide quickly between my eyelashes and a smoke; the way my hand was shaking I couldn't have both. The vanity in me won and I tossed the cigarette and match into a cold-cream jar that served as an ashtray.

It was heaped with butts, so I decided to empty it. Getting up and walking around will help my nerves, I thought, and I was right. By the time I had emptied the tray in a basket at the far side of the room, I was calm again. Calm, but just a little weak.

I sat down and readjusted the blue velvet under the needle of the machine. Before I had a chance to start the motor, I heard footsteps on the stairs. At first I thought it was my imagination. Then I saw the latch of the door move!

They say that when a person sneezes they are closer to death than at any other time. That is, of course, without actually dying. It may be true, but at that moment I still feel that I came closer than any sneezer could. I don't care what anyone says, my heart stopped beating.

There was a voice yelling through the door, but I couldn't answer.

"Hey! What's with the barricade?" Then, "Open up!"

The latch jiggled and the pressure of someone pushing at the door made the chair under the knob creak.

"Open the door!" The voice was loud and agitated. It was Gee Gee.

"Just a moment." I managed to reply and my rubber legs carried me to the door.

Gee Gee had a wild gleam in her eye when I finally managed to throw open the door. "Thank Gawd you're all right," she said with a heavy sigh. Then her mood changed.

"Why in hell didn't you answer?" she demanded. "You scared me half to death."

"I didn't hear you at first," I lied, "and the wind kept blowing the door, so I just put a chair under it."

Gee Gee looked from the bolted window to my face. "Yeah, I know," she said, "and you probably felt a cold coming on from the draft."

Then she saw the blue velvet on the machine. "Oh, Gyppy darling, you did work on mine first!" She clapped her hands happily. "Oh, lemme try it on?"

If I do say so myself, it was a perfect fit. The blue was wonderful with her hair and the rose had just enough color for contrast. I was as pleased with it as she was.

"I love it, Gyp," she said as she lifted the front panel. Then I explained how she could strip from the skin out.

"Yeah," she agreed, "and these splits in the skirts are swell for my bumps." She hummed "Black and Tan Fantasy" as she paraded around the room, and I cautioned her about the pins while she went through her routine.

First the underskirt came off, then the bolero. With long strides her legs darted in and out of the panels.

"You ought to wear a rose G-string!" I exclaimed as the inspiration hit me, "and glue on two more for a brassière."

"Wonderful! And for my last trailer, I'll use 'Only a Rose.'"

She was still rehearsing when Sandra and Jannine came in. I pushed Sarah Jane out of the way and started cleaning up the room. The ashes I kicked around so they wouldn't be too noticeable, and I covered the sewing table with a sheet.

"You make such a mess when you sew," Jannine complained. It was obvious that she was annoyed because I wasn't making anything for her. Even before she took a good look at Gee Gee showing off in the new blue, I knew that.

"Hmm, pretty," she said when Gee Gee asked her if she liked it. Then she added, "A little like my green satin, isn't it?"

Gee Gee went "miaow" and we settled down to the business of getting glamorous for the evening performance.

Dolly was the last one in. Alice asked if she had looked at the house.

"Yeah," she said. "Stinks! Half full." Then she flopped in a chair. She put on her powder base and under rouge before she spoke again. While she was still blending the rouge, she turned around in her chair and said," I guess it's awful to say so, but I'm a little glad the notice is posted. I'm getting tired of working this far downtown."

She started powdering her face with a huge powder puff. "And anyhow, I got a chance to open at the Eltinge the day I close." Then, with elaborate unconcern, she added, "They want Russell, too."

"How nice," Jannine said laconically. "Nothing like a change of scenery when things get hot."

"Whadda you mean by that crack?" Dolly snapped. Her eyes were the only feature that showed through the powder.

Jannine deliberately turned in her chair and faced the fury. "I wasn't referring to the weather, if that's what you're in doubt about." Then she smiled and shrugged her shoulders. "Skip it," she said. "It's none of my business, anyhow, and I'll be damned if I'm going to take La Verne's place as your sparring partner."

It was enough of an apology to satisfy Dolly. She let the subject drop as though it were a red-hot stove. In a moment she meditated aloud about the virtues of playing in a Broadway production, "like the Ziegfeld Follies, for instance. I'd really like that better than the Eltinge."

She lit a cigarette and let it hang from her mouth while she melted her cosmetic over the guttering candle. "One show a night, Sundays off. Boy, what a racket."

Sandra stopped massaging her breasts long enough to snort, "Racket is right! You rehearse four weeks, spend four more weeks on the road, then come into New York and run four days." She pushed her chair back and put her feet on the makeup shelf. "Nope, I'll stay in burlesque."

"Damn right you will," Gee Gee giggled under her breath. Sandra wasn't sure how Gee Gee meant that and before she had a chance to decide, Biff came in.

He headed straight for the army cot and after moving the magazines, sheet music, crochet work, and extra street clothes, he made himself comfortable.

"Nice little place you got here," he said, staring at the cracked ceiling.

Then I saw the envelope sticking out of his pocket. I recognized the address; it was from the Ringside Bar and Grill.

"The Ringside send you another bill?" I asked.

"Oh, this?" He took the envelope from his pocket and handed it to me.

It was an announcement for a beefsteak party they were having that night. I looked at the date on the envelope; it was several days old.

"Wanna go?" Biff asked. His eyes were still on the ceiling and I felt Gee Gee give a little start at the invitation.

"You mean me?" I asked.

He nodded, but very slowly. I knew he didn't want me to say yes. For that very reason, I was going to, when Gee Gee spoke.

"Gyp, you promised to finish my costume." For a moment I thought she was going to cry. "If you go carrying on at the

Ringside, you'll have a hangover tomorrow and I won't have a damn thing to wear."

She would have protested more but I stopped her. I looked first at Biff, then at Gee Gee.

"All right, I'll finish it tonight," I said.

Biff didn't say a word. He might have coaxed me a little with the whole dressing room listening in. Instead he got up from the cot and walked out of the room.

I looked from the door he had disappeared through to Gee Gee. She was so guilty she couldn't face me. She bit her lip and tossed her head. That was all. It was enough, but if she thought I was going to give her the satisfaction of accusing her in front of all the girls, she had another guess coming.

I went right on with my makeup as though it was an everyday occurrence for my best girl friend to make a date for the Ringside with my boyfriend.

I didn't mention anything during the show either. When I played the two scenes with Biff, I kidded and clowned as I always did. In the finale I took Gee Gee's hand and we both closed the curtain in as usual. But as soon as the show was over, I made a dash for the new blue bathroom so I could cry. Not loud, just the kind of crying that makes your chest hurt.

In a few minutes I came out and started to take off my makeup.

"What's the matter with your eyes?" Gee Gee asked. "You aren't crying, are you?"

"I got cold cream in them," I said stiffly, "and what would I be crying about?" I rubbed the Turkish towel across my face so hard it's a wonder I didn't take the skin off.

"I sent for a container of beer for you," Gee Gee said in a small voice.

"Thank you," I replied without glancing at her.

"And, Gyppy, there's something I want to tell you. It's about…"

"There's nothing you can tell me, Gee Gee, that I don't know already," I said, but I've never been so mistaken in all my life.

SEVENTEEN

GEE GEE WAS THE LAST ONE TO LEAVE THE DRESSING room. Through the corner of my eyes I watched her put the finishing touches to her street costume.

Over her blue serge dress she wore a simple, tailored coat. A red, patent leather belt was the only hint that she wasn't a stenographer or a shop girl out on a spree. Her carrot-colored hair was pushed under a blue felt vagabond hat. The small red feather stuck in the crown matched her belt.

She looked at me. "Sure you don't mind sewing tonight, honey?" The freckles showed through the thin rice powder on her nose.

"Positive," I said with one of those "don't worry about me" martyred faces. Just to give her something to worry about, I added, "Tell Biff I'll meet him there later, will you?"

Gee Gee stopped fumbling with her gloves and opened her mouth to speak. With a grim little face she changed her mind and threw her arms around me.

"We'll always be friends, Gypper." With an abrupt motion she turned and ran down the steps.

I followed her to the balcony and watched her go through the stage entrance. There was a sound of footsteps behind me, then heavy breathing. As I turned, my eyes met Russell's.

"I thought you left with Mandy and Joey," I said quickly. I was irritated. He startled me and perhaps my voice wasn't friendly.

"Forgot something," he replied curtly. "Went back to get it."

His mouth twitched. There was a piece of cigarette paper stuck to his lip. As he tried to pull it off, I saw that his fingernails were dirty.

"What's the matter, Russ?" I felt that he needed sympathy.

The last few days had changed him so. Instead of the well-dressed, suave straight man, I looked at a bleary-eyed, untidy bum. From the pink grease paint on his collar to the frayed bedroom slippers on his feet, he was dirty.

He bit his lip savagely. The cigarette paper stuck there. Before he answered me, he glanced into the empty room.

"You gonna sew tonight?" He closed one eye as though he couldn't focus one of them.

"Uh-huh, promised Gee Gee." Even mentioning her name made me jealous.

To change the subject, I invited Russell to have a drink. As soon as the words were out of my mouth, I regretted them. After everything that Biff had told me about Russell and after all that Jake had told me, I had to go and invite him to drink with me!

While he was making up his mind, I remembered the day after La Verne's murder; how I'd found him sitting on that tree stump as though he'd lost his only true love. Then admitting that the main thing he was worrying about was La Verne's money.

I was glad when he refused the drink and started downstairs.

I backed into the room and closed the door. I had a strange feeling that he was still there until I heard the stage door slam. I propped the chair under the knob again. The window was still bolted and, stuffy as the room was, I wouldn't have opened it for anything in the world. I lifted the cretonne draperies and looked under the makeup shelf. Then I felt behind the costumes hanging on the far wall and, for luck, tried the window. It was secure.

While I was maneuvering Sarah into a better light, I thought of Biff. It was hard for me to believe that he could be so unfaithful. Maybe it wasn't with Gee Gee at all. I used that thought for consolation for a little while. Somehow I wouldn't have minded so much if it had been anyone else but Gee Gee.

I unfolded the white satin and began pinning the wedding gown on Sarah. She didn't look too well in white. The black stocking material showed through and the places where her stuffing was coming out seemed to be increasing. The gold knob wobbled back and forth and she creaked in every joint. It was about time to pension her off.

My thoughts went back to Biff. "He might have waited until we were alone and then told me," I said. "He's sat around with me when I sewed before. He could have tonight, of all nights."

I punched in the side of the container so the beer wouldn't spill and took a long drink. I felt betrayed, so I took another drink. Then I felt abused, so I took another.

"Maybe it wasn't Gee Gee," I said again. "Maybe it was Sugar Bun Kelly, or that Joyce Janice."

That made me madder than ever, so I put the container on the shelf and began stabbing at the wedding gown with the scissors. They went clip, clip and the white satin fell on the paper-covered floor. With blue chalk I outlined the seams to be sewn and stripped Sarah of her finery.

I don't know if I nudged her when I sat down or if the vibration of the sewing machine did it, but with a screeching, snapping noise Sarah collapsed. Her wire bottom sprung open like the innards of a clock and the buxom top went sprawling on the floor.

The gold knob bounced like a golf ball across the room. Sarah was no more. Like a half woman in a side show she rolled over on her back and was still. The whir of unsprung metal still sang as I looked at her.

I picked her up and carefully sat her on a chair. It took a little balancing, but she finally became steady.

"You can't do this to me," I said to her. "You're the only one left. Everybody went to the Ringside but you and me, and now you have to fall apart."

I took another gulp of beer and looked at her again.

"You know," I said eyeing her intently, "with the right clothes and a little makeup you'd be a damn fine-looking woman."

My coat was hanging behind the chair. I took it down and placed it on Sarah's strong shoulders. It covered her to the floor. I stood back and appraised my handiwork.

"But you gotta have a face."

I took just a sip before I wadded a clean makeup towel into a large ball. With a piece of string I tied it on to the screw the gold knob was fitted for. Then with a lipstick I gave her a mouth. A little rouge on the cheeks with Gee Gee's rabbit's foot.

"That's for luck," I said, as I gave her a healthier blush. An eyebrow pencil made eyes and lashes, long lashes.

"Now for a touch of eye shadow to make you mysterious."

I took my hat from the hook and put it on her, punched the extra part of the makeup towel into the high crown, and pulled the brim down over one unblinking eye.

"Madam, it makes you look ten years younger." I pulled the brim down a little lower. "I bet if Biff saw you right now he'd take you to the Ringside. Not that the one he's with is any more intelligent."

I had another drink.

"Or witty, or adorable, or something."

The container was empty. At the bottom was a brownish, frothy leftover. I scooped it out with my fingers. It tasted bad, so I brushed my teeth, washed my hands, and started back to work.

The wedding gown seemed to leer at me. I thought suddenly of how many wedding gowns I'd worn; the Polish wedding finale, the bridal-night scene, my own number, "Always a Mother But Never a Bride," and now, another finale. Some people wear wedding gowns to get married in, I thought bitterly, and the only guy I ever wanted to marry has to go out with somebody else and leave me all alone.

It must have been my imagination, but I thought Sarah gave

me a sympathetic glance. She didn't speak, though; I'm sure of that.

To keep from crying, I buried myself in the business at hand. I stitched up one side of the gown, then the other. My foot pressed so hard on the pedal that the machine raced along.

A light was shining in my eyes and I remember throwing a scrap of dark material over the guard. Then I moved the table a little so the light would come from over my shoulders.

As I sat facing the doorway, every now and then I glanced at the door to assure myself that it was firmly closed. Sarah was sitting in Gee Gee's chair, staring at herself in the seasick mirror, and the room was hazy with smoke.

It was cozy, I decided. I felt very safe, quite secure. As a matter of fact, I was safe and secure—until I opened that door.

But that was later. How much later, I don't know. I do know that once or twice I got up to stretch my back and legs. Then I played a couple of victrola records. Maybe the selection was bad, but to this day I can't listen to a victrola without thinking of La Verne's blue, swollen face.

That night it was worse. I kept seeing my own face on her body. They were carrying me out of the toilet room and I was dead. The wedding gown wasn't for a wedding; it was for a funeral.

I lifted the needle from the record and began sewing furiously.

That's when I feel asleep. Beer always makes me sleepy and I really just meant to rest my eyes. Just for a moment, just put my head on the shelf and rest my eyes…

EIGHTEEN

THE PAIN IN MY BACK AND NECK AWAKENED ME. When I first opened my eyes, I wasn't sure just where I was. Then it slowly dawned on me.

I looked nervously around the room. The door was still closed, the chair propped under the knob; the window was bolted, Sarah continued staring at her unlovely towel face in the mirror, and I was still alone.

Something besides my stiff back had awakened me, though. It was a voice. Or had I dreamed that I heard someone singing?

I got up from the chair and let the cold water run in the sink. Then I scooped up handfuls of it and splashed it on my face and head. With the water still dripping from me, I went back and sat down. I lit a cigarette and glanced at my wrist watch. It was one-thirty. I must have slept for an hour or more.

Suddenly I heard the voice again. It was coming from the stage!

I was so startled that I dropped the cigarette. It rolled down my chest and onto my lap before I realized that I had been burned. I shook my apron and when the cigarette fell to the floor I quietly pressed my foot on the lighted end. Then I waited. I waited for the sound of footsteps on the iron stairway, the rasping noise of someone lifting the latch of the door, the groan of the chair as it would give way.

The voice had stopped, and still the sounds I expected didn't come. It's easy enough for people to tell me now that I should have stayed in the room; in a way I agree with them. But I couldn't stay. There was no doubt in my mind that I was alone in the theater with the murderer. I just couldn't sit in my room and wait patiently for him to break in and strangle me. No, I had to open the door, walk down the stairs, and say, "Here I am!"

I turned off the lights, leaving just the covered one burning. It made the room quite dark and shadowy. I wanted to fix it so that when I opened the door I wouldn't throw a streak of light on the stage, but I was too afraid of total darkness.

When I pulled the chair out from under the knob it made a slight noise, so I waited a moment. Then I heard the voice again. It was almost like someone vocalizing, but the sounds were guttural and harsh. As long as I could hear it I felt safe. The stage door was straight ahead. All I had to worry about was getting down the stairs without being caught. Then I could run for the door.

I unlatched the door and slowly opened it. It didn't creak that time and as I left, it closed behind me. The stage was in darkness; not a gleam of light. Just the sound of a voice to convince me I wasn't alone.

My slippers shuffled on the landing while I grabbed the iron banister. If a person can be glad about anything in a moment like that, I was glad—glad I had left my soft bedroom shoes on, and glad I was out of the room. I felt the top step with a cautious toe, then the next. It suddenly occurred to me that I had never counted the steps leading to the stage. Twenty-eight weeks in a theater and I didn't know how many steps there were!

A cold draft of air hit my face and I pulled my robe around me. Maybe the stage door was open! The thought made me hurry. Then, maybe the stage door was locked! I hadn't considered that at all and when I did, I wanted to turn around and rush back to the dressing room.

Why hadn't I thought about the window? It led to the roof and maybe there would be some way to the street. But something kept me moving forward. I'd lost count of the stairs. Was it twelve or one hundred and twelve?

Then the banister ended. "Straight ahead is the stage door," I told myself over and over. I touched the call board and felt the thumbtacks that held the two weeks' notice sign, then another piece of paper.

That would be the B.A.A. announcement, I thought. "Are you paid up on your union dues?" it read, and at the bottom was Tom Phillips', the president's, signature.

As I felt the door I realized I wasn't paid up. Maybe they'll think I got myself murdered on purpose so I wouldn't have to pay. My hand touched the latch and I tried to lift it.

It was heavy and wouldn't budge. I tried with both hands. It was locked.

I wanted to pound on the door, to shout and scream, but instead I pressed my face close to the cold iron. I think that is the only thing that kept me from fainting.

I don't know how long I stood there, but suddenly I became aware of a new sound. The voice had stopped. There was a faint, scuffling noise like someone tiptoeing. It was getting fainter, as though they were trying to move away from where I was.

Maybe they thought I was the murderer! Maybe it's just someone who was locked in, like me.

I thought of Russell. It could have been him. I was going to call out when I remembered his dirty fingernails and his bleary eyes. Did he stay on purpose because he knew I was alone in the theater? Did he think I knew something about the murders? Was *he* the murderer?

The tiptoeing sound stopped. I began feeling my way back to the stairway. My breathing seemed to fill the theater, and if I'd worn spiked shoes, I couldn't have made as much noise as I thought I did.

I touched the railing again. Then I decided to try the coal chute. If I went back to the room I was trapped, I reasoned. What if I did get out through the window? Would the Chinese restaurant be open at this hour? Certainly not. The only other exits would be the shops or the florist. They all closed early.

My hand touched the water cooler and it reminded me of the first time I'd tried to get out through the coal chute. Someone had grabbed my throat, thin, strong hands had pressed my vocal cords. It had been dark then, too, and someone had tried to kill me. I was sure of it. Biff had laughed at me when I told him. He should have listened.

My foot found the top step. Then I stopped. Someone had shouted.

"Who is it?" The voice came from the stage.

It sounded familiar, but I was too terrified to place it.

"Who's there?" it asked.

Then I ran. Not downstairs or toward the stage door, but straight for the voice. I bumped into the scenery. It was a plush drop and the stagehands had roped it together for the cleaning women, roped it so that it cleared the floor for the mops to go under.

I grabbed hold of it to keep from falling. I must have been pressing the plush the wrong way because the nap felt like thousands of little needles stabbing me. I tried to breath into the plush so the voice couldn't hear me, but the musty odor made me want to sneeze.

Just a few hours ago I stood on this same stage. The theater had been full of men, slouched down in their seats. Their cigarettes glowed in the dark and a spotlight pierced through the smoke, following me as I walked back and forth. Musicians in their shirt sleeves, with racing forms in their pockets, played "Sophisticated Lady" while I flicked my pins in the tuba and dropped my garter belt into the pit. Then my petticoat. When it fell, it covered the tuba player. He struggled to get it off and the audience laughed. I had thought, I'll keep that in.

Only a few hours ago, and now I stood there with my face buried in the dirty plush curtain, alone with a murderer.

There were so many things I wanted to do before I died. I wanted to live in one of those apartment houses with trees growing in cement boxes in front of it. I wanted to be in a big show so I could have Sundays off, and, most of all, I wanted to be Mrs. Biff Brannigan.

A round circle of light blinded me. It was a flashlight and it was coming nearer and nearer. The voice was nearer too.

"Why didn't you answer when I called out before?" it demanded. I could just barely see the startled face. It was Stachi's. It looked as frightened as I felt.

"You gave me a turn," he said.

I gave *him* a turn!

"How'd you get down here in the dark?" he asked.

Then I found my voice. Not exactly my voice, but a quivery sort of thing that would do for the time being. "I fell asleep while I was sewing and then I thought I heard someone singing, but I guess I was mistaken."

An expression of relief covered Stachi's face and someone giggled stupidly. I realized it was me.

"I'd better get dressed," I mumbled. "Folks are waiting for me." I was still giggling. Stachi threw me a beam from his flashlight and I had an urgent desire to turn and yell "Boo!" as I started to go upstairs.

He held the light until I opened the door and entered the room. It was still shadowy, but I was in too much of a hurry to waste time turning on the lights.

I zipped myself into a dress and stuffed my garter belt, with the stockings still hooked to it, into my purse. Then I stepped into my shoes and took my hat off Sarah Jane. Her round unblinking eyes seemed to follow me when I went over to the mirror.

My hair and face were certainly not looking their best. In fact, I reminded myself a little of Stella Dallas at her worst.

There is some scientific explanation for my next emotion, but I don't know much about it. It's a feeling that I'd lived the moment before. Yet I couldn't remember when; maybe a thousand years ago. When I looked in that mirror to fix my hat, I felt it again. There was something weird about it.

My hand was unconsciously reaching for the closet door; not to open it, but to touch it. My arm seemed to hang suspended in the air. I had no feeling of effort. Then suddenly I remembered!

I knew the door leading to the stage would open, and I knew a man would come into the room. There was nothing I could do. I just waited.

The door opened silently and slowly. Then I saw a hand in the shadows and an arm. A frayed maroon sweater covered it. There was that same odor of carbolic acid.

"You were in the dressing room the night La Verne was murdered," I said without turning.

Reflected in the mirror was the full figure of Stachi, the doorman.

"I smelled the soap. It is soap, isn't it?"

He said yes.

"You said you were downstairs, but you couldn't have been, because I fell over your chair."

He nodded.

"You were watching me when I dressed for the finale, too."

He didn't answer me. The door was closing and I could see both of his hands. Something sparkled in one of them. The other hung limply at his side. I realized that he was closing the door with his foot.

"You murdered them, didn't you?"

The face I saw in the mirror was calm, almost benign. I turned and put my hands on the makeup shelf.

He was walking into the light and I could see the little beads of sweat in his eyebrows. He held the glittering thing close to my face. It swung back and forth on his index finger. The rhinestones hung heavily on the dental floss.

"See?" he said. "On one finger I hold the costume of a lovely lady. Such a little thing," he said tenderly, "and yet so dangerous."

"Then you are . . .?" My mouth was too dry to speak. He had taken a step closer to me and I could feel his hot breath on my face.

"I am the stripper strangler," he said. Then he smiled. "Amusing title: stripper strangler. I like that." He laughed quietly. "I like the other touch, too; strangled with her own G-string."

"But it wasn't her own G-string. It was Jannine's."

He looked at me narrowly. The smile left his face.

"It was her new plush-lined one," I added. "She said she dropped it on the steps and..."

"And I found it."

"You tried to kill me during the raid, too, didn't you?"

He shook his head.

"Yes you did," I insisted, as though it were very important to get that straight. "When the lights went out backstage you tried to kill me with your hands."

"I turned the lights out, but I didn't mean to kill you. Not then. When you screamed I knew I had the wrong neck."

My hands felt wet and sticky. Something pressed hard against my palm. I realized it was my lipstick. I moved my hand and touched my powder puff, an eyeliner. Then I felt the little scissor-like gadget that I used to curl my eyelashes.

My dressmaker's shears! They should be on my shelf! They were strong and sharp. My hand trembled as I felt for them. I was afraid Stachi could read my mind as my hands touched the useless things on the shelf.

"The Princess saw me," he was saying. "She walked by the door as I stood behind La Verne's chair. She saw me with my hands on La Verne's neck, but La Verne was..."

A sudden change came over his face, a startled expression. Then he nodded his head. A strand of dusty gray hair fell over his eye.

"Now I know," he said. He looked at me strangely, as though

he were going to tell me something. Then he changed his mind.

"Where were you hiding?" I asked.

I didn't want to know. I just wanted him to keep talking until I could feel the curved handles of my scissors. The thought of what I'd do with them when I found them frightened me. Would I have the courage, the strength to use them?

Stachi glanced at the wardrobe sheet. My eyes followed him.

"I stood behind that curtain," he said. The costumes made bulges in the cretonne almost as if someone was there then.

Stachi's voice went on. "The body was in the closet when Jake put the wax on the door. I watched him. Once I thought he heard me. Then I would have had to kill him. But he went away and as I was getting ready to leave the room, someone else came in."

From the way he looked at me I knew that I was the someone.

"I thought you saw me," he said, and I shook my head.

There was something cool and curved against my right hand. I moved my fingers until they were close to the handle. My scissors!

"It must have been more difficult with the Princess," I said. The effort to keep the excitement from my voice made my chest hurt. I could feel beads of perspiration roll down my face.

"The Princess was easy," Stachi said.

My hands held the scissors tightly. When he turns his head, I thought, I'll pick them up and...

"I waited until everyone had left for dinner. Then I called to her. 'There's someone here to see you,' I said, and when she got to the top step, I slipped the string around her neck. She didn't even struggle; just gasped and began falling. I had to hold the string tightly or she would have rolled down the stairs. That's when she cut her arm—on a nail sticking up from the floor."

"But the prop-room door was locked," I said. "How did you get her body into the Gazeeka Box?"

He put his hand—the one that nothing glittered in—to his pocket and pulled out a bunch of keys. Without taking his eyes from me, he twirled them on his finger.

"Night watchmen and doormen always have these, you know," he said.

"Of course. How stupid of the police not to think of that."

If only he'd take his eyes from me! If I could distract him in some way! Suddenly I remembered a movie I had seen. An actor was in a spot just like this. He had looked quickly over the man's shoulder and, when the man turned, he struck.

I turned my head and stared past Stachi. I've never tried to act as well before in my life. I think I even opened my mouth as if I were going to speak.

Then Stachi laughed!

I laughed, too, but hysterically. I expected him to say that he had seen the same movie. Then it seemed that there were two murderers facing me. I stopped laughing.

"Have you thought of what you're going to do with my body?" I asked.

"Yes, I have." His words seemed to run together. Or was it because my head was spinning so?

"I'm curious," I managed to say. I thought of what Biff had said when we were leaving the theater through the basement. "It would be a good place to hide a body."

"The coal chute, maybe?" I asked. Stachi shook his head.

"The pile of scenery under the stairs?"

"Guess again. You're getting warm." He eyed me playfully. Then, with a little chuckle, he said, "I'll give you a hint. What is it that stands like a woman, dresses like a woman, but isn't a woman?"

I stared at him silently.

"Oh, come now. Surely you can guess that?" He looked at Sarah Jane sitting stiffly at the makeup shelf.

"Now can you guess?" he asked with a grin.

I nodded stupidly and he told me how funny it would be when the girls found out that Sarah Jane was really a corpse.

"I'll have to brace your body in some way to keep it from

falling, but with the sheet thrown over it, they may not discover you for some time."

My hand dropped the scissors. They fell noiselessly on the shelf and I watched the hands coming nearer to my throat. They were long, thin hands, and they had big blue veins that stood out. Something sparkled in one of them.

From a distance a voice was saying, "You'll be dressed in a white sheet like a wedding gown, and there will be diamonds around your throat, diamonds cutting into your neck."

Then there were many hands, all with big blue veins, and each hand held something that sparkled.

"When the others find you it will be very funny."

I felt something touch my throat very gently. Then I heard a little laugh.

"Very, very funny."

NINETEEN

THE THEATER WAS FULL OF HANDS, THIN, VEINED hands. They were all applauding. I was on.

"Always a mother but never a bride, that is my doleful admission. An actress at heart, I went wrong from the start by giving the groom an audition."

"Stop rehearsing your lyrics, Punkin, and drink a little of this." The voice was familiar and the coat my nose pressed into smelled of tobacco and Old Grand.

"Oh, Biff! He said he was going to prop me up in a corner. He said it was going to be funny…" I didn't want to cry, but I couldn't help it.

Biff patted my face with a wet towel and put a glass of water under my lips. "We heard him, Punkin. He was doing his own version of Uncle Don: 'Now, if little Johnny on his seventh birthday will look under the sheet, he will find a present; a nice corpse.'"

That made me cry louder. "Please, Biff, this is serious."

"OK, honey, you be serious and I'll be Roebuck. Don't cry. It's all over now. No more bodies, no more murders, no more nothing."

"Then you got him?" I couldn't see very well, but I got the impression that Biff was grinning from ear to ear.

"Yes, Punkin, we got him. We were waiting right there and the very minute we thought you were in trouble, we grabbed him."

I became aware of the anxious faces staring down at me. I realized I was on the floor again, and I realized something else!

I stood up and faced Biff. "I want a straight answer, yes or no," I said slowly. "Were you within calling distance when that madman was scaring the pants off me?"

Biff stopped grinning. "He wasn't a madman. He…"

"*Wasn't?*" I looked from Biff to the Sergeant, then to Jiggers. Mike Brannen was there, too. He took up the grinning where Biff left off.

"Yep. He's a past tenser all right," he said cheerfully.

Then I hadn't dropped the scissors!

Mike started giving me a detailed description as I tried to go out of the room.

"You'd never think such a skinny guy could hold so much blood. Boy, it spurted like a fountain. His whole throat was ripped wide open."

When I reached the landing, Biff held my arm. "Don't go out there, honey," he said. "You had enough excitement to last you for a while. They're carting the body off to the morgue and, well, it ain't pretty."

Biff still held the glass of water. When I tried to drink it I choked.

Biff said, "We got a full confession before he done himself in. Not that we needed it, but…"

"He killed himself?" This time I almost fainted from relief.

Biff led me back into the dressing room and pulled out a chair for me. Mike was still on the same conversation, and Biff asked him to be quiet for a minute.

"Get Gyp a drink," he said. "Here, honey, put your feet up." He pulled over a chair and put a pillow under my legs.

Mike brought the bottle out from behind the mirror and poured three drinks. Then he looked at the Sergeant and divided his own drink between Biff and me.

I enjoyed the attention; I might as well face it. The drink

made me feel warm and happy. The Sergeant reminded me of my grandfather again, and even Mike Brannen looked handsome.

I had been hoping the Sergeant would take his policemen and go so the three of us could have another drink, when he closed the notebook he had been writing in.

"Well," he said. "that closes the case." Then he held out his hand to Biff. "Thank you, young man."

When their hands met it was a tossup which one was the worse actor. Biff had an expression on his face as though he were screen testing for a Dick Tracy part and the Sergeant was playing "Joe Generous." If he'd rehearsed it for six weeks, he couldn't have read his next line with more hamlike sincerity.

"If it hadn't been for your keen brain and quick eye, this might very well have had a different ending."

They both looked at me significantly. I know I should have given them my sad eye, but I couldn't. The Sergeant was a little disappointed. He wanted a three-cornered scene and I failed him, so he turned back to Biff.

"Remember, if you want a job on the force, get in touch with me." As they shook again, the Sergeant managed a laugh so much like Edward Arnold's that it was all I could do to keep from howling. Then he started for the door.

With one hand on the knob, he turned and paused a moment. Building up for an exit hand, I thought. I was right. The timing was wrong, but the line was there.

"You will be asked to appear at the inquest."

"That does it!" I shouted, hitting the side of my head with the heel of my hand. "What a couple of hamolas! What corn, right off the cob."

I laughed so hard that Mike began slapping me on the back. He waited to speak until the door closed behind the Sergeant and the policemen.

"Aw, Gyp, you shouldn'ta laughed at the chief like that.

He meant it, honest. If it hadn't been for Biff putting two and two together, with that picture, they never woulda caught that murderin' rat." He looked at Biff and his voice was reverent. "He's a hero, that's what he is, a real hero."

Biff, still wearing the Dick Tracy face, shifted his weight from one foot to the other. "Well, Punkin here deserves some credit," he admitted.

"Now, that's damn generous of you."

Biff wasn't sure how I meant it. "I mean, if you hadn't asked him all those questions, it woulda been tougher for us."

"I know how you mean it, dear."

Mike could see the danger signals. His three days backstage in a burlesque theater had taught him not to ignore cues.

"Tell her about the picture, Biff." He turned to me. "Boy, this'll kill ya."

"Oh, that was nothing," Biff began modestly. "The cops just ignored the most obvious clue in the whole case. I—well—I took care of it for 'em." He leaned back in the chair and put his thumbs through his suspenders.

"When the picture of La Verne's mother is missing it gets to be important to me. So in my own quiet way I find out what La Verne's name was. Not that phony La Verne handle, but her real name. Guess what it was?"

"Brenda Goldblatt?"

Biff scowled. "No. It's Stacciaro. Get it?"

"No. Give it to me again. Right from the beginning."

"Stacciaro. Stachi. See?"

"Oh, yes!" I said a little sarcastically. "La Verne's real name was Stacc—something. So that makes her Stachi's relative, daughter. No, granddaughter. He was too old to be her father. Anyway, he's her grandfather. His daughter got in wrong and had an illegitimate daughter and it was La Verne.

"Stachi gets mad and disowns his daughter. Then she and La Verne almost starve to death until La Verne gets a job in burlesque

194

and when Stachi finds out who she is he decides he's got to kill her because death is better than dishonor."

I brushed my hands and leaned back in my chair. If I'd had suspenders, I would have put my thumbs through them. Instead I reached for my drink.

"That's right!" Biff stared at me with admiration. "Howja know?"

That's when I spilled my drink all over my lap.

Biff started drying my dress with a makeup towel. "How did you figure it out?"

I took the towel from him and carefully placed it on the shelf. "Look, Biff," I said quietly and calmly. "I just had a nerve-wracking experience. I just went through hell. I damn near got my neck bent by a guy who has already killed two women. I'm not in the mood for jokes."

Then I turned to Mike. "Hand me my purse, please."

I took out my garter belt with the stockings still hanging from it and began unhooking them. Then I kicked off my slippers and pulled on my hose.

Mike stared at me as though he'd never seen a woman put on a stocking. His face turned red when I straightened a seam.

"It's the truth," he said. "He told me so hisself. Just before he stuck the butcher knife in his throat. You know that knife that hangs in the wings on the tin sign, 'In case of fire cut this rope'?"

I didn't answer him.

"The rope that lets in the asbestos curtain," he added importantly. "Well, that's the knife he does it with. I was right there and he was so calm and quiet nobody had an idea of what was on his mind. All of a sudden-like he grabs it and the blood spurts! Boy, did he bleed! And was we cops surprised?"

Biff spoke up quickly. "Come on, let's get out of here or we'll miss the free feed at the Ringside."

I threw him a look of gratitude and we hurried out of the theater.

They discussed the other aspects of the case as we walked up the alley. I deliberately hurried on ahead of them. It wasn't the talk that upset me so. I can hardly explain it, but my heart hurt for Stachi; the sort of hurt I got when I looked at Dolly.

Biff whistled for a cab, and when it pulled up I started to get in. Then I heard the end of what Mike had been saying.

"Sure enough, the stuff was right there in his pocket."

I got out of the cab. "What stuff?" I asked.

Biff and Mike looked at each other as though they thought I had gone out of my mind. "La Verne's stock in the theater," Biff said.

"Oh. I'm sorry; for your sakes, that is. It would have made a much better script if it had been dope. Now the papers can only say, 'Strangler strips strip of stocks.' "

The cab driver stuck his head out of the front window. "Are you or ain'tchu?" he asked in the same tone I had used with Biff and Mike.

"Are I or ain't I what?" I asked coldly.

"Are you or ain'tchu going to ride in my nice automobile?"

I was being pushed firmly into the cab and Biff was apologizing to the driver. Mike said, "I'll get out of my uniform and meet you at the Ringside. Tell Alice I'll be a little late, will ya?"

"Don't forget to pick up the Chinaman," Biff replied. Then he slammed the door and called out to the chauffeur, "The Ringside Bar and Grill on Forty-Eighth Street."

He pulled down the jump seat in front of me. "Put your feet up, Punkin," he said. "It doesn't make the meter tick any more, so you might as well enjoy all the comforts."

He lit two cigarettes and handed me one. He put his hand through the leather strap near the window and relaxed. Taxicabs always give me a luxurious feeling, but Biff was overdoing it. If he'd had a fat stomach, he would have made a perfect model for a Gropper cartoon of *The Capitalist*.

He chortled.

"What?"

"I was just thinking of that line of yours; 'Strangler strips strip of stock.'"

I chortled too. "It does sound good," I admitted.

"Yeah, it's a damn shame they can't use it."

I had been through too much to get it right away. I puffed away at my cigarette lazily. Then I sat up. "Why *can't* they use it?" I asked.

"It's a swell line. Only you see, Stachi didn't kill La Verne."

TWENTY

"FUNNIEST PART OF ALL," HE SAID, "IS STACHI thinking he killed her, too. Not once does he get wise that he twists the neck for nothing. Not once does he know that she has enough poison in her to kill of an army of..."

"Poison?"

"Sure. Cyanide of something." Biff looked at me, a long, searching look. "Didn't you know that?"

My voice shook, but I managed to tell him that it was a great big surprise. In fact, I was flabbergasted.

"And here I was afraid the Sergeant gave it away," Biff mused. "I was sure of it when he asked Dolly if they didn't have a drink and make up. Then that broken glass he picked up under La Verne's makeup shelf; damn fool puts it right on the desk with everybody in the room."

"Fingerprints, I suppose?"

"Nope, gloves."

"How inconvenient," I said coldly. "For you and the police, I mean. Nice for the murderer."

"It doesn't make much difference. We know who done it anyway." He sat back and relaxed.

I gave him a full minute to tell me. Then I opened the window to the front of the cab. "Pull over here, please," I said with what I thought was great dignity, "I'm getting out."

Biff slammed the window on my dignified nose and pulled

me back into the seat. "You're staying right here," he said firmly.

"I am not!"

"You are, too."

That could have gone on and on. That is, it could have if I hadn't thrown a tantrum.

"Mr. Brannigan, take your hands off my arm," I said.

It was the wrong approach, so I took it an octave higher. "First you leave me alone in the theater with the murderer. Then you tell me I'm not alone. Then you tell me he's not the murderer. You let me make a damn fool out of myself, asking him what he's going to do with my corpse. You must have had yourself a swell laugh! Let go of me!"

Biff got way over in the corner of the cab. I had a strange idea he was laughing. Something was making his shoulders move up and down and funny noises were coming out of his throat.

"If you're ..." I stopped. If he were, it would be too much. "Cyanide of what?" I asked.

After a coughing fit Biff told me he didn't know exactly. "Something that works mighty fast." He said it as though it were explanation enough for one with my limited intelligence.

"And the Chinaman?" I asked, all sweetness and light. "Was he by any chance one of Stachi's granddaughters, too?"

Before he had a chance to answer that one the cab stopped. While Biff dug around for the fare I climbed out.

I was half hoping he'd have to ask me for it, but I was deprived of the pleasure of refusing him. He even gave the driver a quarter tip. Before the cab drove away they had decided that "dames are awfully hard to understand."

What was harder for me to understand was where Biff got the bankroll. It was no Mexican; the twenties went right through to the bottom.

I watched him put it back into his pocket. "Horse come in?" I asked.

Biff eyed me. "Same as," he said. "Russell paid off the dough he owed me for the last three months."

Some of the actors standing under the Ringside canopy greeted us. Stinky, the Eltinge comic, was picking his teeth, so I knew he was on the way out.

"Howzit?" I asked.

"For free, it's good," he replied.

I imagined he meant the beefsteak. From the satisfied look on his face I also imagined there was nothing left but the gristle.

Biff and I peered through the blinds. "The joint's packed," he said. "Let's go next door for a quick one first."

"I'd love it," I said quickly. I wasn't sure if he'd seen Sugar Bun Kelly or not, but she was draped gracefully on a bar stool near the entrance. She was in black satin and she had a generous look in her eye. I was in no mood for primitive business like fighting over a man—not with that audience, anyway—and I know what black satin does to Biff.

Joe's place next door was empty. The boss was behind the bar polishing glasses. He seemed surprised to see us.

"I never expect nobody when the Ringside gives with the free beefsteak," he said rather apologetically.

We didn't have to order. Joe knew what we wanted, and in a minute the brown boys were in front of us.

I poured my rye into a glass of water and raised it to my lips. For the second time that night someone said something that made me spill my drink in my lap. This time it was Joe.

"No," he said, "it didn't surprise me none when I heard that Russell had got La Verne's dough."

He went right on talking, but I was sputtering so over my drink that I couldn't catch all of it, just the end.

"A dame that carries ten thousand bucks around in her G-string deserves to be strangled.

Ignoring me completely, Biff agreed with him. "She was a dope to let him know about it, but he was a bigger dope to flash the roll. He shoulda dug a hole and buried it until the heat was off. Either that, or he shoulda taken the bankbook, too. He mighta known the cops would be lookin' at anybody who got rich sudden-like. Ten grand is..."

Joe had just noticed me. "Wassa matter, choke?" he asked.

"Oh, don't mind me," I replied. "You boys go right ahead and chat. I do this sort of thing all the time."

Biff took me at my word. He went on talking without so much as slapping me on the back. He did throw me an annoyed glance when I coughed on one of his lines, but that was all.

"Russ was so anxious to get started with that play of his that he don't wait for nothing. He pays me the C he owes me just to get me to read it. It's supposed to have a part in it that's right up my alley; that's what he tells me. Alley is right. I've read stinkers before, but this is the one that does it! Anyway, I take me a look at the script and then I ask him where the money's coming from. His own dough, he tells me, an inheritance."

They both found that amusing. "Inheritance is right," Joe said, and they laughed again.

At that point the door flew open and Mike Brannen made his entrance. He had changed his uniform all right. He wore a pinstripe number that was enough to frighten even a hardened trouper. If the suit didn't get you, the tie would. It was like an Easter egg that had gone wrong. The handkerchief sticking out of his pocket was a desert sunset.

I was too blinded for a moment to see the small man who stood next to him. It was the Chinese waiter who had given me the root.

"Well, here we are," Mike said, as though we could miss seeing him.

Biff got up from the stool and signed the check Joe had given him. "Here we go, Punkin," he said gravely. "Play dumb. No matter what happens, don't open your kisser."

"Play dumb? I'd like to know what else I can do. Am I supposed to..."

Something in Biff's face stopped me. I smiled. "You're the doctor," I said.

No one spoke until we reached the door. Then Joe suddenly whipped out his keys and locked up behind us.

"What the hell," he said. "I might as well join you. I can't make a sale with that guy givin' it away." He kept up his complaints until we reached the Ringside.

The crowd had thinned a little, but it was still large enough to make Joe remark, "Son of a bitch's got a gold mine here." Then he left us to check on the quality of the free food.

Gee Gee was at the end of the bar. She had lost a little of her girlishness and her blue hat with the red feather was pushed back on her head. She greeted me uncertainly and looked at Biff.

"Did the big strong man save you from the murderer's clutches?" she asked.

I know Biff wanted to tap her gently on the head with a beer bottle, but he controlled himself.

"I already told Gyp," he said quickly. "Look, Gee Gee, I had to do it that way. If she hadn't been mad at me she never would have stayed, so I ..."

"So you made like we were singing baby shoes," Gee Gee snapped. "You didn't care if that idiot killed her or not as long as you got your old evidence!"

Biff was unwinding her legs from the bar stool as she talked and, before the waiter had time to take our orders, he was leading both of us to the back of the room.

The orchestra, a piano and an accordion, was playing, "When Kansas City Kitty Smiles At Me." The deep sawdust on the floor was mixed with so much beer that walking through it was like plowing through mud.

Sugar Bun Kelly and Joyce Janice were sitting at the Eltinge table, outminking each other. On their arms they wore enough railroad fare home to take care of a stranded Chautauqua. Sugar Bun was too busy telling Rudnick, the manager, about how she broke the Columbus house records to say hello, but Joyce managed a frigid greeting.

"Cute kids," Gee Gee remarked as we passed.

"Kids?" I said, with the proper inflection. Biff was smart enough to keep walking.

I was surprised to see Moss sitting at our table, but there he was, cigar and all. He looked very pleased with life in general and, considering everything, I couldn't blame him.

Sammy, sitting next to him, was trying too hard to enjoy himself. In the time it took us to reach the table, he had downed three straight drinks. His eyes were watering but he kept them on Russell.

So did Dolly. Not only her eyes, but her hands. One held his hand and the other was on his shoulder. She had a ladylike half nelson on him.

He didn't appear to be too happy about it. Maybe because it interfered with his drinking; maybe because he didn't like having the entire burlesque industry know that he was Dolly's. She isn't exactly the Sardi's type, I thought, while I watched her rub noses with him, but if he thought he was going to get rid of her, he was very much mistaken.

With Mike Brannen and Alice it was different. Alice was being difficult. She didn't like being left alone so long, she didn't like the suit, and she wasn't keeping her dislikes to herself.

"I don't go to platheth like thith unethcorted," she said.

The way Mike jealously watched every man who looked at her, she might have tried to enjoy herself while she was still Alice Angel. When she became Mrs. Brannen, I had an idea it was going to be harder.

Moss stood up when we approached the table. It made the other men so uncomfortable that they scrambled to their feet, too.

Mandy almost knocked himself out offering Gee Gee his chair. She stared at him as though he had gone a little soft in the head, but she sat down. Joey, not to be outdone, offered me his.

Biff and the Chinese man stood at the head of the table with H.I. Moss. If they were self-conscious with all of us looking at

203

them expectantly, they didn't show it. Biff introduced the waiter.

"Folks, this is Sam Wing."

The waiter bowed stiffly.

"I've asked him to join us tonight because he has something very important to say; something very important to do."

Mandy started to chuckle. He probably thought it was a gag that Biff was leading up to. Then he realized how quiet everybody was and he lapsed into an embarrassed silence.

Biff waited.

"He's timing this beautifully," I thought with a little pride. Then he dropped his bomb.

"Sam Wing is going to point out Lolita La Verne's murderer!"

Jannine mumbled, "But Stachi..."

Biff heard her. "Stachi didn't murder La Verne," he said.

I had wanted to watch everybody when he said that, but Russell got all of my attention. He grabbed Dolly's hands so tightly she gasped. His other hand broke the glass he was holding. The liquor spilled on the stained tablecloth and a stream of blood dripped from the cut where the glass had gashed him.

Biff couldn't have seen him, I thought. He went on talking too calmly.

"You see, the window leading to the roof was open and the murderer was seen; I knew Stachi didn't kill her because of something that was said during the investigation. Someone at this table said that they saw Gypsy go into that room after everybody had left. They said they were on the stage.

"That was a lie. When someone lies at a time like that they are either lying to save their own skin, or they're lying to save someone else's skin. The murderer wasn't the type to think of any skin but his own!"

I was watching Russell. What I saw in his face surprised me. The nervousness was gone. He was puzzled, then wary.

"But he didn't see Gypsy," Biff said in the same low tone. "He couldn't, because he wasn't on the stage. He was on the landing outside the men's dressing room. He was hiding and waiting for a chance to get down the stairs unseen. To be unseen, he had to be unseeing, too.

"Why would he lie? Because he had just poisoned a drink that he handed to La Verne. He made the appointment with her during the matinee. She was to give him the money for his play that night. Her mistake was in wanting to star in the play. Had she been content with just being the angel, she would be alive right now."

Our table was silent. The noise of the saloon seemed to be coming from a far distance; like listening to the radio when you're alone in a hotel room.

Russell looked at Biff through half-closed eyes. I couldn't see what was in them when Biff began to speak again. Russell dabbed at the cut on his hand with an end of the tablecloth.

"He had no intentions of starring La Verne in the play. There wasn't even a part in it for her. I know because I read it. The lead was a man. Naturally, he'd play it himself. But he wanted the money. Why not get the money and kill her? He had every intention of making it look like a suicide, but he was interrupted. Someone was coming up the stairs. He quickly smashed the glass and left the room.

"The stairway to the men's floor was dark and he stayed close to the door. It wasn't Gypsy he heard; it was the doorman. He didn't know then that Stachi had been in the room. He knew Gypsy was because Mandy and Joey told him how we walked on during their scene and he knew she had to change for the finale.

"He must have been quite surprised when no one screamed that La Verne had been found where he left her; her head on the dressing-table shelf, her body full of poison, and her G-string thrown carelessly on the floor after he had taken the money from it."

Then Biff looked at Russell. "You were surprised, weren't you?"

I'd always thought Russell was a bad straight man, but at that moment I changed my opinion. He was an actor. He took the tablecloth from his cut hand and examined the mark carefully. Then he took Dolly's cigarette from her limp fingers.

"It won't work, old man. Sorry." He inhaled deeply on the cigarette. "I wasn't in the room until her body was found and I can prove it. I was in the Princess' room."

"And you can prove it by her?" Biff asked. His smile matched Russell's.

"Certainly not. I know who poisoned La Verne. I've always known."

Biff turned to the Chinese waiter, who was living up to the Oriental reputation of stoicism. He hadn't moved or changed his facial expression.

"Can you point out the man who dropped the poison in the glass?" Biff asked.

The Chinese faced Russell. "He did," he said, pointing a finger at the straight man.

Russell started to rise. Then he seemed to realize where he was and who he was. He sank back in his chair with his hands holding the curved back.

Mike Brannen walked over to him and put his huge body between the chair and the exit. "Shall we talk this over outside?" he asked. One hand held a pair of handcuffs. Even in the loud suit, he looked like a policeman.

'We'll talk it over here," Russell said evenly. "I said that I knew who killed La Verne, and I do. It's true that I was in the basement room. I was alone, though. The Princess was with La Verne. I heard their voices through the ventilating pipe. They were playing a blackmail scene, only this time La Verne was doing the threatening. She was threatening to…"

Russell stopped and looked at Moss.

"Go on," Moss said quietly. He puffed on his cigar and took a sip of his drink.

"They were talking about you. La Verne knew who the Princess was getting her money from and she wanted some of it. She was trying to blackmail a blackmailer. My play or my name wasn't mentioned once. The Princess knew La Verne had ten grand and she knew her racket with Moss was up. But she was clever and she played her cards well."

A respectful note had crept into Russell's voice.

"Instead of fighting with La Verne, she shook hands with her. She said that they would get together on it. 'Plenty for both of us,' she said. 'Let's have a drink on our partnership.' I heard her get up. I knew she got the glasses because her voice became louder; she was closer to the pipe. Then they clicked glasses and La Verne laughed.

"Then I heard a gasp, the sound of breaking glass, and hurried footsteps leaving the room. The Princess didn't come downstairs. I waited, but she didn't come. Someone else entered the upstairs room. I heard them moving around, the sound of something being dragged. It was probably Stachi. I left the room and stood on the stage. That was when I saw Gypsy go upstairs. She brushed past the Princess, who was on her way down."

"Yes," I said. "It's true. I remember." I looked at Biff and he grinned at me. I felt a sudden wave of nausea. How could he smile at me when I had forgotten a thing like that?

It was Russell he was smiling at.

Russell stared at him. Then, slowly, he understood. "You tricked me, you dirty rat," he said.

"Now Russell," Biff said. "You know damn well you wouldn't have admitted all that if it hadn't been to save your own hide. You knew you'd lose the money, too, if it got out that it was La Verne's. The Princess might even have accused you of being an accessory after the fact."

In my dumb amazement and more than dumb pride, I hardly noticed that Biff was using legal phrases and big words. It sounded quite natural to me.

"When the autopsy showed poison I thought right away that it was a murderess, not a murderer. I suspected Dolly. She had the motive, and the Princess said that she was in the room."

Dolly didn't even look up when her name was mentioned. Her hands were lying palm up on the table and she stared vacantly across the room. I had a sudden urge to put my arm around her, to tell her that nothing was worth the pain that she was suffering. Then I realized that she would always suffer, that nothing I could say would change that.

Biff went on. "The old cut on the Princess' hand made me change my mind. *She* could have cut herself when she broke the glass. The money could have been a motive. She wanted to do a show. If Moss wouldn't put it on for her, why not Russell? Jake told me he followed them to her hotel one night. Couldn't Russell have sold her the idea of the play then? Little by little the whole thing put itself together. She wore long, black gloves in her number. She could have given Russell the money. She was blackmailing Moss. Would she kill to protect that income? Then, when I found the torn glove, I knew."

Russell looked up quickly. "She told me she destroyed them," he said.

"She was new in the theater or she would have known better than to flush them down the toilet. Our plumbing isn't that good. That's what she was doing upstairs in the men's dressing room. When the Sergeant said the murderer had worn gloves, I wondered what they'd do to get rid of them quickly. Naturally the toilet! If she hadn't gone upstairs she wouldn't have bumped into Gypsy. She wouldn't have passed the room while Stachi was supposedly strangling La Verne. She'd be alive today, in fact, if it hadn't been for the toilet."

Russell shuddered. I know he was thinking more of losing La Verne's money than anything else. I wondered a little about it myself. With Stachi dead, who would get the money? Who would get her shares of stock?

Stock! I suddenly remembered the picture and the frame with the hollow back.

"Did Stachi take the picture?" I asked.

Moss spoke up. "Yes. It was found on him. A will, too," he said. "Is that what you were thinking about?"

I felt a little ashamed to be thinking about money and stocks at a time like that, but I said yes. "I was really wondering about the scrap of paper, though. I thought it might have been the share of stock you had given her."

"It was. The other stocks she kept in a vault, but I guess she didn't have time to put that one away. Stachi got everything legally because he was her only relation. He left everything to Daryimple and the Hermit in his will. That is legal, too. Daryimple told him about the value of the stock. His own real estate firm was buying it. That's why Stachi wanted the theater closed.

"He didn't want to make just a small profit on it. There was a chance to make thousands. He probably hoped to buy everyone out. Once the theater was shuttered, well, your stock wouldn't be worth a thing. If he offered you what you paid for it, you'd sell it in a minute. Then he in turn would sell it to Daryimple. He was damn smart. There was only one weak spot in his makeup. Burlesque!

"I don't doubt for a minute that he was crazy when he decided to kill La Verne; not when he killed the Princess—*that* was for protection. But with La Verne he must have gone *non compos mentis*, when he realized that one of the people whose guts he hated was his own granddaughter."

I remembered the look on his face when the fight between Dolly and La Verne took place. Yes, I decided, he was capable of murdering her, and for that reason, too. Russell broke the silence that followed.

"I'll fight it," he said suddenly. "That money was given to me and I won't give it up." He was breathing heavily and his fists were clenched. "I'll fight it."

"After me," Biff said. "First of all we're taking a trip to an alley and I'm gonna beat the damned stuffin' outta you. Not only because you caused me a hell of a lot of extra work by keeping your mouth shut; not only because you put the G-string in my pocket, but because you're a yellow-bellied rat!"

Russell grinned. Then he saw Mike and his mouth trembled. I wondered if he thought the law was on his side. I didn't have a chance to find out.

Dolly suddenly went into action. I knew what was coming; I could tell from the two splotches on her cheeks. They warned me in time to save Biff from the fast one she gave out with.

But there was no way to shut her mouth.

"You keep your name calling to yourself," she shouted. "If you so much as lift a finger, I'll tear you apart. You—you stage wait between stripteasers."

The orchestra had stopped playing. A sudden lull fell over the room. A good fight comes first in any saloon and the Ringside was no exception.

Sammy materialized through the smoke and helped me hold Dolly. Then Russell jumped in. He put one arm around her waist and his hand on her mouth.

"Rudnick, the boss of the Eltinge, is here," he whispered. "If he hears a brawl like this, we won't get the job."

Magic words! Dolly's eyes lost their fire and a calculating gleam filled them. Russell broke his hold on her and the two of them sailed out of the saloon arm in arm, two lovebirds on their way to a four-week guarantee on Forty-Second Street.

Mike followed them at a respectful distance.

I asked Moss if Russell could be arrested and he shrugged his shoulders.

Biff sat back in his chair with a serves-me-right look on his face. "That's the kind of loyalty I expect from you when we're married," he said.

I wasn't sure I understood him. "I got the words, but I didn't catch the music."

"Aren't you ever gonna get smartened up?" Biff asked. "I'm asking you to marry me."

Before I blurted out a too-hasty yes, I thought of the theaters I'd be playing for the rest of my life. Four shows a day; the drugstore food; the second-rate hotels, and the seltzer water in the pants.

Then I said it! Instead of just saying yes, I said, "Yes, darling."

Biff took my hand and whispered, "Punkin," very softly. "Mrs. Gypsy Punkin Rose Lee Brannigan."

I forgot we were at the Ringside, even forgot that we weren't alone. The orchestra playing the "Wedding March." Moss' congratulations brought me back.

Alice was crying softly. "It'th tho romantic. I can't help it," she sobbed.

It *was* romantic. I got goose pimples all over. Everyone in the saloon was kissing me on the head and slapping Biff on the back. Gee Gee was even planning on what she'd wear to the wedding and then Sandra whispered in my ear.

"There was nothing to that romance between Biff and me," she said; "it was really all on my side."

I pretended that I believed her, but knowing Biff, I decided to keep a weather eye on him in the future. Then I sneaked a little peek at him.

He was taking bows already, as though he were the first comic to make an honest woman out of a stripteaser.

Siggy, the G-string man, was making a speech. It was all about wishing us happiness and how lucky Biff was. Then he put his black suitcase on the table and opened it. He brought out a box, one of those that he keeps the best items in, and held up a ruby-studded G-string.

"My wedding present to the bride," he said importantly.

I was beginning to murmur the conventional, "*Just* what I needed," when Biff made a dive for Siggy.

He grabbed the G-string salesman's arm with one hand and snapped the fingers of the other. "By golly, I just thought of something," he said. "Yep, I got it!"

He was so intense that Siggy got a little nervous. "You got what?" he asked suspiciously.

"Did you send anything up to the Hermit the night La Verne was murdered?"

Siggy tried to back away, but Biff held the lapels of his coat.

"Did you send him coffee or papers, or anything at all?"

"Well, yes, I did," Siggy admitted reluctantly. "But that's nothing; I do it all the time, whenever he asks me. All I done was to send him some chewing tobacco, and it couldn't have had anything to do with her because she was alive then."

Biff let go of his coat lapels and kissed him on both cheeks.

"I love ya, Siggy. You cleaned up the one thing that bothered me. That damn fringe on the elevator! It musta been hangin' on you, or maybe hangin' outta the bag. Did you have the bag with you?"

Siggy was still being careful. I could hardly blame him.

"I don't let that bag outta my sight," the G-string man said. "Even when I sleep, it's under me bed."

Biff roared with laughter. We all laughed; everything seemed very funny.

Siggy took one of his hand-rolled cigarettes from his pocket and lit it. Then he reached for Biff's drink.

"For a minute there you scared me," he said. He drank the rye and looked around to see if everyone could hear him. Satisfied that he was the center of attraction, he said: "I was worried right along about the police suspecting me of those murders. You know, me being in the G-string business. I was afraid the cops'd think I done it for the publicity."

AFTERWORD

Does this sound good for a dust jacket; a picture full length, of a stripper? Semi nude. The G-string actually silver flitter. (Very inexpensive, that flitter business.) And a separate piece of paper pasted on a skirt, like birthday cards, you know? The customers can lift the skirt, and there's the G-string sparkling gaily.[1]

Gypsy Rose Lee suggested this delightful idea to Lee Wright, her editor at Simon and Schuster—or "Essandess," as she called it—in 1941, a couple of months before the publication of her first murder mystery, *The G-String Murders*.

Known for her literary tendencies—even before journalist John Richmond coined the term "striptease intellectual" to describe her in the *American Mercury* the same year as *The G-String Murders* was published—Gypsy became famous by straddling the raucous world of showbiz and the tony world of *The New Yorker* and using the former against the latter, sometimes with great charm and other times with teeth bared. In a 1942 "letter to booksellers" that Simon and Schuster sent around to reviewers with her second detective novel, *Mother Finds a Body*, she took on one of the criticisms of her writing—her burlesque argot—which many reviewers claimed was so outlandish that she must

1. Letter from Gypsy to Lee Wright, February 26, 1941. Gypsy Rose Lee Papers, Billy Rose Theatre Collection, New York Public Library.

have invented it. Gypsy insisted she was just reporting the way burlesque performers really spoke. In other words, this was realism and the problem was that snooty, disbelieving editors, in their ignorance, tried to fix her grammar, unsplit her infinitives, repunctuate her, not unlike the way in which some editors and reviewers had responded to Damon Runyon. "The worst one is, 'scare off the pants from me.' Why didn't people tell me about this fancy talk years ago before I got in a comfortable rut?" she wrote.[2]

Of course, the "letter to booksellers" was a publicity gimmick, inspired, as all publicity gimmicks are, by an earlier publicity gimmick—"Letters to my editor"—that Gypsy had written to accompany *The G-String Murders* a year earlier from the hinterlands (see the selections that follow this afterword). In "Letters to my editor" she amused Lee Wright with her exploits in America's burlesque theaters, somewhere at the carnivalesque intersection between performing striptease and signing books. She stripped! She wrote! She smiled at her fans! "Letters to my editor," with its carefully contrived confection of high/low, was wildly successful as a publicity tool. Journalists adored it. Reviewers quoted from it. The letters got almost more attention than the book itself. But the letters also spoke to the central question that trailed Gypsy her entire life: Was she really erudite? Garden-variety smart? Or just a wise girl full of gimmicks?

Gypsy spent her career kidding the uptown crowd, which explains partway why many of them liked her and even sometimes kidded her back. But the fact that Gypsy stole lyrics from the naughty cabaret songs of Dwight Fiske and dialogue from the hoity-toity Café Carlyle set produced not only a celebration of the striptease intellectual's talents, but also a persistent skepticism about those talents' authenticity. In fact, the kind of thing that people said about Gypsy often had to do with the idea that she became famous precisely for lacking talent.

"Although it takes Gypsy Rose Lee only seven minutes to go

_____

2. John Richmond, "Striptease Intellectual." *The American Mercury*, January 1941, 36-44; Letter from Gypsy to Lee Wright, August 26, 1942, GRL Papers.

through her celebrated striptease, she admits that it took her fully seven weeks to go through Karl Marx's *Das Kapital*," Richmond wrote in his *American Mercury* article. There is lurking below this simple report something not so nice: seven minutes / seven weeks, well, it sounds plausible. But look again. There is the reminder that she's a stripper; there is the comedy of juxtaposing Marx (and not the Brothers) and striptease. This swipe emerges in nearly every article about Gypsy. You could say that it was a kind of running joke. It reflects something deeply ensconced in the American public, something unflattering in terms of who gets to be a writer and who does not. The prevailing view (then and now) is that if you take off your clothes for a living there is something suspect about you, certainly something less than writerly. You could not possibly be an intellectual if you were a striptease woman.

Instead of flattening Gypsy, such sentiments impelled her to strike back. And in hindsight, her public quarrels with those who challenged her on her brains always reveal the other guy's American snobbishness. So that even if she failed to convince skeptics about her writerly talent, she succeeded in getting publicity, which for her was almost as good. Take, for example, her public quarrel in 1941 with H. L. Mencken: when Simon and Schuster was publishing *The G-String Murders*, Gypsy was scolding the great pundit for his creation of the word "ecdysiast" in the second volume of *The American Language*—this was a scientific term he had coined to describe a stripper. Besides the fact that the word came from the term for molting, Gypsy felt that it expressed something disrespectful toward her profession: whatever Mencken was talking about was not what strippers do. Strippers strip and she was just the person to say so.

> Ecdysiast, he calls me! Why the man is an intellectual slob. He has been reading books. Dictionaries. We don't wear feathers and molt them off...what does he know about stripping?[3]

---

3. H. L. Mencken, *The American Language, Supplement I*, New York, 1941, 587.

What's funny here is not just the idea of the famously cranky Baltimorian thinking about stripping. It's that Gypsy inverts with gentle irony the entire skepticism some wags had directed at her own career and the way she hoisted herself to fame. For by this time Gypsy herself was reading books and perhaps dictionaries (or at least so she said), and of course stripping.

Or take her 1942 "Letter to Booksellers," written backstage at the Music Box Theatre while she was in rehearsal for Mike Todd's Broadway show, *Star and Garter*. Gypsy used her status as striptease intellectual to ridicule "real" intellectuals even as she claimed to be one of them, managing to be both funny and accurate. "Of course, the articles haven't paid enough to put me in the higher income tax brackets, but with *The New Yorker* and the *American Mercury*, who counts? Their abacus only goes up to fifty. From then on they have to count on their fingers."

She went on: she was as much a writer as anyone, since she had published ten articles in 1941. But—back to the bottom line—a couple of years earlier, in the midst of the Depression, she had pulled in $2,000 a week in burlesque. Of course, stripping subsidized her writing. Writing always has to be subsidized by something, why not taking off one's clothes? Thus in her playful send-ups of literary New York as well as of downtown burlesque, Gypsy captured something crucial to the American Dream.

GYPSY ROSE LEE wrote The G-String Murders when she was already a show business celebrity, and from our media-saturated perspective there's nothing extraordinary about a celebrity writing a book. But in the case of Gypsy, there was nothing ordinary about this endeavor, for there was nothing ordinary about anything she did. Gypsy is best known to Americans as the subject of the eponymous 1959 Stephen Sondheim musical. But the musical painted her as the victim of a conniving mother, a hapless girl who happened to be the daughter of a woman who had wanted to be in showbiz and never achieved that goal. Her real life, though, is more extraordinary than that musical ever made it out to be.

Born in 1914 in Seattle to the famously disappointed mother played to perfection by Ethel Merman in the 1959 version of *Gypsy*, Gypsy and her family toured in vaudeville until the crash. During the early 1930s, Gypsy made her reputation as a stripteaser in burlesque theaters, which were then the lowest form of theater on the theater food chain. From the first, Gypsy's numbers involved descending from the runway and flirting with men in a way that was less raunchy than cute. Sometimes for example, she kissed their heads, especially if they were bald. Asked how she became a celebrity in the world of burlesque, she said, "I kidded the audience."[4]

Gypsy wound up in New York in 1931 and debuted in the burlesque theaters there when Mayor Fiorello La Guardia was trying to close them down. She performed at the Irving Place, on 14th Street and at Minsky's Republic, in Times Square. She wore extravagant gowns and *Variety* compared her to Mae West and Mary Pickford.

She first began to do her "striptease intellectual" numbers sometime in the early thirties while living in New York. There are different theories about where she got the idea to mix culture with stripping. In her autobiography, Gypsy alludes to her affair with Eddie, an aristocratic guy who bought her both diamond bracelets and copies of *The Waves*, a novel by Thomas Mann, and a deluxe edition of Audubon's *Book of Birds*. Sometimes Walter Winchell is credited or Louis Sobol, the press agent, or any one of the members of her entourage, the idea being that Gypsy could not have possibly come up with the idea by herself.[5]

Yet in articles and interviews, Gypsy would claim that she had generated the idea all by her lonesome, that, though she lacked

4. "Home Movies with Gypsy Rose Lee," author's private collection.
5. Gypsy Rose Lee, Gypsy, New York, 1957, 273.

formal schooling, she had read widely while on the road. In any case, by the mid 1930s, she was enhancing and embellishing her story, giving interviews to reporters about reading Marcel Proust and Karl Marx. Her house on East 63rd Street included Dreiser's *The Genius*, Sherwood Anderson's *Dark Laughter*, and Vincent Sheean's *Personal History*, as well as Proust.

To what extent was her love for literature real and to what extent was it propelled by our Pygmalion/Galatea fantasy? At the very least, it contained elements of reality, but the more important fact was that Gypsy wore her reputation lightly and the fad of the striptease intellectual caught on. "Gypsy Rose Lee . . .put the accent on her IQ as well as s.a.," wrote *Variety* editor Abel Green, using the contemporary Broadway slang for sex appeal. Other journalists blamed her cocktail of beauty and brains for the death of striptease. H.M. Alexander wrote, "there was a stripper and she had a mother, and that killed striptease."[6] By which he meant that striptease belonged downtown in burlesque—not uptown on Broadway, where it cost $4.40 a ticket. But Gypsy was not the only one in love with the "oxymoronic" in culture: striptease intellectual, sex and Matisse, jazz and Stravinsky, and so on. Beginning in 1935, this myth caught the public imagination in many different ways and many different venues. To name just one example: George Balanchine choreographed "Slaughter on Tenth Avenue," a ballet within the musical *On Your Toes*, which used burlesque. Everyone wanted a piece of her action.

Still, Gypsy exploited her striptease intellectual status to do what few other strippers of her era—or any era—were capable of doing: she crossed over from burlesque to the 1936 Ziegfeld Follies, a fact she herself was blasé about. Again it boiled down to economics and to the taste of her uptown customers, which, she often suggested, was more vulgar than that of the working class

6. Abel Green, *Showbiz from Vaude to Video*, New York, 1951, 450; H. M. Alexander, *Burlesque: The Vanished Art of Striptease*, New York, 1937, 8.

stiffs she stripped for downtown. She noted that uptown at the Follies, not only did she have to take it off more quickly, she also got paid about a third less.

Like all great showbiz successes, the Follies happened by accident. Josephine Baker, the original star, became unavailable, and the Shuberts, casting around for someone to fill her place, settled on Gypsy. In the Follies, Gypsy did more than strip. She did some comic parts, like Baby Snooks's mother, and she also played the woman in the "Pickle Persuader," in which she resisted being seduced by a man who had been tricked into believing that a pickle was a kind of aphrodisiac. So she cemented her reputation as a performer whose allure rested on more than just stripping.

From the time of the Follies, *Vanity Fair* and other highbrow magazines began to cover Gypsy as a phenomenon, and the press referred to the striptease intellectual aspect of her persona with a wink, as if to say, how could a stripper possibly be more than just a dumb brunette? Gypsy was friends with many members of the intelligentsia and wealthy New Yorkers, and yet not only was she aware of playing tricks on them, she never hesitated to reveal how the tricks were played. When the Otis Chatfield-Taylors came backstage to invite her to supper at the Oak Room, she pleaded fatigue, saying she has an "ethnological dance lesson." "When the door closed behind my guests, I was exhausted. It was like giving a performance, I thought, only harder. I was pleased with myself, though. Especially the ethnological dance lesson. I wasn't sure what it meant, but it sounded good."[7]

Her signature number, which she probably invented around 1935, and which became the center of the Follies, focused on the titillating tension between books and stripping and between the idea of thinking about sex and pretending you're not.

---

7. Lee, *Gypsy*, p. 284.

Have you the faintest idea about
The private thoughts of a stripper?
Well the things that go on in a stripteaser's mind
Would give you no end of surprise
And if you're psychologically inclined
There's more to see than meets the eye.
For example,
When I raise my skirts with slyness and dexterity
I'm mentally computing just how much I'll give to charity
And though my thighs I have revealed
And just a bit of me remains concealed
I'm thinking of the life of Duse
Or the third chapter of *The Rise and Fall of the Roman Empire*.

The number went on from there, celebrating Edith Sitwell, Racine, and others. And although Gypsy varied the cultural references over the years, she would do the same thing for the rest of her life. In 1936, her stage attire was a large picture hat and an enormous Southern hoop skirt in matching polka-dotted tulle, and by contemporary standards she hardly got undressed at all. "Her striptease has been influenced by her intellectual bent," Richmond wrote. "She scorns the bump or the grind..."[8]

Her "striptease intellectual" number was such a hit that Daryl Zanuck at Twentieth Century Fox tapped Gypsy and she went West. But the sojourn in Tinseltown was a disaster. The Hayes Commission lacked love for any stripteaser, intellectual or otherwise. The censors insisted that Gypsy perform under her original name, Louise Hovick, and banned her from doing the one thing that she did best—strip. Although Zanuck had signed her to make five movies, *Battle of Broadway*, *Ali Baba Goes to Town*, *You Can't Have Everything*, *Sally Irene, and Mary*, and *My Lucky Star*, in not one of them does her talent shine through.

8. Richmond, "Striptease Intellectual," 38.

Gypsy returned to New York in 1938, having made her way back from Hollywood by headlining in various vaudeville theaters around the country. She performed in burlesque and in some revues; but while she was in Hollywood, La Guardia had succeeded in closing many of New York's burlesque houses. The scene was completely different from the one she had left.

With theaters closing every month, Gypsy was at loose ends. When she was in Hollywood she had guest-written a column for Walter Winchell. She guest-wrote another one during the 1939 New York World's Fair.

And then, somehow, Gypsy got the idea to do a book. In the fall of 1940, she moved into the house of her friend George Davis, the failed novelist and magazine writer, at 7 Middagh Street in Brooklyn Heights. Davis's house served as a flophouse for many literati. W.H. Auden, Carson McCullers, David Diamond, Paul and Jane Bowles, and Janet Flanner, whom Alexander Woollcott referred to as Gypsy's "boyfriend," all lived and worked there during 1940 and 1941.[9] Gypsy worked at a typewriter in a bedroom on the second floor.

On Christmas night 1940, *Pal Joey* opened on Broadway and the number "Zip" sent up and celebrated the striptease intellectual. Perhaps it spurred Gypsy on to work harder to sell her own story. Meanwhile, in real life, in the winter of 1941, she fell in love with Mike Todd, the impresario, and she went to the Midwest to perform in Todd's Chicago nightclub, Michael Todd's Theatre Café.

Todd billed his club as "the world's biggest nightclub for families." The mob-funded club served champagne cocktails for twenty-five cents and Gypsy repeated the Ziegfeld Follies act, which she had also done in Todd's Streets of Paris show at the 1939 World's Fair. The nightclub was a smash hit. When she wasn't performing, Gypsy holed up at the Ambassador Hotel at

9. Letter to Gypsy from Alexander Woollcott, August 20,1941, GRL Papers.

1300 North State Street and continued to work on her book.[10]

It was around this time that Janet Flanner sent Gypsy's manuscript to Simon and Schuster. And Gypsy began to correspond with Simon and Schuster mystery editor Lee Wright. The two hit it off. From the first Wright flattered Gypsy but also expressed concern about the book—particularly about Gypsy's inexperience as a mystery writer. "I am especially anxious to know just how you have planned your plot, which is especially vital in a mystery story," Wright wrote on January 8.[11]

As to the enduring question of how much of *The G-String Murders* Gypsy actually wrote, there is no doubt that Craig Rice, the Chicago mystery writer with whom Wright paired Gypsy, helped her significantly. The two women met regularly and worked on the book. Rice, who was known in Chicago as a bon vivant and spent a good deal of time in Rush Street cafes, edited and re-arranged Gypsy's prose and worked with her on structure. Many editorial conferences followed by mail. George Davis also helped Gypsy with some aspects of the book. And Wright made pages of editorial suggestions. One early concern was that the G-string murderer not be a madman, but operate psychologically from some motive that readers could understand. But I don't think that the book was written by either Davis or Wright, nor by W.H. Auden, as some historians contend. It was Gypsy alone who was, as she often said, "making the book words."

THE G-STRING MURDERS marks many firsts besides the obvious ones of being the first best-seller and the first best-selling detective novel written by a stripper. The book presented the world of burlesque in a way that the American public had never really

---

10. According to Gypsy, Mike Todd's Theatre Club made $55,000 a week. Quoted in *A Valuable Property, the Life Story of Mike Todd*, New York, 1983, 70. Letter to Gypsy, GRL Papers.

11. Letter from Lee Wright to Gypsy Rose Lee, January 8, 1941, GRL Papers.

seen it. That's not to say that descriptions of burlesque in newspapers and in the theater were entirely lacking prior to 1941. George Manker Watters's play *Burlesque* opened on Broadway in 1927 and drew back the curtain on the seedy backstage atmosphere that Americans seemed to adore. But *Burlesque*, set in the Midwest before burlesque became synonymous with striptease, would have seemed tame and old-fashioned by the time *The G-String Murders* appeared. In 1937 H.M. Alexander's *Burlesque: The Vanished Art of Striptease* took readers backstage and presented the "real" private lives of strippers. But even Alexander's realistic approach is limited by its genre, much like the newspaper journalism of Damon Runyon. Until Gypsy published *The G-String Murders*, strippers for the most part only existed either as journalistic creations or as "fallen women." They were never characters, much less heroines or real women trying to make ends meet.

Because *The G-String Murders* was the first long novel about burlesque written by someone on the inside—the first memoir of burlesque, really—it presented a much broader, more detailed view of the world than anyone had seen. But even when Gypsy renders burlesque's details lovingly, she is rarely romantic about its seediness. Here Gypsy introduces readers to the ad hoc backstage scene at the Old Opera burlesque theater: "a gazeeka box, loaves of papier-mâché bread strung together, dozens of bladders, all sizes, hanging from the ceiling, a chandelier made of wood with leather braces for the chorus girls to cling to, a park bench, a fireman's helmet, and the constantly used bedroom suite" (p52).

Writing during the first great era of hard-boiled detective fiction and hard-boiled writing, Gypsy, although no one observed so at the time, stole from the argot-drenched, tough-guy prose of Damon Runyon, Dorothy Parker, and John O'Hara. In *The G-String Murders*, she was wreaking her own variations on it. The heroine, "Gypsy Rose Lee, star of the Old Opera," tells the story using that hallowed detective story technique—from a point somewhere in the future. Here is the first sentence of the book: "Finding dead bodies scattered all over a burlesque theater isn't the sort of thing you're likely to forget" (p1). But although the book shares many stylistic tics with Runyon and Co., one way it differs is in the narrator's voice. With a clear sense of herself as the star of her own drama, Gypsy often referred to herself in the third person as "the naked genius"—she sometimes signed letters that way—or as "the woman with the diamond in her navel."

Then there is the distinctive way Gypsy uses the metaphor of the theater. The theater is everywhere in *The G-String Murders*. You could almost say that the book wants to be a play or, at the very least, a burlesque show. In the pulp edition of the novel, the characters are listed in front of Chapter One under the heading "Cast of Characters in Order of Their Appearance" with a list of page numbers indicating when each first comes "on stage." Gypsy writes in dialogue, and many scenes seem like burlesque skits. The types in Gypsy's supporting cast would have been recognizable to anyone who had ever gone to a burlesque show. They included a lesbian policewoman, back-stabbing strippers, snooty ones, and a murderer who dreamed of the days when he worked somewhere more respectable than burlesque.

Insiders would have known that the cast was based on real-life figures from Gypsy's life. Biff is Rags Ragland, the burlesque comic whom she was in love with and almost had a child with. H.I. Moss, the theater owner, is one of the Minsky Brothers, probably Harold. (Another possible referent is B.S. Moss, a Depression-era reformer in La Guardia's New York.) Gee Gee Graham was Georgia Sothern. Princess Nirvena was modeled after a stripper who did a Russian countess act.

But *The G-String Murders* is more than a mystery à clef. It reveals many facets of the burlesque world from the inside. The labyrinthine plot includes a police raid, several terrific—and unique—descriptions of different acts in burlesque shows, including striptease. Gypsy is never romantic about burlesque: "I really didn't want to join a burlesque troupe. No vaudeville actor does" (p3). But she is equally deadpan whether describing the countless rounds of drinking between shows and the violent relationships strippers sometimes get themselves into, or sending up the kind of performer who gives himself airs: "He was our new straight man a 'Meet chu in the moonlight, m'boy' type" (p7). And long before silicone and botox, *The G-String Murders* describes strippers' eternal ministering to their own bodies in numbing detail—wax implants and bras soaked in cold water then worn overnight to perk up sagging breasts. The strippers' allure on stage, in other words, is nothing more than illusion. However, when Lee describes the striptease numbers, if they are not always sexy by our standards, she communicates the strippers' distinct personalities, their business with the audience, and the louche quality of their acts. Here, for example, is the striptease of the much-hated Princess Nirvena:

> Then she began slowly lifting the skirt of her evening gown with a dark-gloved hand, the other covering her breasts. A long, thin tongue licked the purple lips and the music built up to a crescendo. She flashed a rhinestone G-string, and with the same sensual, expressionless face, she threw her torso into a bump that shook the balcony. The audience went mad. She dropped the skirt and waited for them to stop applauding. (p58)

The G-String Murders provides many other details about strippers' everyday lives, including a raid, a jailhouse scene, an impromptu spareribs dinner on the theater roof, a celebratory booze-feast at the joint next door, and an after-hours party. The theater is their family, and *G-String* makes strippers sympathetic as Lee takes readers into backstage reality. The novel tells the stories of the ailing parents or hungry children the strippers support with their "wages of sin." Some of the performers have wasted endless nights in rural theaters in the Midwest and had to reinvent themselves before arriving in New York. Dolly has been in prison—surely not a unique experience.

Plot, ultimately, is not *The G-String Murders*'s strong suit—the scenes are strung together with nothing more than the straight pins Gypsy herself liked to use in her act instead of zippers. But Gypsy captures the down-and-out quality of life in a burlesque theater—the way everyone had seen better days, and camaraderie reigns. "In places, the marble had cracked and had been repaired clumsily with plaster" (p5). And the theater boasted a toilet that was "probably the first one to be built indoors" (p6).

At the same time, *The G-String Murders* is critical of both the American public's attitude toward striptease and its suspicion of any display of open sexuality in the late 1930s and 1940s.

"'I'm an actress. A stripteaser,'" the Gypsy character protests when she gets dragged to the police station and booked for prostitution. "'What's the difference?' said the matron" (p21).

Gypsy wrote *The G-String Murders* at a time when there was a surge of nostalgia for burlesque, after La Guardia had closed most of the theaters in New York. In 1941 there were only three burlesque theaters left out of the twelve that had flourished in the mid-1930s. In 1942 La Guardia would close these as well. One of the reasons for this crack-down was the sex-crime wave of the 1930s—something that may also have inspired Gypsy.

The G-String Murders describes a woman's world—their rivalries, their obsessions with their bodies, their dreams. The men are incidental. They are just something to hang the strippers on (or that the strippers hang on to). Just as Gypsy describes the burlesque theater in its decrepit glory, she is very clear about the fact that the strippers are not all beauty queens. "The bags were under the eyes and the neck hung like an empty salt sack," she writes about Lolita La Verne, one of the Old Opera's stars (p7). Gypsy, of course, as the heroine and amateur detective, never reveals her own physical defects—she is a sexier version of Agatha Christie.

But the striptease intellectual also displays a bushel of irony about nearly everything in her world. Here she is, for example, imagining the hackneyed way the newspapers will report the murder of one of her striptease comrades: "'stripper strangled. brunette beauty bumped off.' In my mind I wrote all the headlines. The pictures would probably be old ones, lots of leg showing, and the captions would all declare we were beauties" (p104). Which is to say that she is a self-conscious narrator, and one aware of the way the reader might be skeptical about her world.

Another fascinating aspect of the book is Gypsy's choice of title, and, of course, murder weapon. Using the word "G-string" in print at all was relatively new. Although female dancers had worn G-strings in the most risqué Broadway shows of the jazz age, the word first began to appear in the entertainment trade newspaper *Variety* sometime in the late 1930s. Striptease shows were defined in the 1930s and 1940s by whether the stripper stripped down to her G-string or not. A "strong" show was one where the stripper did, usually when the police were not in the audience. In "weak" or "sweet" shows, the stripper wore "net panties," and the police were often present. Particularly after La Guardia started his series of burlesque raids in 1936, it became rarer for strippers to strip to G-strings—they would only strip down to brassieres and panties.

Gypsy's use of the G-string here is more than merely titil-lating. The G-string takes on the same richness for this author as the madeleine does for Proust. Her description of this skimpy part of the stripper's costume reveals the homespun aspect of burlesque—she refers several times to the dental floss that she, in real life, used instead of elastic for the string part. The G-string was important economically as well as visually, as it held in place the grouch bag, the place where old-time strippers stowed their money. Siggy, the G-string salesman, with his conniving ways, is tender rather than repulsive or amoral as he sells the tools of the strippers' trade. At the denouement, Siggy gives Gypsy a G-string with a ruby in it as a wedding present.

For all of its underworld atmosphere, *The G-String Murders* ends like a conventional detective story/romance. The police catch the murderer and the Gypsy character marries Biff. Gypsy gives up her dreams to play on Broadway for love and stripping in crummy theaters. The raucous burlesque pair move to the country and, in a twist on the American Dream, wind up in an idyllic house with a white picket fence. Real life, of course, worked out differently for our heroine.

WHEN SIMON AND SCHUSTER published *The G-String Murders* in October 1941, the *New York Times* panned it, suggesting that the book needed a glossary and that the so-called striptease intellectual could not actually write—"In her case the zipper is obviously mightier than the sword." This, according to the *Times* was fitting, since her audience, burlesque theater-goers, were illiterate: her book would appeal to "the patrons of the strip-tease shows—or such of them as are able to read."[12]

Many other reviews were mixed. *Life* ran the headline "Gypsy Rose Lee turns mystery author" and wrote, "As a mystery story, *The G-String Murders* is only third-rate. But as a picture of the . . .striptease profession . . .her novel is a rich and lusty job, brimming over with infectious vitality and a hilarious jargon of her own."[13] But if some critics resented Gypsy's intrusion into literary life, as if there was not room enough for a stripper to crash the party, other magazines were kinder. Some treated the book less as a literary debut than as a successful gimmick, which maybe it was. John Mason Brown, the theater critic, praised it, as did many others in the theater world. In the *New York Herald Tribune*, humorist and critic Will Cuppy celebrated the realism

---

12. *New York Times*, October 12, 1941, br 24. The head of Simon and Schuster wrote, "Don't worry about the *New York Times Book Review*. The guy is an old maid and should have retired long ago" (Letter from Charlotte Seitlin to Gypsy Rose Lee, GRL papers).

13. *Life Magazine*, October 6, 1941, 110–11.

and the smartness with which Gypsy captured the world of burlesque. "This book is the high spot of the season," he wrote.[14] The ever-skeptical *New Yorker* declared the book "Recommended for readers who feel better when their eyebrows are raised." *Time* defended Gypsy, writing that she "has no need of Proust—or of ghosts."

Always in love with the PR stunt, Gypsy wrote her own review, which summed up *The G-String Murders*'s charms pretty well. "It isn't as breezy as Craig Rice's *Trial by Fury* and the plot isn't as well constructed as Harry Stephen Keeler's *The Man with the Wooden Spectacles*, but I liked it."[15]

Her friends, showbiz people, the literati, and her public went further. "You're even better in print than you are on the runway," wrote the producer Jerome Weidman.[16] Craig Rice proclaimed, with a hint of self-praise, "The book leaves me breathless. It is really that swell. How do you do it, you smart girl?"[17] Lawrence Lipton, at the time married to Rice, wrote Gypsy a long congratulatory letter. *The G-String Murders* quickly went into five printings, exceeding the number of copies sold by *The Thin Man*. It eventually went to eleven printings in hardcover and has seen many pulp and paperback revivals before this edition.

From the beginning, journalists cast doubt on whether Gypsy had actually written the book. Some of the early press alluded to the idea that a stripper, even an intellectual one, could not possibly have written anything. Undeterred by these rumors, Gypsy focused on one thing she knew how to do: publicity. After the book came out, she promoted it from burlesque theaters, signing copies from the lobbies, and anywhere else she could. In Youngstown, Ohio, for example, she did a signing from the local department store. She often would complain, while traveling in

---

14. Will Cuppy, New York Herald Tribune, October 5, 1941, GRL Papers.

15. Clipping, n.d. GRL papers.

16. Telegram from Jerome Weidman to Gypsy, October 3, 1941, GRL papers.

17. Telegram from Craig Rice to Gypsy, October 3, 1941, GRL Papers.

the hinterlands, if the local paper lacked a book review section that could feature *The G-String Murders*.[18]

But whatever the obstacles, she was not yet finished with her role as the striptease intellectual.

IN 1941 LONG-TIME MGM producer Hunt Stromberg, who had just left the studio to form an independent company, bought the film rights to *The G-String Murders*. He signed Barbara Stanwyck to play the role of Gypsy, renamed Dixie Daisy in the film. At first the fact that a young movie star played a stripper (even though the camera panned away from Stanwyck every time she undressed) suggested a new leniency in Hollywood and a fading of the Hayes office's censorial powers. Stromberg hired a number of well-known writers to do the screenplay, including James Gunn, Ben Hecht, and Craig Rice, who had helped Gypsy with the book. William Wellman directed.

But when *Lady of Burlesque* was released in 1943, the National Legion of Decency condemned it. "The film contains double-meaning lines, salacious dances and situations, and indecent costumes presented against the background of a sensuous form of entertainment."[19] Still, the film provided Stromberg and his distributor, United Artists, with a major hit. *Lady of Burlesque* is charming and includes several wonderful musical numbers including "Take It Off the E-String (Play It On the G-String)," which Stanwyck performed at the Academy Awards when the film was nominated for Best Scoring of a Dramatic or Comedy Picture. The film's reception history suggests Americans' refusal to accept their pervasive fascination with burlesque and striptease even as it proves how quickly a bout of censorship can turn the obscene into popular success.

THE SUCCESS OF *The G-String Murders* propelled Gypsy to pen a second murder mystery, *Mother Finds a Body*, which appeared

18. Letter from the Palace Theatre to Gypsy, September 25, 1941, GRL Papers.
19. *New York Times*, June 17, 1943, 16.

exactly a year after the first. She wrote it backstage while she was starring in Mike Todd's Broadway show, *Star and Garter*. *Mother Finds a Body*, which Rice also assisted on, was less commercially successful than *G-String*, although the *Times Literary Supplement of London* commented that Gypsy's new novel was "the 1943 version of Scarron's Roman comique."[20]

As the title suggests, the novel features Gypsy's mother as a prominent character. This anticipated her 1957 memoir, *Gypsy*, but for many reasons, *Mother Finds a Body* was less successful than this later effort. Set in and around a seedy burlesque nightclub in Yseleta, Texas, the novel lacks the dynamism of New York's burlesque scene. Moreover, the facts of Gypsy's life post-Ziegfeld Follies reflected in *Mother* are somehow less interesting than those from her life on the way up, which one finds in *G-String*. The plot is, if possible, even more labyrinthine than that of *G-String*, so that emotional realities take a back seat. Then too, in 1942 Gypsy's mother, Rose, was still alive and (in theory) looking over her shoulder while she wrote. Gypsy needed freedom and the forum of memoir, as opposed to fiction, to tell her story more truthfully.

Another writing project Gypsy began backstage during the run of *Star and Garter* was an autobiographical play, first titled *The Ghost in the Woodpile*. "Ghost" refers to "ghostwriter," and the play tells the story of Honey Bee Carroll, a stripper whose manager, Mike Hannigan, gives her the idea to write a book. In *Doll Face*, the movie version of the play, Honey Bee gets the idea during a backstage tête-à-tête with Hannigan.

MIKE HANNIGAN: What's the most cultured thing a person can do?
HONEY BEE: Read a book... Write a book?

Honey Bee hires a ghostwriter, a blue blood who changes her entire life story. She was born in Brooklyn; he moves her to

20. Letter from Lee Wright to Gypsy, November 24, 1943, GRL Papers.

Park Avenue. Her father was a plumber; he makes the man an engineer. Soon the truth wins out: you can take the stripper out of Brooklyn, but you can't take Brooklyn out of the stripper. At the last minute Honey Bee marries Hannigan and becomes a Broadway star.

Looking over Gypsy's oeuvre, a critic might begin to see each piece of writing as a kind of wish fulfillment or a way to even the score. Thus, if *The G-String Murders* is Gypsy's revenge on burlesque, and *Mother Finds a Body* takes on her mother, perhaps *The Ghost in the Woodpile* gets even with Mike Todd. While stripping in *Star and Garter*, Gypsy had fallen madly in love with the married impresario, who refused to get a divorce for the striptease intellectual. He continued to work with her, producing *Ghost*, whose title Gypsy changed to *Seven-Year Cycle*. The title became *The Naked Genius* when Todd decided that any play by a striptease author should have the word "naked" in it.

Meanwhile, Gypsy married the society blue blood Alexander Kirkland. Until the very minute she marched up the aisle, she thought that Todd would come charging in to save her from the marriage. The wedding was a media circus. But Todd did not play the role Gypsy had intended for him. Instead, in one of those bizarre twists of fate, he would marry the woman playing Gypsy in *The Naked Genius*, the comic actress Joan Blondell, who had not appeared on Broadway in over a decade.

Perhaps Gypsy's jealousy stifled her creative ability. It's certainly true that *The Naked Genius* is a worse piece of writing than *The G-String Murders*. It seems slapped together. The characters are cartoonish. The plot lacks the zing of even a lesser murder mystery like *Mother Finds a Body*. Also there is a kind of shift in worldview. In *The G-String Murders*, the heroine gets the guy and is happily ensconced in the burlesque community that she came up out of. This community is not incompatible with her little white-picketed house in the suburbs. But in *The Naked Genius*, the world of burlesque and the world of Park Avenue are completely irreconcilable. When Honey Bee Carroll goes back to Mike Hannigan, she's going up in the world to Broadway. But she is clearly choosing showbiz over high society (and literature).

From the first, *The Naked Genius* teetered. Rehearsals began in August, 1943. George Kaufman directed and provided script-doctoring services. Gypsy and he rewrote the first act entirely. Whole chunks of the play were discarded and rewritten. The plot was filled with fanciful business. But even Kaufman's legendary comic timing failed to save the play, as did changing Blondell's costume from a terry robe to a diaphanous negligee. The play ran to terrible reviews out of town (although good business, especially in burlesque strongholds like Baltimore and Philadelphia) and then played for one month on Broadway before stumbling to a close. Neither Kaufman nor Gypsy wanted it to open, but Todd had sold the rights to Twentieth Century Fox for $350,000, a fee which was provisional on a thirty-five-day run on Broadway. Kaufman and Gypsy stayed away from the opening and Todd closed the show after thirty-six performances.

Operating on the "all publicity is good publicity" theory, Todd used two phrases to anchor his PR campaign: "It ain't Shakespeare but it's laffs" and "Guaranteed not to win the Pulitzer Prize."[21] "The boys mashed it to a pulp," Gypsy's editor Lee Wright wrote, trying to console her.[22]

Still, in 1946, Twentieth Century Fox made a film out of the play, *Doll Face*, with Vivian Blaine as the Gypsy character. It is a charming movie, if hackneyed, but Gypsy refused to have her name on it (she had also taken her name off the play) and the movie is credited to Louise Hovick.

If Gypsy flopped on the stage, during this same era, she did well in magazines. In the 1940s, she published three articles about her show business childhood in *The New Yorker*: "Mother and

---

21. Maurice Zolotow, "Genius with its Clothes On," *New York Times*, November 7, 1943, xi.

22. Letter from Lee Wright to Gypsy, November 14, 1944, GRL Papers.

the Knights of Pythias"; "Mother and the Man Named Gordon," and "Just Like Children Leading Normal Lives." These were really out-of-town try-outs for her memoir *Gypsy*, which was eventually published in 1957 to rave reviews. She also wrote for *Harper's Bazaar*, the *American Mercury*, *Variety*, *House and Garden*, *Flair*, and *Parade* as well as the new men's magazines, including *Swank* and *Go*.

In the late 1950s, Gypsy moved to California, hosted a talk show, got involved in charity work, and went to Korea. She bred Pekinese Crested dogs. And then she wrote *Gypsy*.

When *Gypsy* was published in 1957, it was a smash hit. Perhaps Gypsy telling her own story, without the accompaniment of a plot, was what made it a success. In the *New York Times* review, Abel Green described it as a "valentine to the nomadic little people" of show business. "This book is an honest, unsparing document, extraordinary Americana, a close-up on a doughty tribe, and on the vaude personalities, great, and small, who had immediate bearing on Miss Lee's life and times . . .the book puts Miss Lee into sharp focus as a skillful writer."[23]

In one way at least, *Gypsy* retreats to a device she had used in *The G-String Murders*. Just as the murder mystery opens after the story is over, so her memoir starts after her rise to fame is complete. The book opens in 1957 as the heroine is en route to Vegas, where she will be doing yet another farewell tour. She is incredibly wealthy and famous. She walks along a street in Chicago where twenty-odd years earlier she performed. And that is the impetus for her to flash back into her life on the road in the 1920s and 1930s with her mother, Rose, and sister, June Havoc.

Though *The G-String Murders* ends with the Gypsy character getting married to the comic Biff Brannigan, domestic bliss eluded her in real life, and thus *Gypsy* needed another ending, one with showbiz and glamour in the forefront. "I closed my eyes and along with the familiar noise of the train Mother seemed to

23. *New York Times*, April 28, 1957, BR 4.

be telling me again how lucky I was. 'What a wonderful life you've had—the music, lights, applause—everything in the world a girl could ask for.'"[24]

In her writing, that was exactly the way it was.

Rachel Shteir
DePaul University

24. Lee, *Gypsy*, 319.

LETTERS TO MY EDITOR

Selections from a 1941 publicity pamphlet for
The G-String Murders

A NOTE FROM THE PUBLISHERS OF
*The G-String Murders** BY GYPSY ROSE LEE

FOR THE PAST six months, The Inner Sanctum has been enjoying a new recipe for laughter. The explanation is simple: somebody has just received a new letter from Gypsy Rose Lee.

We (Lee Wright, editor of *Inner Sanctum Mysteries* and Charlotte Seitlin, Essandess Publicity Director) started corresponding with Miss Lee back in January when Janet Flanner tipped us off that the Belle of the Bistros was writing a mystery story. As can be seen at a glance, the correspondence began on an extremely polite and formal plane. Like Miss Lee's celebrated specialty, however, it gradually built up to a stunning climax.

These letters have given us (not to mention all our friends who have seen them) such fun that we consider only fair to share it by reprinting them here. The contents of this booklet represent the extracts from as gamey a correspondence as a publisher is likely to receive.

To all the skeptics who are constantly coming at us with: "Say, I hear you're doing a book by Gypsy Rose Lee. Off the record— who's the ghost?" we say: "Read these letters." If, after doing so, you still think that Gypsy doesn't know from writing (Gypsy's accent rubbing off on us), we will stake you to diamond-studded plush-lined G-String—complete with grouch bag.

> Lee Wright
> Editor of *Inner Sanctum*
> *Mysteries*

* Publication Date: October 10th, 1941

January 4, 1941

Dear Miss Seitlin:

Thank you for your letter. I was very happy to know that you and Mr. Weidman[1] approve of the background for my story. (I am quite a fan of his.)

About a skeleton:[2] It hadn't occurred to me but I will try to beat one out this afternoon. There is a possibility that I will stay in Chicago for some time and would like to get this publishing business off my mind. It's like being all made up, ready to go on . . . and not knowing what theatre you're playing.

Sincerely,
Gypsy Rose Lee

1. Jerome Weidman, author and editor.
2. Refers to skeleton outline of the plot of *The G-String Murders*.

January 13, 1941

Dear Lee Wright:

Thank you for Craig's book.[3] It is my favorite.

I did want to get a clean copy of the manuscript for you. I dropped the original in the bath tub and most of my notes were on it. The carbon (in all colors) was fuzzy, forgive me.*

Would ten thirty Monday be too early to see you? I have so damned many things to do, my plane arrives at nine something. I'll go directly home and wait for a call from you. I hoped to squeeze you in between my dentist and my agent. They're both nice guys but if you'd rather there's an hour and a half between Mike Todd[4] and J. P. McEnvoy.

Gypsy

*That bath tub line reads badly now that I look it over. You see it takes almost an hour to soak off my body paint so I do my rewriting while I wait.

---

3. Craig Rice's *The Wrong Murder*.
4. Producer and impresario.

HOTEL AMBASSADOR
CHICAGO, ILLINOIS

January 20, 1941

Dear Miss Wright:

Thank you for the books, I finished the last one yesterday. My first reaction was to tear my own manuscript in many small pieces.

The murderer in *G-String* is not a mad man. That annoys me too much when I'm reading a mystery. I did think that X would be the logical guilty party. He wouldn't have to be insane to want those women out of the way. I wanted the reader to sympathize with him. A great many will probably think it's a good idea to clean up the Burlesque theatre, anyway.

As for my cooperation on promotion of *G-String Murders*—if and when—I'll do my specialty in Macy's window to sell a book. If you would prefer something a little more dignified, make it Wanamaker's window. There has been so much publicity about it already that I'm a little embarrassed. (The book I mean—not the specialty.)

I do want to finish it before I leave Chicago and I'm certain that I will.

Sincerely,
Gypsy Rose Lee

February 2, 1941

Dear Lee Wright:

Instead of trying to rewrite these few pages I'm sending them on as is. The publicity boys here have me booked solid for a week and I'd like to know if this is the right approach. (This rented Royal is about as unregal as the Princess.[5])

It was swell talking to you the day I left. I have worried about the book, and you cleared the air.

When Biff[6] comes in—start of the next chapter—he says, "This is a hell of a way to get your name in the papers." I'll be talking about the wedding gown and then he says, "Why didn't you tell me you wanted me to make an honest woman outta ya?" Would it make Dolly[7] more of a character to have her a belly roller? I don't have one and what is home without a mother? What is Burlesque without a belly roller? If I take Dimples[8] out of the first chapter . . . the white henna and etc. I can use her for Jannine.[9] Alice[*] I'll sweeten a little more, the Princess you said was set. How is Gee Gee?[†] Sandra[‡] with the ice on the breasts can be in a frozen condition every time we see her. The sink is full of ice for her breasts and the cocoa butter and etc.

My masseuse just made an entrance so I'll get my ass pounded a little and while she's working I'll try and figure a couple of good places to dump the corpse—mine that is.

Regards,
Gypsy

---

5. The female menace in *The G-String Murders.*

6. The hero (first comic).

7. Better known as "Dynamic Dolly"—a fast stripper.

8. A first draft character, later dropped from the story.

9, *, †, ‡. Strippers

February 19, 1941

Dear Lee:

Thanks for the long letter; I got so excited about your suggestions that I bought me a new typewriter. They told me the small type was more dignified—so—naturally Lady Lee had to get it and now I'm damned if I can read the print. (I thought the blue ribbon was sexy.)

If any agents call you about me, I have no agreement with them. They would like to think so but I'm up to my ass in agents and I'll be damned if I'll let them walk in here. They have been calling me long distance and sending me wires about publishers wanting the book. With their ten percent in mind of course. I don't want to know from agents.

Five of them took me into court four years ago—when I was in burlesque not one wanted a piece of me. When I got the Hollywood contract—and I do mean when I got it—they all sued! In the four years they've handled me they haven't gotten so much as an Elks smoker! NOT ONE DATE! The real laugh is that when the story broke that I was writing a book one of them called me and said that they wanted me to do a murder mystery with a Burlesque background. It's a wonder he didn't tell me that he had a terrific little title—The G-String Murders.

I think that's all, gotta make with the book words.

The naked genius,
Gypsy

RIVERSIDE THEATRE
MILWAUKEE, WISCONSIN

February 26, 1941

Dear Lee:

How do these chapters sound? I've tried so hard to make the characters different but I don't like to draw a picture of each one; there are so many and I'm afraid the descriptions would slow up the works. The new gimmick about La Verne[10] is wonderful. I have her singing a little more often so the readers won't forget that she is the Prim.

Does this sound good for a dust jacket; a picture full length of a stripper? Semi nude. The G-string actually silver flitter. (Very inexpensive, that flitter business.) And a separate piece of paper pasted on as a skirt, like birthday cards, you know? The customers can lift the skirt, and there's the G-string sparkling gaily. It is strictly gag business but it might cause talk.[11] More than the *Fortune* painting. I asked Vertes[12] if I could use the drawing he did of me for the back where they say: about the author . . . it is like drawing of me, half dressed pounding on the typewriter between shows. Just in case you liked it. He said he would be delighted. Dammit I love furriners! Aside from the hand kissing they really make like gents.

Is Louie[13] "in" the raid scene enough now? It seems to me like he is definitely La Verne's lover now, which gives him a motive, jealously, for the murder. As for Russell,[14] he has his little reason, too.

---

10. The Golden-Voiced Goddess and corpse No. 1.

11. This hasn't been done.

12. Marcel Vertes.

13. Louie (The Grin) Grindero—gangster and La Verne's saloonkeeper friend.

14. The Company's straight man and tenor.

Moey[15] COULD be hired killer, couldn't he?

Any way I know you are a busy girl so I'll write it first, and discuss it later. Keep this copy, in case I lose mine and if you have time write me to Riverside Theatre Milwaukee about changes you want made in the second draft.

Love,
Gypsy

---

15. Candy butcher at The Old Opera—scene of the murders.

BOOK CADILLAC HOTEL
DETROIT, MICHIGAN

July 21, 1941

Dear Lee:

When your letter arrived I got ambitious. I always do, for that matter. Being so far away from people that I can discuss plot, motive, blood and bodies with, I get stale. I really have finished the last of it but I wanted to wait until I got home and copied it before I showed it to you.

These inserts are rough but I'll clean them up later. Couldn't you hold off with the editing until I get home? I have fifty pounds (weighted by T.W.A.) of new words. None of them are sacred to me but in some cases there is an improvement.

When the coffee is good and we sell out the night before I find that I can write better. If I have night lunch with a smarty pants like Saroyan, I want to spit on the whole damned manuscript. (The coffee was good, and we sold out, but it didn't work this morning.)

Some stupid son of a bitch dropped in yesterday and killed a quart of my good liquor while he told me that HE had the idea of doing a murder mystery with my title! He tops it off by telling me how well I look! "You know," he says, "I know your age, and believe me you look swell!" Am I glad that I keep myself prepared for people like that. I tell you, I wouldn't be without those micky finns for anything in the world! You will rue the day that you brought the Belle of the Bistros into your fold. (His name is X in case anything happens to me.)

I'll call you Monday.

Love,
Gypsy

247

CONTRABAND 🔒

Contraband – the crime fiction imprint from Saraband – publishes an eclectic range of crime, mystery, noir and thriller writing, from dark literary titles to pacy detective novels. Contraband books have proved to be incredibly popular with critics and readers alike since the imprint was launched in 2014. Graeme Macrae Burnet's *His Bloody Project* was shortlisted for the Man Booker Prize 2016 and won the Saltire Society Fiction Book of the Year Award, and two further books were shortlisted for the Bloody Scotland Crime Book of the Year (in 2014 and 2015 respectively): *Falling Fast* by Neil Broadfoot and *DM for Murder* by Matt Bendoris. Several of these titles have already been translated into a number of different languages. Saraband was the inaugural Saltire Society Scottish Publisher of the Year in 2013, and was also shortlisted in 2015 and 2016.